HESHAYOL

THE BLOOD OF DRAGONS
BOOK 2

THRICE NINE LEGENDS

Joshua Robertson
&
J.C. Boyd

Acknowledgement

For those who struggle with their demons.

There once was a time when the gods were gods without question. When men were men without example. When heroes were only the frivolous dreams of lurid mortality. It was a time when truths and untruths were indistinguishable, hatred and love were equally excusable, and life and death regaled all of humanity in the same breath. Myths of old were realized and legends were born from the very dust man was formed of, to be told and retold until the grace of time altered them beyond knowing or forgot them completely. Still, some tales were preserved deep within the hearts of mankind, for reasons that could not be fathomed. Perhaps bearing the fruit of some profound truth or kept alive merely by the strength of the men who lived them. Some tales would never be forgotten.

Table of Contents

Thrice Nine Legends Saga

Legacy Series by J.C. Boyd & Joshua Robertson
BLOOD AND BILE*

The Blood of Dragons by Joshua Robertson & J.C. Boyd
ANAERFELL*
HESHAYOL*

The Kaelandur Series by Joshua Robertson
MELKORKA*
DYNDAER*
MAHARIA*

Other Thrice Nine Legends Saga by Joshua Robertson & J.C. Boyd
STRONG ARMED*
WHEN BLOOD FALLS*
THE NAME OF DEATH*
WARDEN OF THE ASH TREE*
THE SKINCUTTER'S DAUGHTER**
THE HIGHBORN LONGWALKER**
DEATH AT DUSK**

*Published by Crimson Edge
**Forthcoming by Crimson Edge

HESHAYOL

THRICE NINE LEGENDS

Month of Harvest

Fourth of Warmth

1352 CE

Prologue

The rusted iron manacle clasping Drast Kaligula's wrist against the mountainside creaked as he tried to shield his eyes with one hand from the torrent of wind. With a snort, he lifted his eyes to see the white dragon descending through the open ceiling of the ruined temple called Anaerfell. The beast's wings propelled the warm gust to wisp the silvery hair fringing Drast's balding, splotched scalp, and pressed the feathery strands of his beard against his desiccated frame. The distinct brawn in his chest and shoulders had long ago withered to nothingness, much like the lower half of his severed right arm.

With little success, he twisted his head in annoyance, unable to properly shield himself. His other arm, clinched by a similar iron loop around the bicep, was entirely useless in protecting him.

"The bitch has returned." Drast coughed, biting off the beginnings of a chuckle and peering at his younger brother through the dirt stirred up by the blast, now clouting him across the face. Secured in a similar manner, though with decidedly more hands, Tyran looked little better. His skin had shriveled with age, sagging against his bones with only the barest hint of his former sinew.

"Mm." Tyran grunted weakly, hardly wincing at the uninvited dust storm. The younger brother's blue eyes flashed in the midday sunlight and hung on the leviathan, their eternal sentinel, with unmasked hatred. For thirteen hundred years and more, Lahmia and the Wardens of the Ash Tree had guarded them in their solitary sanctuary in the north, a place lost to the world of men.

Drast grimaced. He and his brother were as forsaken as Anaerfell, doomed to live without living. They were not immortals like the gods, but ageless, except for the steep cost in years when casting their magic, *Koldovstvo*. Neither could touch the ancient craft of the Stuhia while hooked on the mountain beneath the engraved mark called *Znaki*—a crude eye with a moon and cross.

A familiar, imposing timbre resounded in Drast's ear, which nearly caused him to jump out of his skin. He never could quite discern from where exactly it came.

She has come to finish what I could not, Drast.

He echoed the voice. "She's come to do what her god could not, no doubt." He snarled, clenching his teeth to keep back a giggle that threatened to steal his breath. "We have to fight, brother. We cannot let her take my other arm."

That is why she has come.

"That is why she has come. To take it. She wants to see what the left hand tastes like, just like when Wolos took my right." He smacked his lips. "To taste it."

She drifted downward, extending the two large feet tucked near her round belly, folding her thin, large wings over her coiled body. Her three cone-shaped heads snaked at the end of long necks, the cold eyes of each fixated on the two imprisoned brothers. Her icy breath could kill them at any moment, yet she let them live.

Drast waited until her feet touched the weathered stone of the temple before speaking. His sunken stomach rumbled with such vitality that he could feel the vibration through his spine. "Any update on the whereabouts of our caretaker? Our Warden?"

She will not say.

"No?" He raised his eyebrows.

No.

"Fascinating. I would expect no less from the brainy beasts who follow you. Well, if such is the case, please tell us if we are to eat or be eaten."

I'm hungry.

"I have been positively giddy awaiting her return." A smile he could not control split his face in twain. "I will not die here without fighting. I have broken a Znaki before and I can do it again!"

One of the heads zipped toward him, displaying rows of bloodstained razor teeth while issuing the familiar high-pitched screech. Drast's ears rang. He reared back from the dragon's bell-shaped nostrils as it took a step closer, swirling its other heads above the first.

His shoulder blades scraped against the rocky wall. The deteriorating fabric covering his chapped flesh might as well have not existed. Sneering, he leaned toward the dragon and screamed back in defiance with all that he could muster, his thin frame soon trembling from the effort.

The dragon's shriek echoed against the stone walls, shaking loose motes of dust from the few columns holding up what was left of the ceiling. The vegetation that had overrun the temple did little to dampen the sound.

Drast ended his wheezing cry and began to laugh, breathlessly, having outlasted the dragon to win the contest.

As the cry faded, Tyran blew the long white strands of hair out of his face, wafting them loose from his thick, tangled beard. He seemed irritated, casting a hard, wordless look at Drast, who could not contain his giggles.

With the faceless voice conversing with him, Drast sometimes forgot Tyran existed. He wished Tyran would speak with him too, but his brother had not spoken in hundreds of years.

He has no tongue.

Drast nodded to himself, shifting his eyes from his silent

brother. The voice made perfect sense. Reasonable, really. That is what the Wardens had done. They took Tyran's tongue.

Drast squinted at Tyran, curious, almost as if staring hard enough might allow him to see past his brother's lips. *Was all of it gone? Maybe just the tip?* He peered so heavily at his brother's chapped lips, he nearly missed the fact that Tyran was licking them.

Drast blinked. "I thought you said he did not have a tongue."

I never said that.

"Yes, you did." Drast scrunched his face, looking down at his arm. He idly wondered if the Wardens took his arm or if it was missing at all. Maybe if he stared long enough his arm would come back too.

Yes. The Wardens took your arm. No amount of wishing will bring it back. You are lucky that is all they took.

"Lucky?" Drast cast a blurry squint back at Tyran, at the dragon, and then at a speck on the wall. "I want to know where the hooded Warden went. We have never gone so long without silent judgment; I am beginning to forget how bad I am supposed to feel for trying to kill their precious god."

You didn't kill me.

"Well, of course, I know that now. You won't shut up about it." He squinted harder at the speck. "Is that you?"

No.

"Oh." Drast blinked. "So, *are* you Wolos?"

I didn't say that.

"You didn't *not* say it either."

So.

"Can I call you Wolos?"

It's a fine name.

Drast stopped squinting at the speck, somewhat certain it was Wolos. Maybe.

Lahmia twisted her leftmost head toward Tyran to

deliver his meal. Drast heard the babble of regurgitated food rising from the depths of her throat before she spewed a stream of brownish muck like a waterfall over his brother. Despite the acidic stench, Tyran gulped ravenously at the watery substance washing over his face, further discoloring his mustache and beard.

Drast fought back his churning stomach, jerking his head sideways to dodge the droplets spraying against the side of his face. He considered slamming his head against the stone wall in hopes of losing consciousness before receiving his own meal. Long ago, he tried to kill himself by splitting his skull open but simply woke hours later with a dented head and a brutal headache. If that were not bad enough, he also suffered Tyran's wrath.

The incident occurred during the earlier years of their captivity when Tyran spoke more than five words a day. He did not talk much after.

The bobbing, crowned head of Lahmia returned Drast to reality. Lahmia expectantly recoiled and rose inches above him. His stomach ached for sustenance, beckoning him to do as he had done the last few days, if only to survive.

"Or you could kill me today," Drast proposed, squinting his eyes shut and reluctantly lifting his chin.

The last syllable fell from his tongue with the first splash of dragon vomit. He stretched his mouth wide, swallowing as swiftly as he could, tasting the slight flavor of bloodied venison through the bitter bile. He did not stop until he had nothing to gulp but air. He did not want to think about the pieces of the meal he missed, already crusting to his skin and clinging to his clothes.

His belly still rumbled.

Tyran's voice croaked, and he hung his head despondently to stare at the stinking mess on the floor.

Drast grimaced trying not to think about his meal. He coughed again and muttered, "Sadly, it is worse going out than coming in."

"Mm," his brother responded, using what little strength he had to kick at the pile of filth gathered around them. Drast luckily stopped smelling their combined stench years ago.

"Tyran." Drast glanced at his brother before looking to Lahmia. The last few days, the dragon tore from the temple after feeding them, staying no longer than needed; yet now she remained. "Something is different."

What?

"Maybe the Warden has been replaced," Drast said.

And I was just getting used to the other.

Tyran hummed with disinterest.

"You know it was a joke, Tyran?" Drast raised an eyebrow, leaning closer to his brother with a weighty sigh. When Tyran did not reply, Drast dejectedly turned to Lahmia too and waited.

Over the years, neither he nor Tyran could identify any Warden from under their hooded robes. Yet he knew several had come and gone over time. The bastards never said a word, but he knew someone had appointed them to guard Tyran and him. Since defeating Wolos beyond the temple, a single guardian had come regularly to spoon-feed them, clean their clothing, or even build a fire during cold nights. He could not remember when he stopped asking why the Wardens wasted their time to keep them alive.

The gods knew Tyran and he each had their fair share of suicidal attempts, from starvation to inciting either the Wardens or Lahmia to end their life. Nothing worked. In addition, by some peculiar fate, Tyran unearthed the clarity to provide reason to Drast early on during his darkest days and vice versa; for better or worse, they were one another's saviors. However, after Drast's last attempt—smashing his head into the wall—Tyran had stopped speaking. Drast had lost count of the long years that since passed.

When the green light suddenly gleamed between Lahmia and the brothers, tearing through the fabric of the air,

Drast's jaw fell. From the glow, a recognizable woman, Erzebeth Navenka, materialized in a ghostly form. Her emerald eyes, round as the fading sun, shown with more brightness than humanly possible.

Tyran's gasp barely took form, though no words came out.

"Erzebeth?" Drast supplied, drawing a confused glare from his brother. "What trick is this? You cannot be alive," Drast hastily said, his tongue swelling in his mouth. He twisted his neck to see the Znaki scratched into the wall. He was powerless with the sign above him, not that he had the strength to wield Koldovstvo anyway.

The woman was a Vucari, a skin-switcher, the sworn enemy of his people, the Stuhia. Memories raged in Drast's mind against Erzebeth, who ultimately had been the one who left Tyran and him bound here at Anaerfell. She healed their wounds, brought them back from the brink of death, and committed them to this horrible existence.

She isn't alive.

"I am not alive," Erzebeth admitted slowly, shifting her eyes from Drast to Tyran, "or, at least, I am incapable of living as I once did." Her essence brightened shortly, reflecting off the white scales of the looming dragon behind her. Lahmia rested her body against the stone flooring of the temple, her three heads perched over Erzebeth like guardians.

"Good," Drast hissed.

Tyran exhaled loudly, his expression unreadable. Drast gave his brother a sidelong glance. The dragon's vomit already had begun drying in Tyran's beard and mustache.

Centuries have passed since she left you here to rot. A swift death would have been merciful. But you have been allowed to linger on like a fart in a closed room.

Drast stifled a giggle, snorting, doing his best to glare at the wispy woman. "Why are you here? Are we to finally die?"

"No," Erzebeth said. Her eyes held little life, piercing through them as she spoke. "Death will not come so easily for you."

Drast muttered. "Nothing about what we have endured in our lives has been easy, I assure you."

"Good," she responded without emotion. "Rabid dogs should not be coddled. Consider yourself fortunate I kept you alive."

She is dead. How has she done anything?

"The Wardens kept us alive," Drast corrected.

"At my command," Erzebeth said.

Drast kept his eyebrows angled at the Vucari. "For what purpose, skin-switcher?"

"To undo what you did," Erzebeth answered.

"Undo what we did?" Drast echoed.

Undo what you did to me.

"So we did kill Wolos?" Drast jerked his head, twisting toward the southern stone wall as though he could see through it. "I remember the decay we smelled when you first left us chained to this wall. We thought the body decomposed out there, but we thought the spirit survived. We have wondered for so long—"

Drast felt a weight lift from his shoulders, one which he had not realized he carried. Hundreds of years passed since they fought Wolos, the God of the Dead, in the clearing beyond the temple, and still the battle was fresh in his mind. He had lifetime after lifetime to replay the dreadful event that resulted in him losing half of his right arm.

To keep himself from gawking at his missing appendage, he looked to Lahmia uncertainly, a so-called *child* of Wolos, the Horned God, who had been caring for them in this prison. Lahmia must have known her *father* was killed by them, yet she helped keep them alive.

I'm not dead.

"She said you are."

And you believe her?

"About as much as I believe you."

But you are talking to me.

"I am also talking to her."

So you think.

"Shut up! You're dead."

"I am, Drast." Erzebeth said with no small amount of confusion on her translucent features.

"Not you. Him." He responded in a murmur, his mind racing with the implications of the God of the Dead being gone from Aenar. "If Wolos is dead, then our father must have achieved immortality?"

"No, young Red. Dagmar Kaligula is dead," she said, the epithet far from accurate, given his advanced age. Before Drast could consider whether he was comforted or distraught by news of his father's death, Erzebeth persisted, "Killing Wolos did not give mortals immortality. Instead, his death forced the dead to pour from the Netherworld and walk among the living. You have brought an imbalance to the cycle of the gods, which nearly annihilated the Ash Tree and returned power to the *old-dark.*"

The old gods.

Drast gulped, being familiar with the name but not much more. The old-dark, also called the Likhyi, were said to have existed not only before the world had fully formed, but before the gods of mortals became gods. They were said to hold no love for the living.

Erzebeth went on, raising her voice, "For the past era, heroes have struggled to keep the old-dark weak enough so you might resurrect Wolos and restore order. Though the world will not survive much longer."

"You think we can save Aenar? It sounds as though we brought about its destruction." Drast snickered.

Tyran glared at him, grunting and flapping his lips.

Erzebeth frowned, floating closer to Drast. "You will journey to the Netherworld and return with Wolos. Without him, the Ash Tree will die and the old-dark will destroy the pantheon of the gods."

"And why should we care?" Drast sneered.

"Have you learned nothing during your time here? Is it so hard to be moral and decent?" Erzebeth responded, unblinking.

Drast met her wide eyes and smiled. "I am not sure how well those glowing eyes of yours work, but Tyran and I are more hanging here than standing. We only breathe because we cannot touch Koldovstvo to end our pathetic existence. We are frail. Brittle. The only journey we have left is death." He began to laugh, his voice cackling. "He can't even talk!"

"I would free you," Erzebeth argued.

"And I would kill myself at first chance," Drast said.

I could help.

"Death has become a cruel adventure. All the dead have become twisted by Marheena's death magic and then they return to this world to feast on the flesh of the living. Without Wolos, none can reach Thrice Ten Kingdom." Erzebeth paused, letting her words hang in the air.

Drast swallowed hard at the unwelcome thought. The lingering taste of dragon vomit in his throat caused him to gag unexpectedly.

"Mm," Tyran filled the silence.

You were never destined for Thrice Ten Kingdom. You failed your charge in life. I told you that.

"That's right. I remember. We failed our charges. I was supposed to help Tyran, and Tyran was supposed to have sex." He grinned at Erzebeth. "We were never going to Thrice Ten Kingdom."

"You have been given another chance!" Erzebeth cried in desperation, her translucent features a mockery of life.

Drast felt a spark of life, grinning again at her despair. He suspected his few teeth looked more like jagged rocks sprouting from the sea than anything close to a smile. "You are claiming we will be given residence in Thrice Ten Kingdom if we free Wolos from death? Who gives you the authority?"

"I am a Warden of the Ash Tree. I speak for Wolos who leads the dead to their resting place," Erzebeth said. "Would you rather stay fastened to this wall than do a good deed?"

Good deeds have a way of multiplying. Before you know it, you will be protecting the innocent and making sweet, timeless promises like a rainbow.

"You're a rainbow!"

I never said that I was.

"You didn't say you weren't either."

"What?" Erzebeth asked.

Drast blinked at her, uncertain what she was asking.

She wants to know if you are going to release me from death, even though I am alive and decidedly not dead.

Drast pursed his lips, trying to muddle through the mess in his head. "By what means do we release a god who does not have the power to free himself?"

Lahmia rumbled behind the skin-switcher. The center head opened its mouth, revealing an unusual gem with a strange blue light illuminating from within.

"This is *Ojenek*," Erzebeth said. "Not only will this stone allow you to speak and understand any strange tongues heard in the Netherworld, but it is also the key to Wolos's chains."

"We still do not have the strength to travel," Drast said, weakly flailing an arm and a half.

"Restore what strength you can," Erzebeth replied briskly. "And then Lahmia will carry you to the Kalinov Bridge. I will meet you there."

Tyran's forehead wrinkled temporarily, then he dipped his head with a reluctant grunt.

"Sure. I have been growing a bit restless anyway," Drast said with a half-smile, bowing his head at Lahmia. "Besides, we have surely overstayed our welcome."

Month of Rutting

Second of Frost

1352 CE

Chapter I

The dragon nosedived alongside the snowy crag, painted as white as its scales, clasping Tyran Kaligula in her curved black talons. He inhaled a lungful of frosty night air, holding his breath until his cheeks burned with the same fervency as his chest. With an exasperated breath, he peered through watery eyes at the fading fog and tangled treetops whipping beneath him in the strange, flushed light.

He was helpless, hanging with his arms wrapped up in the dragon's scaly grip, his skull nearly crushed in the limited space. For days, the mountain range was as soundless as a grave and, in the silence, Tyran's mind quieted. He did not need his voice or even his thoughts to occupy the time; he was a *master* of emptiness. Nonetheless, by and by, he eventually came to think about the last time he ventured into the Shade to steal a young dragon for his father's blood ritual, which eventually gave his brother and him more power than any Stuhian man should possess. The journey had been arduous at best, made even more difficult in the company of his ignorant soldiers.

Ser Tyran is what they called me. I was the son of a Serder who became Arkhon. I was the commander of armies. And now, I am what…a dragon's plaything…

His upper lip quivered under his faded mustache as he

strained to see Lahmia, the winged serpent who carried him in her grasp. Everything was a blur. The beast was nothing more than a hoary blotch blocking all the other blotches of color.

Lahmia was a stupid, fat beast. She should know he and Drast were *dragon-men* and *god-killers*. By the gods, they still had dragon's blood flowing through their veins.

He forced his head sideways to peer at his older brother, squished in a similar fashion in the adjacent claw. Like himself, Drast was little more than wrinkles and timeworn hair sprouting from parchment-thin, mottled skin. Dark brown spots and blackened bruises dotted Drast's exposed flesh, all muscle, fat, or sinew seemingly boiled away to leave only bone beneath. Tyran was certain Drast would not know the origin of any of the bruises. Not only did a contusion surface on either of them from touching an object more solid than their flesh, but they frequently woke to discover blood welting beneath the surface of their skin like they were suffering from internal wounds.

His brother's half-arm drooped at his side, twitching slightly, while he slept. Tyran once thought the entire arm was torn off during the battle against Wolos, but later learned he simply could not see what remained of the appendage through all the blood.

Drast swayed in the adjacent claw, snoring soundly, looking old enough to be a long-buried corpse.

"Wake up!" Tyran heard himself holler. His tone sounded as profound as a strapping man, a tone powerful enough to command nations. The wind whistled in his ears. The cursed dragon seemed to be picking up speed as they descended through the Shade Fells. He huffed in and out, regaining some strength before yelling again. By the gods, his voice was immaculate. *"Drast, wake up!"*

Drast snorted, his eyes fluttering for a moment before widening in excitement. He croaked, twisting in the talons as though he could free himself with a simple tug. He chuckled, the sound carried away with the wind. "Nine Lands!" Drast mumbled, barely intelligible.

"Calm down. We are finally here." Tyran said aloud, ignoring his brother's muttering.

Lahmia screeched from one of her many crowned heads and fanned out her leathery wings, rearing up to bring them to a halt before dropping them several feet above the ground. Tyran's gut roiled and his head spun as he heard Drast's wild shout nearby. Falling onto his weak legs, he crumpled to the dirt and rolled over and over. Drast flailed next to him in attempts to regain some sense of balance.

After several rotations, Tyran finally stopped on his back and groaned. Lahmia flapped her wings above him, rising back toward the darkened sky, flinging dirt and dust at them in her departure.

"I want to kill that pretty dragon." Drast found the energy to sit up and shake his fist in the air at the serpent as she flew away.

"She probably feels the same way about us," Tyran remarked, pulling himself up onto his haunches to see the small clearing among the snarled trees and jagged rocks. *"How many years did she protect us at Anaerfell knowing we drank her kin's blood, murdered her father, and all the while, called ourselves dragon-men? Keep your vengeance for someone worthier, hm?"*

Drast whipped his head around, bloodshot eyes watching Tyran. "Admit you want to kill her, too. I do not remember Father's spell, but maybe her blood would ripen us right up. Or it might kill us!" Drast cackled, twisting his hand over and over in front of himself as though he were spinning yarn. His grin split his face until the laugh completely faded. "Ah. The days since Erzebeth visited us at Anaerfell have already turned to months and Wolos remains dead. I really expected this little escapade to move a bit quicker. What took Lahmia so long to bring us here?"

He touched the wrinkles on his cheek, searching for an appropriate response. Finally, Tyran muttered, *"I do not know.*" Even at a whisper, he sounded hearty, unlike Drast's nasally drawl.

Drast chortled, shaking his gaunt bare foot at Tyran. "Can you believe this? Look at me! My thighs are as thin as my ankles. My muscles can barely hold my frame upright. I nearly break my own knees with the pendulous sack flogging between them." He smirked. "By the gods, Tyran, I can only shit water. I wish we were but a bit stronger than when Lahmia was spewing down our gullets."

"We have had a few good meals in us," Tyran said.

His brother rattled on before Tyran even had his say. He was not sure Drast was even listening to him. "We do not have any weapons with us. I am telling you, we are not going to last long in the Netherworld wearing these rags either, not that you have the strength or I have the appendages." He waggled his stump. "You do remember I lost an arm, right?"

"Yes," Tyran replied, pushing himself from the cold, hard ground to his feet. He lifted his eyes to the crimson glow emitting from the sky. *"What do you make of that?"*

The dark red moon hanging in the night sky had been hidden when they were cusped in Lahmia's talons, but now the ruddy ball was unmistakable. The light defiantly danced amid the shadows on the ground through the naked boughs of the trees. A subtle wind stirred the dusty ground into small whirlwinds reminding Tyran of the intrinsic death Erzebeth said clung to the world. He was reminded that, instead of dust, the land should have been covered in red-gold leaves from the maple trees, which now stood stripped of fronds. The branches were stained red in the light of the moon, taking on the forlorn image of crimson-clawed fingers reaching for the meager white light of the stars.

Like ashes, the dust drifted through the air, illustrating images. Tyran strained, his frame rigid with shock. *"Are you seeing this?"*

"Are you seeing this?" Drast repeated softly, the stupid smile still planted on his face. Tyran wanted to turn and glare at Drast, frustrated that his brother would mock his honest question. Yet he was too caught up in seeing anything after his eyes had failed him for so many years.

The wind swirled and a stone statue of the Horned God appeared before being crushed under the massive weight of a dragon's claw. The ash-like dust eddied and the walls of the great city unknown to Tyran gave way under the onslaught of a hundred legions of troops. Then the earth seemed to bound into the sky, knocking Tyran back to his knees. The dust churned into the image of a score of gods, all once worshipped throughout Aenar; the image was then swept away by a great darkness. As the sights played through the arid powder, it was almost as though the cry of the wind became the sound of the gurgling screams of women and children dying beneath the weight of the draconic breath. The rustling of the barren branches bespoke of the clattering shields and axes of battle-worn warriors; then came the sudden silence of the night as though the gods were emptied from the heavens.

"I didn't mean…this. We didn't know. Did Father know what could happen?" Drast's voice was a whisper. "We aimed for everlasting life, and instead, we invited eternal death." Tyran watched Drast blink several times as the images dispersed, passing before them. Although Tyran understood he and his brother held similar ambitions, the methods in reaching these ambitions knew different boundaries. From this knowledge, he wondered if the apparitions blurring in his mind's eye corresponded with Drast's visions.

From the corner of his eye, Tyran saw something move in the distance near the mountain edge. He turned from Drast's angular face to peer along the ghostly dark trees, ready for any evil that would come for them.

The light figure that emerged from the shadows appeared like rain from a cloudless sky. Tyran fought against the dim light to make some semblance of who the person could be, but he quickly realized the individual was cloaked in hooded robes—too-familiar hooded robes.

Drast tittered, throwing his head back in amusement, confirming Tyran's own suspicions. "Would you look at that, Tyran? We found the missing Warden. What is he doing here?"

"Sent by Erzebeth, no doubt," Tyran said, inspecting the Warden as he approached. Tyran knew this Warden was smaller in stature than the others who had guarded Drast and him over the past millennium, but in the shadow of the mountain under the wretched, decaying trees, he looked all the slighter, as though he may have been drowning in his robes. Tyran could not see much of the frame or face, but the shoulders were narrow enough to belong to a woman. Yet he could not see much beyond the typical grey robe securely fastened by a brown belt notched around the skin-switcher's scrawny waist. He squinted to better see some sort of axe hanging from an iron ring on the belt. The handle seemed to be fashioned out of what may have been a man's leg bone.

Tyran toppled forward, hardly able to hold his head upright, skimming over the shadow of the Warden's hood. He drew closer, close enough to feel the breath of the skin-switcher, noticing the Warden carried more objects. Drast's bow was slung over the man's shoulder. He held the quiver in his hand along with a large cloth sack. In his other hand, he held another pack and what looked to be Tyran's cherished mace, forged long ago by the giants of Tundris Mor. The two-foot yew haft had a heavy bronze ball at the end, the size of his fist. Tyran weakly reached for the weapon, wishing he had the power to pull the mace to his hand with Koldovstvo without cutting the remaining thread of his life. He stopped mid-reach, catching sight of his large rectangular shield—once made from yew and hardened bull's hide, now forged from an unknown alloy—shimmering over the Warden's shoulder.

Tyran had to blink to keep his eyes from watering.

He sidestepped around the Warden, his knees popping, swinging his hand at Drast with a relieved smile. *"Look. He brought our weapons. They were kept all these years."*

"Tyran, he brought our weapons. Probably to kill us with." Drast dropped his head to acknowledge his half-arm, then bobbed his head at the Warden, who unslung his bow. His lips became a snarling grin, revealing the handful of crooked, stained tines lining his bloody gums. "I suppose I *could* use my teeth." He snorted. "Those I have left."

Tyran grumbled deep in his chest, reaching for his mace again and missing. He could feel the soreness in his body. He was tired, drained of strength, and ready to be at an end. But the memory of past glories danced between his ears. He craved to have his weapon in his hand or the shield on his arm again.

"Are we not here for blood? I cannot remember. Did Erzebeth not come for us? Was it an illusion?" Tyran rumbled, his deep tenor ringing in his eardrums. *"I could have sworn we had a newfound duty to uphold."*

No one answered him. No one even looked at him.

The Warden slung the bags to the dusty ground with an extended whine, the weapons, too, tumbling from his hold.

When the shield clamored with a loud thud, Tyran opened his mouth to say something, but the Warden spoke first, tossing back the grey hood of his robes. The boyish face, flat nose, and shaved head took Tyran by surprise, but not nearly as much as the soft-spoken, young tenor of the near-child. He barely heard the words. "I am Kam Artur of Raccassi, a Warden of the Ash Tree, the kin of Jersi Artur. In your packs, you will find suitable clothes, a month's worth of rations, and filled water skins. Your weapons have been refastened, reinforced, or restrung to withstand the journey ahead. I will be accompanying you to ensure Wolos is reborn and balance is restored to Aenar."

"He is using big words, Tyran. Do we know these

people or places? I do not think I do." He paused, cocking his head. "Oh, yes, I am sure he sat here among the decaying trees, practicing his little speech to perfection. I suppose we should clap or something?" Drast raised one hand, his half-arm moving as if he still recalled having an arm. Both arms swung, but lacking his right hand made his clap decidedly one-sided. He paused, a confused expression on his face as he looked down before hooting with laughter. Just as quickly as the merriment began, he stopped and tilted his head, speaking to something unseen. "I will ask him."

Tyran dropped to his knees and clawed for his mace and shield. He could not believe the foolish Vucari would throw his items down.

Drast scuffled behind him, nearing the Warden while looking down his long nose. He smacked his lips. "You *do* know you left us in Anaerfell with a dragon who fed us with its own vomit?"

Kam crossed his arms, dipping his chin to his chest. "I am aware. Lucky for you Lahmia did not feed you from her other end."

"Oh? Luck—are we—" Drast coughed on spit catching in his throat. Fumbling for words, Drast stalled to reach for his bag, eyeing the longbow but keeping his hand a distance from the smooth wood. He regained his composure. "What makes you think we would allow you to come into the Netherworld with us? Hardly a place for a boy! Did you hear that, Tyran? The boy thinks he is coming with us."

"He is not coming with us."

Kam opened his mouth, then quickly shut it again as Drast kept talking, laughing loudly as though he was telling the best of jokes. "You—you are not coming with us!"

Tyran reached for the sack on the ground, flipping it upside down to discover the contents were as the boy had suggested. He soon discovered a fresh pair of pants. *"I will not have any more blood on my hands. Any fool knows we will die before we reach…wherever we are going. We can hardly walk."*

"I am coming with you whether you want it or not," Kam asserted. "It is not a discussion, and by your own admission, you have little strength to stop me."

"You are talking, and then I am talking. It sounds like a discussion," Drast said, casting aside his rags and pulling a brown tunic over his head before peering down at the boy with condemnation. "Tyran and I have led many soldiers to their deaths. Soldiers who, I might add, earned the right to fight alongside us. Now, any other day I might drag you to the grave with me, promising you glory and riches and the finest of women. But you—*clearly*—have yet to even touch a woman. So go embrace your life a bit before you seek death."

"The skin-switcher is puny. He should stay here and guard our rags," Tyran suggested, pulling the pants over his bony legs and fastening them with a belt. He then searched the ground, trying to see his mace through the thick cataracts blurring his vision

Kam snipped at Drast. "While I am glad to hear the infamous Kaligula brothers carry some guilt for past transgressions, I will be guiding you and watching over you through the Netherworld. You will find my knowledge crucial in surviving the frozen darkness."

"What? Was there not a skin-switcher with more hair on his chest?" Tyran located his mace. He grabbed at it and pulled it closer. The weapon was heavier than he remembered.

Drast crowed to the skies with laughter. "Why would they send you?"

Drast echoed him again and again, endlessly running his mouth. Tyran frowned at the heavy mace.

Kam scoffed. "There was no one else. Without me, you will likely die."

"We will die regardless," Drast said. "But we might die in silence. By the gods, you ramble on like a woman."

Tyran grunted. Drast would not have the sense to call the kettle a kettle, or whatever people said. He pulled at his mace again. With a grunt, he slipped it into the loop on his belt. He squinted at Kam. *"What do you know, exactly?"*

Kam curled his lip. "You two old men would do well to listen to my rambling. Might help you to know the *Alatir Stone* is kept by Zyem and, if retrieved, the artifact will return you both to your youthful vigor."

"You expect us to *kindly* ask the *dragon-god* for this magical stone?" scoffed Drast.

Tyran struggled to lift his shield from the ground and finally let it down where it was with a pained grunt. The new forged metal was glimmering, solid. Impressive. Too heavy.

"I expect you to take it," Kam said, answering Drast's question while staring at him in the eye. "In the Netherworld, Koldovstvo is limitless."

Drast lifted his bushy white eyebrows at Tyran in surprise. "You mean to say we will not grow older in the Netherworld? What do you think of that, Tyran? You surely have something to say to that?"

Kam nodded. "You will be ageless, even when channeling your magics."

Drast took a step back, taking a long look at Kam. "I suppose you can come along, but keep your little orations at ten words or less. I'll be counting."

Tyran pointed at the newly crafted ward. *"If the skin-switcher is coming, he can carry this. He clearly ruined my shield with this metal, this—"*

Kam followed Tyran's finger with his brown eyes, filling in the blank. "It is called steel. Much has changed since you have been in the world."

"—you can carry it." Tyran finished, hefting the shield at him.

Chapter II

"Keep walking," Drast rasped, hoping to incite some response from the Warden. The voice in his head had not appreciated being told it was dead.

To your death and the death of your little brother.

He could not evoke the deep, commanding tone of his younger years, but the narrow, lightless tunnel angling beneath the mountain carried his voice well enough. Kam had taken Drast's warning about talking too much to heart, apparently, giving Tyran a run for grunty and unsatisfying responses. After being stuck for a thousand years with only Tyran to speak to, Drast already regretted shutting the boy down. He would kill for a little conversation.

Kam peered over his shoulder, the reflection of the firelight flickering in his brown eyes. He held his torch in his right hand, lighting the path ahead as he guided them ever farther into the musty darkness. Drast knew the skin-switcher did not need the light to see in the dark, which meant that he brought the torch for their benefit.

If only the poor sap knew how useless his and Tyran's eyesight had become. The Warden himself was a bit of a blur and the path ahead looked like a fuzzy hole that he could only chuckle at any time he thought about what it resembled.

I would walk if you had not taken my legs with death. You are cruel, Drast Kaligula.

"I used to think so," Drast grumbled, "until I met your Wardens and a thousand years of imprisonment. A thousand years of half-starvation. A thousand years of pain and hatred. Not all your Wardens restrained themselves to simply keeping us breathing. Many felt life was not torture enough."

He squeezed his eyes shut, trying to push back the flashes of cutting knives and hot pokers from those Wardens who thought Drast and Tyran had secrets to tell. He stumbled to a stop to prevent himself from falling.

At least such wounds heal.

Drast began to giggle, breathless and feeling as though his grin would split his face in twain. The image of the top of his head falling off from laughter sent him doubling over, unable to stop.

After a moment, he realized that Tyran was by his side, pulling him straight. Catching sight of his brother's sagging features, he blinked away the tears, trying to sober his merriment.

Delaying the inevitable. You, Drast Kaligula, are a coward.

"Do not worry," Drast said, still smiling so much it hurt. "My brother and I are not cowards. We will not be running back the way we came like frightened hounds." He paused. "Maybe crippled hounds. With two legs."

Tyran gave the barest nod to Kam, who turned to face forward again, no response or reaction given. Tyran awkwardly stumbled forward to take his place between the two, saying nothing.

Drast squinted at the back of Tyran's head, wishing his brother would say something to fill the void. Say something to shut the voice up. Dead gods were not gracious speakers.

Tyran's blob of white hair, more than what covered Drast's scalp, bobbed with each clumsy footfall. He watched the muddled mess bounce, having little else to admire in the blackness. Despite the withering of muscle and flesh from age, Tyran's broad shoulders grazed the walls, intermittently catching an outcropping and drawing grunts and groans. In addition, the low roof of the narrow passage presented plenty of opportunities to knock their heads against jagged stones, which would illicit winces and sharp cries. Drast tried to watch closely in hopes of dodging the rocks Tyran whacked, but rarely was he successful.

"My knees went numb an hour ago, if anyone cares to know," Drast rasped, his feet loudly scraping against the rough terrain, lacking the strength to lift them beyond an awkward shuffle. He wondered how long the leather boots Kam had provided for each of them would last. Longer than his knees, he imagined. The thought was brief, interrupted by Tyran's grunts while fumbling to grip at the rocky walls as he nearly went tumbling head first down the tunnel. While his brother regained his balance, Drast paused in his tracks, recalling what he had been saying. "But it is no matter to me. When I get to the Netherworld I will simply use Koldovstvo to float around like a cloud. Nice and easy. Until then, consider yourselves lucky I have the fortitude to willingly skid along behind here, never mind the fact I am but a simple sheep being led to slaughter."

Kam looked over his shoulder again. Drast squinted at the Warden, blinking against the light of the torch to try to make out his expression. His lips were pursed. No smile, that was for certain. He had to be breaking the boy's resolve.

The resolve of my Wardens is not so easily broken.

"I could collapse at any moment," Drast persisted. "And if I were to tumble, you do realize that *you*—Kam— would cushion our fall. It is probable Tyran and I would crush your spine. I mean, how much deeper does the mountain run? How much momentum would be gained? Really, what is the likelihood of you surviving if we spill down the path?"

About as likely as you surviving, ancient one.

Drast chuckled, nodding at the fair point. A moment later, the three of them were moving again when the ground beneath their feet leveled. "Oh! You have been saved!"

Drast's exaggerated exclamation was drowned out by Kam. "We have reached *Babejega*." Drast hurried to count the four words on his fingers, listening eagerly for more. Instead of talking, the Warden raised his torch higher to reveal the great expanse in which they suddenly appeared. No breeze greeted them in the cavern, yet a cold chill crawled along Drast's cheeks and nose. He squinted against the dark, seeing little more than pitch, when a twinkling above caught his eye.

"Are those stars?" Drast squinted. He cleared his throat. His constant chatter down the tunnel seemed to have left him hoarse.

White dots danced across the wide open stretch above them, pulsating with light as though they were breathing. Drast adjusted his eyes, recognizing spirals of dark blues and greys beyond the *stars*. If he strained hard enough, more colors seemed to appear in the far distance.

Drast asked, "What is this place?"

Your doom. The beginning and the end for mortal kind.

"Babejega," Kam repeated, touching the torch to a pan of oil hidden in the gloom.

The lantern awakened in a torrent, temporarily blinding Drast. He blinked, hardly realizing what was happening. The fire from the pan ricocheted a bolt of fire, no bigger than his fist, into a second pan, and then a third. The coppery discs holding the oil were strategically placed around the cavern—hundreds of them—seemingly hanging from nothingness in the chasm. The bolt of fire was a flash of light, bounding about the cavern, controlled by some magic beyond his knowing. He could only think the power came from Koldovstvo, but neither he nor Tyran were controlling the flame, and the Vucari would not have the ability.

The thought was fleeting when the speckles of light stopped dancing across his vision, and he saw what more the hollow in the mountain held. Ahead of him, a bridge made completely of rope, from the interwoven base to the taut guardrails, stretched across an immeasurable void, leading to a floating isle of land, only large enough to fit a handful of people. Interconnected around the island were similar bridges constructed of rope leading in all directions. Drast counted twenty-seven.

He shuffled forward so he stood shoulder to shoulder with Tyran. His breaths suddenly felt strained, either from the journey through the mountain or from the unexpected nexus displayed before them. "What exactly is Babejega?"

Kam replied, taking the first step onto the rope bridge leading to the center landmass. "All worlds connect here at this single point, a place between life and death, youth and old age, human and animal, male and female, good and bad—Babejega is everything and it is nothing. This is the yoke that births all, connects all, rescinds all."

Forty-five.

"That was more than your allotted ten words," said Drast, finally taking his chance to scold the skin-switcher.

"You asked," Kam curtly replied, adjusting his own bag and the shield over his shoulder. He shuffled ahead.

You did ask.

Drast tailed Tyran, tracking behind Kam cautiously, surprised the walkway did not sway in the slightest. Still, he held on to the rope to keep his feet underneath him. In the expanse around him, he saw nothing that resembled the mountain they had trekked down. Even when looking over his shoulder, the ingress they had exited moments before had entirely disappeared. Nothing remained but the many bridges drifting into space.

He peered over the edge at the eternal darkness beneath them. The void was unquestionably chock-full of distant stars and faraway worlds.

Tyran grunted and murmured incomprehensibly.

How many worlds? How many lands?

"Twenty-seven worlds total," Drast answered, pointing

out the bridges branching off the irregular piece of earth in front of them.

"No," Kam said. "Come and look."

Tyran stumbled from the bridge onto the solid ground, and Drast shuffled behind him. Almost immediately his eyes seemed to turn inward as a spectrum of rope bridges appeared around him, blanketing the one they had just withdrawn from in countless multitudes. Thousands, if not tens of thousands, of mirrored passageways forked in all directions, each one a hair to the left or right of the other. Like a pond rippled by a tossed stone, the walkways blurred across his vision, holding no evidence of a clear path.

"It has to be an illusion." Drast blinked, trying to focus his old eyes.

You are too old to believe in magic.

Drast snickered.

Kam's boyish intonation echoed across the abyss. "Thrice Nine is three multiplied by three, nine times over. Nearly twenty thousand lands exist beyond our own."

And which leads to the Netherworld?

"And which leads to the Netherworld?" Drast repeated.

Kam scrunched up his face, creases forming around the edges of his brown eyes. The expression appeared even more detailed with the boy's lacking hair, his thin, arched eyebrows, and small, flat nose. Before the Warden could provide a response, the familiar green light flashed behind him, and the faint, ethereal ghost of Erzebeth emerged from nothingness. Her glimmering figure rippled inches above the ground, mouth twisted awkwardly as she attempted to make sense of her surroundings.

She indifferently studied the three of them standing in the nexus. "I trust you still carry Ojenek?"

A moment passed before Tyran reached into his pocket to reveal the smooth stone in the palm of his hand. Drast had forgotten they carried the thing. The faint blue light glowed from within the gem. Drast faintly recalled Erzebeth mentioning that the stone would be the key to freeing Wolos.

Erzebeth dipped her chin. "Come. I know the way." She drifted away toward the flowing footpaths flickering around them.

You cannot trust her. She is dead.

"So are you."

But I'm on your side.

"Why?"

Because I am in your head. Self-preservation.

"Oh." Drast nodded. "That makes sense."

Stumbling forward, he tugged at Tyran's shoulder as his brother returned Ojenek to its resting place. The boniness of his younger brother's shoulder caused him to swallow in realization. Neither of them was ready for this adventure. He tightened his grip on Tyran, and despite his words, he laced his tone with concern. "After what she did at Anaerfell, you cannot trust her again."

Tyran grunted.

He will trust her. He doesn't think either of you has a choice. Look at his eyes. He is mad. The only things he thinks about are love and duty.

"We have plenty of choices," Drast muttered. He hesitated, hoping that Tyran's infatuation with love had, perhaps, changed even if his obsession with duty had not. He decided to press a more concerning thought. "She said Father was dead." Drast held on to him while he slowly inched his way along behind Erzebeth and Kam. "What if we come across him in the Netherworld?"

Drast could nearly sense Tyran's panic, his body growing tense under his hand, but he still said nothing, despite his teeth clenching followed by the issuance of a deep-throated growl.

"I suspect he will find a way to torment us," Drast said with an exasperated breath, somehow twisting his unease into sounding like a jest. "No matter what he *thought* he was good at doing, ruining our lives was the only skill he managed to perfect."

Yes, he did a rather bang-up job of it, did he not?

Tyran rumbled with a nod. "Mm."

Erzebeth redirected their attention back to her as she neared the wavering bridges. If she had been listening to what Drast had said, she gave no sign of it. Neither did the young Warden. "Be careful where you place your feet," she said. "Hold fast to Kam so you do not slip beyond reach."

Yes, hold on to the young boy.

Drast snickered.

Before either could reply, Kam reached back and grabbed Tyran's wrinkled fingers, which Drast suspected felt like a fish too long out of water. From the looks of the Warden's smooth-looking hand, he suspected the young man had never swung a weapon in his life. The Warden would not last long in the Netherworld.

Keeping these troubled thoughts from his expression, he reached for Tyran's other hand with his remaining one and held fast.

Drast's voice splintered. "Out of all the stupid things we have done—"

"Mm."

Drast winced, thinking about the days ahead in the company of his grumbling brother. With a long sigh, he conceded, "Kam, if we survive this, I will stop counting your words."

You are going to regret that. Mark my words.

His voice trailed off as Kam shadowed Erzebeth while tugging Tyran along. He did not realize they were stepping off the chunk of earth into the empty space, and suddenly they were on another bridge, identical to the first, trekking into an atmosphere as cold as Anaerfell during late winter. The icy air stung at his nose and ears, promising to chill his bones before the day was done.

Drast glanced over his shoulder momentarily to count

twenty-seven bridges, including the one they passed over, beneath the fading light illuminated from the fiery copper pans. Babeyega disappeared.

Chapter III

The cold of the Netherworld bit into Tyran's face, causing him to hold his breath. The chill clung to his cheeks. Ahead of him, Kam stepped off the bridge, letting go of his hand almost as quickly as he had grabbed it. At first, Tyran thought the boy was reacting to the cold too, but Kam seemed unaffected. Tyran had to remind himself that the Warden was a Vucari. The skin-switchers did not feel the cold or heat like regular mortals.

"By the gods, Tyran," Drast said, pulling back to adjust the quiver of arrows at his side. Tyran stretched out his fingers, already feeling the soreness from gripping Drast's hand. His brother waited a moment with him on the end of the bridge while Kam and Erzebeth moved farther ahead on land, and then said, "This is not a welcoming place to die. We best keep breathing a bit longer, eh?"

Tyran strained, gripping the heavy mace at his belt. The weapon threatened to jerk his pants to his ankles. His mind swirled. *Breathing is about all I am doing. Why are we here anyway?*

Drast flashed his teeth, or what was left of them. "I know we have spent a lot of time together—probably saying all that would ever need to be said between two people—but you cannot grunt at me all the way through the Netherworld.

Do not leave me having to talk to the skin-switchers."

Tyran cocked his head, raising his voice at Drast. He was not certain he could yell any louder. *"I am talking to you, and I would appreciate it if you answered the question."*

Drast snorted, smiling wryly and rocking his head. "You may not say a word, but I know you want to be here. This is already far better than being chained to a stone wall. Besides, you would not deny the backstabbing skin-switcher. I know you and your endless pledges to duty."

Tyran scrunched his face, feeling his mustache meld with the overgrowth on his chin. He leaned closer to try to make out his brother's facial features. All he could see was the blasted grin. *"What do you mean duty? And why should we be here?"* He took another step closer. *"I do not know that I want to be here. I definitely do not want to hear your tireless rattling. You ramble as much as Kam."*

Drast widened his mouth to the point that it looked painful. Of course, he would smile and answer nothing. His brother was hopeless.

Tyran twisted away to leave Drast alone with his ridiculous grin. He sucked the cold air through his nostrils, feeling the burn in his chest, and scanned the nonstop landscape ahead of them. The topography consisted of blackened, jagged rocks irregularly sprouting over the frost-laden ground. From what Tyran could tell, the entirety of the earth could have been a frozen sea, forgotten to time. An ice-blue haze clouded in subtle bursts across the horizon, hanging midair, like fog might over a millpond in the early morning. Tyran was hauntingly certain the mist could darken while giving no promise of diminishing.

The sky, if it could be called such a thing, appeared to be eternally overcast, but a gleaming indigo-infused light brightened this outlandish world in equal measure. No sun, moon, or set of stars could be seen, only the soft ruddiness of the strange hue emanating from the heavens.

"At least we have some light." Tyran eased his tone, stepping

off the rope bridge to the ice. He immediately slipped and had to grab the bridge post to stay on his feet. Once his legs were locked into place, he peered back over his shoulder. *"Be careful."*

"Do not be an ass," Drast said, the smile frozen between his wrinkled, pale cheeks. "Tell me something worthwhile, like why the skin-switcher is here. By the gods, I cannot think of any good reason." He eased himself onto the ice with more care than Tyran had applied. "What? You cannot either? Well, someone has to know."

Tyran hobbled on, wondering if Drast was talking to him or someone else entirely. He spun around to see if Erzebeth had snuck up on him, but she was a good distance away—a green blur—standing next to Kam. They both gazed across the breadth of the region.

He mumbled under his breath, *"No matter why he came, the Warden will only find death."*

Erzebeth spun around in flight, as though she were propelled by a gentle breeze. Her voice carried across the distance. "Ready yourselves, Reds. We draw close to the Kalinov Bridge and the dragon-god will be near." In the gloom, Tyran could see her softening her features as though a sneer may have coated her expression a moment ago. "Though I can guide you to Wolos's prison, I have little power in this realm."

"Ready ourselves? Dragon-god? What are we doing?" Tyran asked, inching closer across the icy terrain. He could not remember if they had discussed battle. His mace was certainly too heavy for him to fight anything.

"You need to use Koldovstvo," she said with a tilt of her head, indicating she was repeating herself. "Your life will not be forfeited here as it was on Aenar. In the Netherworld, you can cast your magic freely."

"I already told them," Kam chimed in, reaching for his hood to cover his shaved head.

"The hell he did," Tyran muttered. He remembered the

Warden talking a lot but could not claim he heard the boy say anything useful.

"Go ahead," Erzebeth encouraged. "Give it a try."

"Come on, Tyran. Worst case scenario, we die, and we can be done with this little trek." Drast smiled. He then turned his head to the side and mumbled over his shoulder.

Tyran hesitated, knowing the slightest trickle of Koldovstvo would steal breath from him as swiftly as a hard fist to the gut. Except in this instance, he would not breathe again. A thousand years and more passed since he last welcomed the power of Koldovstvo into his thoughts, shaping the will of his mind upon the physical world. Yet now, as he finally gave in to the watchful eyes of the Vucari, the effort was as natural as his beating heart.

Forgetting the pain in his joints, Tyran used elemental magic to lift himself from the frozen ground. The chilled air rustled his hair as he slowly rose several inches off the ground, matching the height of Erzebeth's ethereal form. Taking the weight from his knees and hips immediately eased some pain from his aching bones. He sighed in relief. He was not dead.

With a gasp, he suddenly fell to the ground. The sting of the hard ice on the soles of his feet shot up to his hips.

Drast hooted from behind him, drawing Tyran's attention. He twisted his neck to see his brother grinning from ear to ear, his few teeth flashing between his beard and mustache. Where the missing appendage had been moments before, Drast had created a spectral hand, a shimmering sapphire color—partially transparent—which he used to pull an arrow from the quiver at his side. His wraithlike fingers twirled the arrow around as he let out a booming laugh.

"Looks like I can use my bow after all. Can we kill the brown-eyed bastard now?" Drast laughed, nocking an arrow and spinning the weapon at Kam. The skin-switcher stepped back, raising his hand in alarm. Drast pulled the string back and forth playfully, as though he might release at any moment, then noticed Tyran. He relaxed the string. "Are you okay?"

"*Yeah.*" He groaned, rubbing his sore hip. "*My mind wandered, and I lost concentration.*"

"What happened?" Drast asked.

Tyran scowled. "*I just told you.*"

Embracing Koldovstvo again, Tyran pulled himself from the ground and floated back into the air, finding no reason to stay on the rough terrain. Though he may have felt some joy for Drast reforming an arm with magic, he did not share his brother's enthusiasm. With his age, his thoughts were too broken to maintain his hold on Koldovstvo for long.

"Where is Zyem? Where is the dragon-god?" Drast puffed, pointing his arrow at Kam with a wink.

"*No matter how much power we can wield with Koldovstvo, you cannot believe we have the capacity to kill a dragon-god.*" Tyran lowered himself back to the ground, feeling his mind wander off into memory. The mace at his side grew heavier. "*How long has it been since I was called Ser Tyran? How many Vucari did I slaughter with my weapon?*"

"They are mad, Erzebeth," Kam said. "You should not have brought them here. We could have done this alone."

"Careful with your words, skin-switcher. Do you know who you are talking about?" Drast hysterically shouted between chortles. "Tyran and I slaughtered Wolos while our blood was draining from our bodies. That is right. A god! We killed a god! By the gods, we killed a god! If anything, we can do this without *you*, but you can do nothing without us. We are untouchable."

Erzebeth interrupted Drast, addressing them all without any hint of emotion. "We cannot do this without them, nor are they unrivaled, which they should not soon forget." She rushed to Drast, shining brightly. "While channeling Koldovstvo will not kill you outright, you can very well die here in the Netherworld. Whether engulfed in fire or crushed by boulders, or cut down by an axe or spear, you are still living. Make no mistake of your mortality."

"I will kiss the demon who rids me of it." Drast threw his head back, tapping his temple. His laughter rang with amusement. "No, no, I will not use tongue."

"You will survive." Erzebeth ignored his strange comment. "Now listen. When Zyem appears, you will not harm him. We came here to restore balance to the world, not further disrupt its order. The dragon-god's role in guarding the Kalinov Bridge cannot be overlooked. He does not only keep the living from entering, but he keeps the dead from leaving."

"I thought the dead were spilling into Aenar," Drast challenged.

"They do not cross the bridge," Erzebeth said.

Kam entered Tyran's space suddenly, causing him to jump. The Warden's face twisted with determination. "Zyem has the Alatir Stone. You need it if you wish to survive the Netherworld. Do you understand?"

Tyran's unfocused mind scarcely understood the seemingly jumbled speech coming from the boy's thin lips. "*What?*"

Erzebeth said, "The stone is an eye found on one of Zyem's three heads. Once it is retrieved, we must flee from him as swiftly as we can. He is bound by the bridge and can only roam so far."

"We have to *pull out* his eye? Like pluck it out?" Drast snorted.

Tyran lifted himself back into the air with Koldovstvo. He had no idea what they were talking about and was tired of being ignored every time he asked a question.

"Like Ojenek, you cannot use your magic to manipulate the stone or retrieve it," Erzebeth said.

The world quaked, knocking Drast and Kam to their hands and knees while Tyran and Erzebeth remained hovering above the trembling earth. Tyran whipped his head toward the Netherworld, searching for the source as the ice and rock around them crumbled away into an unseen chasm. His concentration slipped momentarily, causing him to fall inches before he quickly regained control. He hoped if he were high enough, he would have plenty of time to catch himself before smacking into the earth.

Drast used Koldovstvo to join Tyran in the air, his left hand gripping his bow and stringing an arrow with his translucent fingers. Tyran floated into an open expanse as the soil milled into nothingness, save a thin strip of land adjoining the ever-expanding spread.

Tyran gritted his few teeth, the dentin cutting into his gums. He could taste blood in his throat, but he hardly cared. His attention was on the so-called bridge, standing no wider than his foot. A moment of clarity struck him. *That is the Kalinov Bridge.*

"Ah, yes. The bridge is awfully narrow," Drast spoke to the wind. "I am flying, though. The skin-switcher is the one who has to tiptoe across."

"Do not worry about me," Kam said, backing away as the limited land space around him continued to rattle. "Worry about the dragon."

"Dragon? Dragon!" Tyran rang out. *"Who said anything about a dragon?"* He inhaled sharply, fighting to see his brother and the skin-switcher beneath him. The silver of his shield glistened in the blurred colors.

A deep-throated reverberation thundered from the hidden depths, soon followed by another screech—ringing in the hollow—higher-pitched than the first. Along with the sound came a voice in Tyran's head, unlike anything he had ever heard before.

What is that we smell? Mortal blood? Who tries to creep into the land of the dead?

Tyran considered reaching for his mace, but instead stuck out his shaking hand to retrieve his guard from Kam. His shield rose from the Warden's back, pulling Kam from his feet, tugging him closer to the gap.

"Wait!" Kam shouted in alarm, jerking at the knotted leather strap across his chest that held the shield in place. The knot gave way, sending the shield straight to Tyran's arm. The Warden landed on his feet, bending his knees slightly with impressive agility. "If you are not going to carry it, at least tell me when you want it!"

He paid no attention to the skin-switcher, feeling the encumbering weight against his deteriorated muscles; he quickly used Koldovstvo to support the mass. He slipped in the air with the reallocation of magical energy but hastily readjusted before dipping too low.

He smacked his lips with satisfaction. The square of metallic grey covered him from knee to shoulder. He lowered his head and peered over the ridge of the shield as another rumble echoed from below.

The first greyish-brown claw surfacing from the chasm and clamping onto the ridge did not surprise Tyran, though the sheer size gave him pause. The limb had five digits, each of which ended in a massive nail, long as his forearm, and seemingly made from bone. A second claw slammed into the earth, cracking the foundation, followed by the expected three heads of Zyem. Each horned skull was attached by a long, thick neck to a colossal body covered in coarse skin with a crystal ridge running the length of its spine.

Tyran gawked at the two fat, warped nostrils directly in front him, wide enough for him to walk inside without so much as dipping his head, before following the row of small horns spread over the dragon's serpentine head to the large teeth poking out from the side of the mouth, previewing the terror hiding inside. A forked tongue slithered out inches from Tyran before darting back between the off-colored scales.

The other two heads whipped around to gain better sight of Drast and Erzebeth, while Kam huddled down beneath Tyran. Zyem reverberated in the throat nearest Tyran and pushed off the inside of the chasm, flapping leathery wings starting from just above its shoulders to the middle of its back. The wings were bladed with spiked scales patterned along the visible bone between the taut skin. The wide tail, ending in a mace-like growth, flapped beneath the dragon like a pendulum ready to strike. One of the heads screeched, the terror-inducing sound echoing off the oversized abyss, causing chunks of rocks to break away from the opposite edge. The noise prompted the voice again in Tyran's mind.

God-killers!

"Oh! He does not look pleased to see us," Drast said, flying to Tyran's right side.

Tyran pressed his lips together, uninspired by his brother's humor. *"I heard him well enough, Drast."* He steadied his breath, scanning the dragon's many amber eyes elegantly sitting within the creature's three skulls.

"I wonder if we should tell him we are expert dragon-killers," Drast smirked. "Let us see, the first dragon you killed was but a baby. We probably should not mention that. The second we fought was Torn'ash, but we did not kill him, did we?" Drast looked over his shoulder for a moment, scratching his scalp in confusion. "No, I do not believe we did. But…Wolos…Wolos… Is Wolos considered a dragon? He looked like a dragon when we killed him…"

"The stone," Erzebeth said solemnly, flittering closer to them. "Go get the stone from Zyem. Center head. Left eye."

Tyran strained to see what the ghostly skin-switcher referenced, barely seeing a white stone hovering by some unseen magic in the socket. He was thinking how the gem resembled a glistening eye when bursts of flame spewed from Zyem's three heads. Forgetting his shield, Tyran lifted his hand and used Koldovstvo to raise a field of energy between himself and the dragon breath.

Drast mirrored him while giggling uncontrollably. He kept trying to open his mouth to speak but only started laughing harder. In short spurts, words eventually escaped between his wheezing fits. "This…this is…so…hot!"

Kam shouted as red-hued flames whipped against the two wavering walls of magical energy. Tyran peered down at the young Warden scrambling for the bridge, jerking their packs along behind him.

The cowardly boy was not even in danger but was screaming like a frightened girl.

"Grab the stone," Erzebeth commanded once more. She rotated around until the dragon fire was tearing through her backside, having no impact on her ethereal form. "And then get across the bridge."

The flames desisted. Tyran fumbled to hold his steel shield and hurriedly used Koldovstvo to keep the heavy guard steady. He then looked to Drast for an explanation. He could not remember if they discussed the importance of this white artifact yet. *"Why do we want the stone? What does it do?"*

Drast turned his nose up at the skin-switcher. "I will pull a hundred stones from dragon skulls if it means being younger again."

"The stone makes us younger!" Tyran swelled his chest with excitement, pulling his mace free from its loop. The weapon felt like it weighed a thousand pounds, pulling his arm down straight next to his side. His mind swirled with magic trying to lighten the weapon, keep his shield steady, and himself hovering above the ground. All the while, he did not want to forget the purpose of the blasted stone. Though his voice sounded as vibrant as ever, he could tell his body was not what it once was. *"The stone makes us younger. The stone makes us younger. The stone makes us younger."*

Zyem's rage rebounded off the chasm's wall as Tyran advanced with Koldovstvo. Drast grumbled something about drawing fire, circling wide to Tyran's left, the blue fog swirling from his path as he pushed ahead.

Zyem's three crowned heads met each of them with fire and fury far more powerful than the initial burst. The lashing flames danced over the heavens adding their own shade to the purplish sky. Tyran clenched his fist with concentration, pulling the particles of cold together to form a wall of ice in front of him, widening his distance from Drast. Two of the heads followed his movement, the heat tearing through his defense mercilessly but keeping him safe from the flames.

Lightning blasts tore through the fog from nothingness, directed at the behest of Drast. White as sin forgiven, the light repeatedly struck along the stretch of Zyem's back between his beating wings. The beast screeched in what may have been pain, but when the attack halted, Tyran saw no injury.

Erzebeth appeared between them in a flash of light. "I told you the stone keeps him from physical harm."

"You did not tell us anything!" Tyran cried.

"You can shut your two-faced hole, skin-switcher." Drast smirked despite his reddening cheeks and elevated tone. "Do you think I am blind to your poetic justice? We kill a god who turned into a dragon and then you have us killed by a dragon-god. Oh ho! But we will win this fight too! Go float about somewhere else and watch us escape your little trap."

Tyran watched Drast rush Zyem with a grin, hitting the dragon with another bolt of light for good measure, ignoring Erzebeth as she disappeared again. The rightmost head twisted to face Drast, opening to either deliver another round of fire breath or eat his brother whole. Drast did not slow his speed. At the final moment, as Zyem swooped to catch Drast in his teeth, Drast used Koldovstvo to leap between time and space, dipping beneath the coiling neck. The second head met him, whipping sideways and connecting with Drast, a blue shimmer of energy outlining his brother's form at the last moment.

Drast flipped head over heels backward through the open space as though he had been hit by a mountain.

Tyran tensed, his heart crushing against his chest, as

Drast disappeared from the scope of his vision. His instinct was to check on his brother, but Zyem could not be ignored. Using the same tactic as his brother, Tyran embraced the entropic magic of his bloodline, folding space and time, and quickly closing the distance to the leftmost head.

Even a taste of Koldovstvo would have warmed his bones, padding his veins with magical energy and stealing away the cold of the Netherworld, but the amount he embraced now was deafening. His ears buzzed and his eyes ached; the world appeared to vibrate around him as he hurdled at his enemy.

When Zyem finally roared, fire forming along the edge of his forked tongue, Tyran could have sworn time had stopped indefinitely. He spun to his right, the dragon fire harmlessly scorching the empty space. He drew back the arm with his mace and slammed the iron ball into Zyem's center head.

The scaled triangular head rocked backward, the white stone remaining fixed in the eyehole. Tyran screamed in agony, the magic-infused attack ripping his shoulder from its socket.

He awkwardly passed his mace to his shield hand, holding them together, and twisted his neck in time to see the third head rounding on him with fangs revealed.

He gritted his teeth and braced for impact as he writhed in pain.

Drast came seemingly from nowhere, lifting his hand from his ribcage and jerking Tyran's mace to his own hand with Koldovstvo. Quick as an arrow, he pummeled the weapon into the crown of the beast, interrupting its attack. Drast remained balanced, lifting his free hand toward the Alatir Stone. Tyran could see Drast's fingers quaking with energy as he tried to pull the gem to his hand. With horror, he watched the stone sink deeper into Zyem's socket.

"Why is it not working?" Tyran cried.

Erzebeth popped in front of them again. If she was

frustrated with them, she did not express it in the slightest. "I told you retrieving the stone with magic would be impossible."

"Shut your mouth," Drast snapped, lifting his finger at her. Drast then flung the mace back to Tyran, shouting his name.

He barely saw Zyem attacking in his periphery. He tried to dip slightly in the air but lost his hold on Koldovstvo. Roaring in desperation to stay afloat, his throat burned with the effort as the mace flew off into the empty space over his head.

In an eyelid's beat, Tyran released the shield, to hover around him with Koldovstvo and pulled the mace back to his left hand. With a roar that reminded him of his days on the battlefield against the Vucari, he lashed the mace in an upward arch striking the nearest head beneath the jaw.

Erzebeth materialized next to him, blocking his ability to see Drast, who dived from his perch to elude razor-lined jaws. "Kam is across the bridge and legions of demons are coming this way. You need to finish this."

"Finish what, exactly? Is Drast right?" He strained to see her expression. *"Do you really hate us so much you want to see us ripped apart? Gods know I have not fought more than hunger and exhaustion in a thousand years, and you dragged me down here to wrestle a dragon."*

"Get the stone," Erzebeth said.

Tyran scowled at the Vucari, dropping his mace into his belt loop and reeling back from Zyem, who bit at him with the intensity to shatter teeth. He looked for more words to say to Erzebeth, but she dispersed as the dragon lunged at Tyran through her incorporeal body. Tyran backed farther away and reached for the shield fixed in front of him, only to realize his dangling arm would not move.

Drast hit Zyem with another lightning bolt, pulling attention away from his brother.

Grumbling, Tyran lined himself up with his floating

shield and impelled it into his arm and chest. The sickening snap of his shoulder realigning filled his ears, spotting his vision.

His brother's voice cracked in what may have been a poor attempt at a battle cry as he spiraled down from Zyem, who twisted his own body to give chase, with all three necks reaching out to swallow Drast whole.

Tyran sped after them, seeing his opportunity to flank the dragon. He pushed ahead with Koldovstvo, dodging the large whipping tail and beating wings. Aligning himself with the center neck, he kept tight beside it, careful not to make contact and give his position away.

With a quick peek over his shoulder, he saw the Kalinov Bridge disappear behind him as they entered an abysmal cavern. Darkness met them in the depths, the light of the Netherworld behind them faded.

The Alatir Stone glowed a pale white in the heart of the dragon's eye. Tyran inched closer, reaching the curved horn on the dragon. In his peripheral vision, he saw the other adjacent head staring back at him with a glowing amber eye.

"Grab the stone, Tyran!" Drast shouted, twisting around in the air.

With a heavy breath, Tyran moved his shield behind him with Koldovstvo at the same time as he reached for the Alatir Stone. His right hand touched the spongy substance surrounding the white gem and dug into the soft flesh. Zyem screeched, swinging his other head at Tyran with the clear intent of smashing him between the beast's hardened scales. The dragon struck the suspended shield instead, which only drove Tyran's hand deeper into the socket.

He grabbed the shield with his left hand as though his meager strength might hold Zyem back from crushing his mortal body between the creature's two horned skulls.

As his fingers clung to the magical stone and yanked it from its pulpy bed, his entire frame from wrinkled toes to wrinkled brow bursting with an inner light. The power was unlike anything he had known before, churning through his veins like liquid courage. Any physical ailment, including weariness from age or battle, fled his senses like shadow from light. Where holding on to Koldovstvo took endless concentration before, he hardly considered it an effort now. The mace at his side was only as heavy as a feather, the shield as light as the wind.

Zyem thundered, stirring about in the air, snapping and screaming in a frenzy. Through the chaos, Drast emerged from the swallowing darkness, grabbing Tyran by the arm and pulling him to the light with their prize in hand.

"The rift is closing in on us!" Drast shouted over the defeated dragon.

"Hurry," Tyran said through his gritted teeth.

Drast's mouth hung open, his perpetual grin stretching the width of his face. "You spoke!"

Chapter IV

Drast groaned, his feet hitting the ground too hard before he fell to his knees, pain racing through his bones. Even as he sought to close his eyes and curl up on the jagged stone beneath him, the sound of heavy footfalls clattered small rocks about him.

Something is coming.

Erzebeth emerged in a greenish burst. "Your fight is not done. Demons approach. An army marches toward you."

She summoned them, no doubt.

Drast wheezed a laugh that shook his distended belly. "An elaborate plot to kill us."

The Kalinov Bridge vanished the moment he and Tyran cleared the shutting chasm, which had swallowed Zyem whole. The land rumbled, the pieces realigning to hide the Kalinov Bridge as though nothing had happened.

"We need to move," Tyran growled.

Drast closed his eyes for a moment, listening to the forgotten sound of his brother's voice. The low hum was familiar despite the raspiness of old age.

Tyran hovered over him, still flying, as though he were asserting the seriousness of their need to move, yet he said nothing of his abrupt ability to speak. Drast deliberated whether Tyran recognized the significance of this moment.

He sighed. Of course they had to keep moving. He did not want to be sitting here when Zyem burst back through the crust of the earth, but his body was not quite responding.

"Kam has gone to meet the demons to buy you time, but the Warden cannot face this foe alone." Erzebeth flitted to and fro.

The boy is a fool. He should have stayed near. What can he do alone?

"He shouldn't have run off." Drast groaned, turning his head one way and then the other to crack his neck. His eyelids were heavy, but he forced them back open again. Ahead of him, he studied the awaiting Netherworld with broken rocks and layered frost, mostly hidden by the bluish mist that clung to the landscape. Nothing about what he could see was inviting.

The sound of the approaching army grew louder with the clinking of armor and weapons pinging against the endless, irregular stamping.

The ground rattled beneath him, bespeaking of the scale of the approaching army. He had survived enough battles to know that armies who rattled grounds were poor conversationalists.

"Come on." Tyran landed softly, the sound of his boots swallowed by the din of a threatening battle ahead. Kam was hidden somewhere in the mist that filled the Netherworld, waiting for them to accompany him against the demons.

Drast sighed heavier than he intended, his lungs burning from the thin, icy air. "Remember I am older than you, brother. You need to give your elders a chance to recover."

You are lucky you're not dead.

"Tell me something I don't know." Drast paused, trying to catch his breath. "What makes you think so this time?"

No one on Aenar could cast that much magic. It is no wonder you exhausted yourself, slinging so many spells. We have our health to think about after all.

"Ah. Good to know." Drast bobbed his head. "Which

one gets rid of you?"

"What?" Tyran asked.

If you destroy me, you will destroy yourself.

"Tempting," Drast said, "but if I have to suffer you for another thousand years to keep breathing, I will."

"Are you alright?" Tyran asked.

Since he found his voice again, maybe you will find your arm?

"Maybe." Drast looked at the nub where the spectral arm had been moments before. He was too drained to keep the ghostly limb indefinitely. He addressed Tyran. "Tired is all. I don't remember Koldovstvo being so draining. How about you?"

"Surprisingly well," Tyran said.

Drast twisted to gaze at his younger brother in disbelief. Catching sight of the Alatir Stone made him pause in consideration. Tyran held the artifact firmly in his shield hand, the white gem barely fitting in the curve of his palm.

A slight glow outlined the stone, mirrored by a strange glowing aura surrounding Tyran. "The stone has taken the ache from my knees and back. I can almost feel my insides restitching themselves. It is like using Koldovstvo, but in reverse. It does not feel as rapid as channeling such magic, but it is working."

"The fight was not in vain, then." Drast smiled, pulling himself upright. His own knees popped from age, loud enough to give away his position if he were hiding.

Tyran reached out to help steady him. "Do you want to hold the stone for a while?"

Yes!

"No." Drast grunted, eyeing his brother's decrepit figure. Tyran's appearance was a hard thing to stomach with his sagging muscles and stringy hair. After all they had been through, he wanted to see his brother young again before himself. No small amount of guilt wormed its way through his mind for the things he had done at the behest of their father. He tore happiness from Tyran's grasp more times than fate itself. "You hold it a bit longer and regain some more of your strength. I will have my turn."

Tyran narrowed his gaze as though he wanted to say something, but the death cry of a demon rasped ahead and pulled Drast's attention. Tyran said, "We better go before we are blamed for another skin-switcher's death."

You could just let him die. No harm in that.

"You must go!" Erzebeth cried louder before zipping away toward the fight.

"Mm," Tyran rumbled. With a dip of his head, he thrust ahead of Drast with Koldovstvo, vanishing into the murkiness.

Drast followed, using magic to hurry himself along, attempting to ignore his fatigue. The shadows moving upon shadows against the obscure landscape were initially misleading and hard to make out. Though, at last, his breath caught when recognizing the armies of the dead scattered ahead of him without formation. He could not see the end of the ranks and hoped against hope the thick fog misled his senses.

Each demon stood twice as tall as Tyran or him, their skin glassed over and colored like snowfall, their blue-grey eyes glimmering. Each held some type of weapon—long axes, hulking maces, and double-edged swords—between their three fingers and thumb; they growled menacingly through pointed fangs. The front line already advanced forward, attacking the— Drast's jaw fell.

A hundred paces away, a hulking beast standing a head taller than himself, roared and barreled into the line of bulky demons. He recalled seeing a similar creature during the battle against the skin-switchers outside of Lairhein when he and Tyran commanded their own armies. His people had no name for the beast, only knowing it walked among the armies of the Vucari.

Disheveled hair covered the *thing* from its horned head to its massive hooves. Beady brown eyes sat behind the wide black snout. The monster was something between a bull and a man with the muscle of an ox.

"Kam?" Drast said in disbelief, finding no resemblance between the monstrosity and the scrawny boy who traveled alongside them. Yet the scattered robes and bags leading to the path of the Warden gave away his identity.

In shock, Drast watched the skin-switcher leap into the larger demons, biting down into the nearest demon's shoulder with bestial fangs. Black claws covered in demon-blood raked into his foe, tearing away chunks of flesh. The enemy swarmed in, the skin-switcher thrashing among the many, ripping at flesh and sinew.

No fear. He has courage, you have to give him that.

Erzebeth screeched near Drast's ear, giving no explanation from where she had come. "Fight the Bukavac, Red! Protect the Warden!"

Tyran reacted quicker than Drast, hovering feet above him, flinging flames from his aerial vantage point at the so-called Bukavac, careful to miss the skin-switcher in the mix. Fire rained down, burning the demons where they stood. The immediate roars dwindled to low hums.

"By the gods! There must be two hundred of them." Drast grinned nervously, reaching for Koldovstvo. The energy filled him, lifting him off his feet and taking the burden from his muscles and joints. With a wave of his good hand, he created a wind to throw several of the attacking Bukavac away from Kam before they could sink their enormous metal weapons into the Warden's skin. The demons tottered into their counterparts, knocking over handfuls. Tyran arched his flames toward the cluttered mess, igniting any in the midst.

"We have no reason to fight them," Tyran cried out, scorching the enemy. "We should pull Kam free and fly to Wolos."

Drast gave a mirthless smile, uncertain if he could keep the pace to outrun the demons.

Erzebeth replied in a hollow, distant voice, "The journey to Wolos is long. Either slaughter them here or have them follow us to the first *Grumadki*. They will not be the last of the hordes to stand between us, and the larger the horde, the stronger the fiends will be among their number."

"Thanks for the uplifting reminder," Drast said, scanning to see if anything more than Bukavac riled the ranks of the army. He saw nothing more. "Try lying to us!"

You are going to regret that request.

"What is the Grumadki?" Tyran shouted, while Drast followed his example with fire. The Bukavac roared in protest, having no way to contend with the endless magic.

"A crossroads, an entrance to a portal tearing through the fabric of time and space to further advance our position," she said. "To simply walk to Wolos's prison would take a hundred lifetimes or more."

That's a long time. But at least you would be walking instead of sitting in a prison.

"True." Drast nodded to himself.

"Drast," Tyran bellowed, redoubling his efforts against the Bukavac. The demons beneath were swarming from either side, encircling Kam. The Warden roared in his bestial form as a blade sliced him above the left knee. "Watch the skies, and I will protect the skin-switcher."

"The skies?" Drast flickered an eyelid. He was unaware a new legion had arrived.

The encroaching shadow could have blotted out the sun, if a sun existed in this forsaken land. He looked up beyond the ghostly skin-switcher to the heavens, where an unearthly sound emitted.

"Nithhoggr." Erzebeth named the fiends orbiting above them. The creatures screeched over and over again, echoing one another. Erzebeth did not wait for the din to subside, saying, "They fed on the roots of the Ash Tree before it was cut away. Now they hunger for anything."

I am a bit peckish myself.

"Enough with the history lessons, skin-switcher!" Drast slung a bolt of lightning at the nearest Nithhoggr, the energy blast ricocheted from its scaled body. The demon spiraled in the air, seemingly unscathed, and dived at him. Drast stepped back with surprise, noticing the creature carried a sickle in either of its humanoid arms.

Without having time to cast another spell, Drast sprang out of the way in the nick of time, the curved blade missing him by a hair.

Too close. Don't kill us.

The Nithhoggr returned to the sky as a second swooped down to attack. The eyeless demon paused for only a moment, swaying in the air as a circular frill quivered like a bowstring around its neck. The taut skin barely stopped before the Nithhoggr charged. Drast flung fire at the beast to no avail, finally propelling himself from the line of attack with Koldovstvo.

Erzebeth appeared from nowhere, speaking dully in his ear. "They are immune to the elements."

Drast blew air from his nostrils, ensuring his bow was secured over his right shoulder. "Lucky for you we are dragon-men."

Two more Nithhoggr came at him. The first swung a sickle at his midsection. Drast twisted, dodging the blade, only to be hit by the underside of the thrashing, barbed tail of the second. He toppled to the side, falling slightly as his concentration was interrupted, and hurried to steady himself again with Koldovstvo. He glanced to his leg for injury and found none. Another few inches and the bone spikes would have been buried in his leg.

Be a dragon-man already.

Before he could act, the first Nithhoggr charged directly from overhead with its arms pulled back, fibrous wings tucked, and bristle-like teeth bared.

Using Koldovstvo, Drast pulled himself through space and time, springing himself from the path of the deadly jaws.

Several more of the flying demons screeched nearer to the clouds, needlessly reminding him of his odds. The several attacking Nithhoggr were circling back.

Any day now.

Drast gritted his teeth. Ignoring the cries of battle beneath him and the orange glow of Tyran's magic burning a path through the Bukavac army, he filled his being with the magic of the void. The cosmos seen at the nexus of Thrice Nine Lands filled his vision as he touched the gap between time and space.

Light blistered through the first Nithhoggr's scaled flesh, tearing the muscle and skin from the demon. Blood splattered, drenching the horde army beneath. The wings fell limp, enfolding the arms and serpent tail, the carcass plummeting to the Netherworld below. As the finite frame of the demon fell away, the blackened soul of the creature ripped from the skin, crying mercilessly at Drast in a hoarse whisper meant only for those already pervaded with decay. The black wraith twisted, a silhouette against the purplish sky, reaching for him with shadowed claws.

Should have seen that coming.

"Stop talking to me!" Drast snapped. "I have enough trouble concentrating without your incessant chattering."

Terror stabbed at his heart, hearing the other Nithhoggr crying for his blood. In desperation, he struck at the approaching ethereal beast with Koldovstvo once more.

His magic dissipated into nothingness.

Erzebeth suddenly shielded Drast from the wraith, an ear-splitting scream pouring from her gullet. "Be gone!" Her green light brightened, piercing through the Nithhoggr's spiritual essence and blinding Drast.

Drast's focus slipped, causing him to fall several feet before regaining control.

"Listen to me. You cannot defeat them alone." The undead Vucari did not give him time to think. "You must use magic from the void. Flame and stone, sky and sea—

these things cannot avail you. Tear them all apart in spirit, Red! I will do the rest.”

Don't listen to her.

“Shut up!” Drast snarled.

“I will not!” Erzebeth cried, her glow swelling again.

“I wasn't talking to you!”

Taking heed of her advice, he reached into the void to find the essence of the next Nithhoggr, tearing it apart. The demon shrieked and dispersed into nothingness. With a cackling laugh, Drast duplicated his feat, reaching out with a dozen tendrils to do the same.

The battle raged as Drast and Erzebeth ripped the Nithhoggr to pieces, both materially and spiritually. One after another, a dozen or more of the snake-like demons emptied from the clouds. Drast evaded the sickle blades and spiked tails until his body ached in equal measure as his skull, a pounding headache stretching to the base of his neck.

When the Nithhoggr stopped coming, Drast joined Tyran beneath him, still waging war against the Bukavac. The young Warden, despite his visible exhaustion, continued to fight them, tearing into every demon that approached. Blood seeped from the wound on the Warden's leg, leaving him slowed in the battle, but not completely useless. When the last demon finally dropped, bones decorated piles of blackened ash alongside small hills of tangled, bloodied bodies.

Drast coughed, grabbing at his chest and falling to his haunches. “On the bright side, if we do not bring Wolos back from the dead, we could stay and clear out all these demons for the centuries to come. How many could there possibly be?”

How many people live and die in a thousand years?

“I promise, you have barely scratched the surface of the darkness in the Netherworld,” Erzebeth said. “Wolos must be reborn.”

“Wolos? We came to give rise to Wolos?” Tyran grunted

in awe, joining Drast where he sat. "Someone should have told me."

Drast blinked confusedly at his brother but did not have the energy to respond. His eyes fell to the Warden.

Kam crumpled to a knee behind them, groaning as the bestial form shredded away. His inner skeleton fractured and popped, realigning itself with the human form. The gristly hair fell away from the exposed flesh, the fangs retracted, and the face readjusted to that of a young boy.

When finished, Kam tried to stand slowly, running a hand along his pale cheek and across his shaved scalp. The wound on his leg caused him to kneel again, eliciting a groan from his thin lips. The Warden's brown eyes began searching for the grey robes about the time Drast recognized something missing from between the boy's legs and the trifling breasts pointing in his direction.

"By the gods, the boy has tits, Tyran!" Drast grabbed at his brother's cloak, ignoring the gash on the leg and instead, staring at the nakedness of the Warden with absolute fascination. Kam was not a boy, but a young woman! "Small tits, but tits nonetheless."

Chapter V

"I am ready to carry the stone," Drast said, reaching eagerly for Tyran.

Tyran ducked around Drast's extended fingers, stumbling over to the Warden's gear. While Kam awkwardly wrapped her robes around her pale skin and tied the belt around her waist, he rushed to hoist her bags over his shoulder. The weight nearly took him to the ground. He rumbled in his throat, straining to keep his knees straight while continuing to hold his focus on his shield, which magically hovered in the air.

Drast followed him, persistent with his request. "This old body needs rejuvenation."

"You are not sleeping with her," Tyran bluntly said, turning around to his brother. His throat ached with the effort of speaking the few words after so many centuries, the splendor of his voice gone while the Alatir Stone repaired it.

"What? Of course not! Her tits are too small." Drast winced, withdrawing his hands. "If you are going to start spouting nonsense, you can go back to holding your tongue. By the gods, I have survived this long with only the sound of your grunting. I can last another thousand years."

"I do not know what you are talking about. I have never stopped speaking to you," Tyran said.

Drast looked over his shoulder at nothing. "Maybe my ears were broken all this time instead of his voice?" He chuckled, shoulders shaking. "Well, that is true. I never stopped hearing you, but who can say if you are real at all?"

"Who are you talking to?" Tyran grumbled.

"Look what you did now!" Drast said, covering his mouth with his hand as though he were sharing a secret with someone other than Tyran.

He was not sure what happened to Drast, but Tyran knew he was the one who had been ignored these past many years and not the other way around. Certainly, old age had done Tyran's memory no good—already the battle a few moments ago was fading like a dream—but it stood to reason that Drast's mind also suffered from some sort of internal rot.

He stifled a groan as the weight of the bags rested on his shoulders. As he stood erect, he realized Kam was staring at Tyran and then at Drast, her mouth falling open in shock.

"He is not getting the stone, and he won't rape you," Tyran tried to assure her.

"Why in the Nine Lands would you say something like that?" Drast huffed, blowing air from between his lips. The act looked like a desperate attempt not to smile any longer.

Tyran gritted his teeth. He was sure Drast's thoughts mirrored his own when seeing Kam's naked body. No doubt, he feigned innocence, and the lengthy explanation that flew off Drast's tongue did not convince Tyran otherwise.

"Listen, I am exhausted from battle, and I wanted to see what the fuss was about with this stone. The last thing I want is to have a run at some *child* out here in the forsaken cold. Have I not warned you often enough about sleeping with skin-switchers?" Drast made a point of shooting daggers at Erzebeth with his eyes, lifting his eyebrows before ending with the biting remark.

Tyran trailed the sharp look, feeling the pang of guilt in

his stomach, though the long-dead Vucari gave no visible reaction. In fact, she hardly paid him any attention.

Drast went on, "By the gods, I would not betray my own advice."

"You might if it suited you," Tyran said when Drast stopped talking. His skin heated. His thoughts raced, admitting to himself, *We both might.*

"That is a boldface lie." Drast ran his fingers through his stringy beard before balling his hand into a fist. He laughed out loud. "I *would* if it suited me. Irrefutably...but it does not suit me. She is a *child*."

Tyran cleared his throat, forcing his jaw to move with his words. "Kam needs the Alatir Stone until her leg heals."

"What?" Kam blurted. She limped forward. "I do not need the stone. Give me my bags. You two are, without a doubt, in far worse condition."

Drast spoke over Kam, ignoring her, the sharpness fading from his eyes. "Why should we care if she bleeds out? My ribs are broken! Are we not the ones who Erzebeth brought to pull Wolos from his grave? The small-breasted tart is the liability here. Ah, look at her! She could not have expected to survive down here."

Tyran scratched his head, faintly remembering why he was in the Netherworld with the Vucari and his brother.

Kam flared her nostrils and stared at the ice-covered ground. Tyran never had the impression she was one to back down from a fight. Something more troubled her.

The pulsating vein in her neck caught his eye. Tyran was not stupid, but he did not know Kam well enough to guess at what upset her. He knew she was Vucari. He knew she was a Warden. And the only other Vucari Warden he had crossed was Erzebeth, who never hesitated to make herself heard, unless duty kept her from it. Kam was surely as strong as Erzebeth, or she would not have been sent to accompany them. If Kam wanted to speak her mind, he doubted there was anything he or Drast could say to stop her.

In the end, whatever thought suddenly riled the Warden was her own to sort out. Just like he and Drast had to sort out their own problems; protected by those who were once their enemies, accompanied by those who were once their captors. And now Kam—man or woman—endangered their quest simply by existing.

Drast was right. Kam was a liability. He did not want to lead another to their death, but the cards were dealt. So whether she hated his and Drast's lack of empathy for her plight as Warden or their shortsighted opinion of her as a woman, he hardly cared.

What he did care about was Drast's words, which he mulled over in his head.

They came to resurrect Wolos. They came to the Netherworld to right their wrongs, to see their duty done so they might die. He was not here to change and, without a doubt, his brother was not either. He did not know when they had talked about the purpose of their journey—or if this was even the first time—but this was significant. He did not want to forget.

Drast interpreted his silence, or maybe he had been talking all the while and Tyran only now chose to listen. "We should save her the trouble and kill her now, and keep the Alatir Stone. She made the choice to come here, knowing who we are—what we are. Nine Lands, we told her to stay behind."

Tyran gripped the Alatir Stone in his hand, his words oozing through his lips with great effort. "We are not killing her."

"I am standing right here," Kam said.

"She will not spread her legs for you any more than me, Tyran. Your love for women will only lead to our suffering," Drast said with a snort. Tyran shuffled a step, considering hitting Drast, but he did not have the energy. Drast went on, "I do not know what made her think a two-legged ox could battle demons and walk away unscathed."

"It is called a *bies*, and it is a blessing to my bloodline, gifted by Wolos," Kam said. "And you would do well to keep your thoughts away from what is betwixt my legs, because if I find you between them, the bies is the last thing you will ever see."

"I am glad you have a name for it. Does not change the fact that you are hurt," Drast muttered, and then came nose to nose with Tyran. He clutched the broken ribs at his side, meeting Tyran's eyes, mocking the Warden. He looked over his shoulder at nothing, and then chuckled. "Fine. If we are not going to kill her, let her carry her injuries like any *mighty* fighter would. You and I need our strength if we are going to reach Wolos."

"She is our charge now. I will not see her die when we hold the means to her survival in our hand," Tyran said.

"Do not grunt at me, brother."

Tyran angled his brow, realizing the words had caught in his throat. Maybe there was some truth to what Drast said of his inability to speak. "She is our charge," he rasped.

"Our charge?" Drast laughed, spinning around on his heel, hands fanning out at his sides. His wild eyes drifted to Erzebeth, who hung back in silence. "Like coming to the Netherworld to raise Wolos was our *charge?* We have done many terrible things. We wrought hell on the world and any who crossed our path, but the burden does not fall solely on our shoulders."

"No, it does not," Tyran mumbled. *"Yet we are the only ones left to lessen its weight."* He pointed to Kam. *"And she is helping us see it through willingly."*

Drast rocked his head, missing Tyran's gesture entirely as he continued to glare at Erzebeth. Rolling his eyes, he spun back around. "I am here for you, brother," Drast said, "but I am only here for you. We cannot make every obstacle in this journey our onus. You and I look like an old man's shriveled bits on a wintry morning. We need the Alatir Stone or we will die—"

"We should already be dead!" Tyran bellowed. His lips quivered with the reverberation of words bounding from his gullet.

Drast rocked back with a hum, shaking his finger at Tyran in appreciation. "You—you sound like Father when you are angry. Hear me, though, when I tell you that I would have preferred we died at Anaerfell than face whatever hellish fate exists here." Drast smiled. "I am here because *you* are here! By the gods, we cannot do this if every problem becomes our problem."

"I am not your—" Kam cried out only to be cut off.

"Shut up!" Drast and Tyran said together, neither drifting their eyes from the other.

Tyran's next words were swift, although his voice was strained once more. "We are bringing our enemy back to life. We will undo what we have done."

"If you say so, brother." Drast grinned, his cheek muscles tightening beneath his white beard. He tilted his head, nodding to himself again. "You are right. This place definitely has more promise than being chained at Anaerfell, but I would expect you to give a convincing argument," Drast paused. Tyran was not sure if he was speaking to him anymore, and then his older brother added, "Alright. Give her the stone, but we are resting here for a few hours. I can hardly breathe."

"No," Erzebeth finally said from behind. "We need to keep moving. Enough time has been wasted and Wolos is waiting."

Drast tittered with amusement, dropping to the ground and crossing his legs. "If you were worried about saving time, you should not have brought two old farts. To remain compliant, we need certain things. Warm milk, our drawers changed regularly, and frequent naps…" He groaned, lying his head back on the ground and closing his eyes.

Ignoring the Vucari, both living and dead, Tyran followed Drast's lead and soon fell asleep.

Tyran could not say if they slept a couple of hours or a full night. From what he could see, the soft hue of purple and blue meshing between the ground fog and the clouded sky did not change. Upon waking, the three of them ate a bit of food from the packs and set out behind Erzebeth.

As they walked, Tyran savored the taste of dried meat and sugared bread on his tongue. The flavor was nearly overwhelming. He could not remember when he last tasted seasoned food. He feared it would make him sick, but he managed to walk on and on without vomiting. And soon enough, his stomach began to rumble, begging for more.

Tyran could not track the time while they walked any more than he could while they had been sleeping. His thoughts were disorganized. He could not pinpoint when he forgot his purpose in this frozen wasteland, and while he asked several times for someone to remind him, no one answered. He eventually decided to simply keep up as best he could and listen for whatever tidbits might give him some idea of why he was traipsing through the cold with his weapons. While his brother chatted almost constantly to some unseen being, Drast rarely spoke to the Warden, and Erzebeth said absolutely nothing.

Tyran was left in dismay, trying to hold Kam upright with his weakened muscles, his shield held up with magic.

Several times his steel guard would drop, clattering to the ice before he lifted it again with Koldovstvo. All the while, Kam hobbled along, her arm wrapped over his neck, clutching the Alatir Stone in her other hand. The white light outlining her lithe body marked the power of the stone working its magic. Occasionally she would moan and jerk as though a needle suddenly punctured her leg to attach one piece of loose skin to another.

He cringed as her voice pitched in pain, fingers digging into his neck. He steadied himself, his old legs threatening to collapse under him. When her whine lessened, he spoke to her. His words came out harsher than he intended. *"Why are we here? Why did Erzebeth have you come with us? Why would she not send someone stronger, someone who knows war?"*

She clung to him a bit tighter, forcing him to hold her upright, but gave him no response. He scowled as she hung from his neck.

He tried again, articulating his words to perfection. *"How long have you been caring for us? Six months? A year?"* He knew he had not spoken as much as Drast while they were imprisoned; such a feat would have been impossible. He hazily recalled hearing his weakened voice but, once more, he heard the commanding tone of his tenor. And the skin-switcher outwardly ignored him.

He had a mind to throw her little body to the ground.

Drast took the mantle, his tone clipped when speaking to the Warden. He could not blame his brother's slight annoyance, no matter his grin. He carried all the bags like a pack mule several feet away. He surely lightened the load with Koldovstvo, but his own grunts did more than hint at his aggravation. "Tyran and I watched your predecessor keel over before you came to Anaerfell, but certainly there was another skin-switcher who could have accompanied us. Someone from a village, perhaps? An adult? Without tits? Who could carry a sword?"

Tyran felt Kam tense her arm over him, refusing to look over her shoulder at Drast. "I may be young, but I am the only one to help you. There is no *village*. The Vucari as you knew them in your lifetime are only stories in mine."

"What do you mean?" Drast replied.

"When you slaughtered Wolos, you destroyed the Vucari civilization," she said. "The Ghan, the Khagan, and the other nobles who reigned over the landless built their laws around Wolos. Without a god to encourage—"

"Fear," Tyran interrupted. He had never known much about the inner workings of the Vucari society, but the tale Kam told seemed straightforward enough. *"Your nobles used a god to force their own people into servitude."*

"—order, everything collapsed," Kam went on, gasping again as the Alatir Stone mended her leg. She stumbled over her words, wincing in pain. "The landless rejected authority and lost hope. My people lost their purpose."

Tyran peered down at Kam's shaved scalp leaning against his shoulder. Her bloodline was clearly from the side of nobility for her to believe such nonsense. He was not ignorant to the power of fear over the masses; his father taught him well, and he had been a scholar in the subject.

"My ancestors were the first to take an excursion to Anaerfell and find the remains of Wolos, which in turn led to finding you and your brother chained under the watch of Erzebeth," Kam said. "While the rest of our people murdered each other or fled for the mainland to find the Ash Tree, my family tended to you."

"Why?" Drast grinned, nodding his head as though an answer were already being provided. "Why would you waste your time on two dragon-men?"

"Because she told us to," Kam replied.

"What a weak, ignorant fool," Tyran said. *"Erzebeth stayed at Anaerfell for less than a year and never returned. She left us to rot while condemning your family to eternal servitude."*

Drast cackled. "Sounds like something a stupid skin-switcher would do. Your ancestors blindly listened to her," he pointed at Erzebeth, "and you simply accepted the drivel passed down over generations?"

"Wolos may have been dead, but our charge had not changed," Kam snapped. "If it were not for my lineage, you would have been twisted by Marheena's death magic a long time ago. Are you not grateful?"

"No." Drast smirked.

Tyran looked at his decrepit skin and the frozen wasteland encircling them. *"I would rather be dead,"* he agreed.

"Then why are you here?" Kam gritted her teeth.

"My silent brother has an inescapable devotion to duty," Drast said, wriggling his white eyebrows, "and women." He dipped his head to Erzebeth. "I cannot deny his insatiable appetite for either."

Tyran felt his thin lips quaking with frustration, realizing he may not have been speaking again. No matter. He did not see the need to explain the importance of duty. The word hung in his mind like an ominous threat, which he feared to forget or ignore.

Kam refocused on the unmarked path ahead. "Seems we have something in common, then."

"I know. I know," Drast said emptily, looking off into the distance. He touched his bearded chin to his chest, causing extra wrinkles to sprout from his neck and face. His smile never waned. "You still have not explained why you were the one to come."

Kam hoisted herself up again. He strained under her weight, her words coming in between heavy breaths. "Only a handful of Wardens remain in the north. An elder impregnated me with a son to continue the line when I was thirteen. I birthed him three months before I took my place at Anaerfell, when the Warden before me died. I should have had another two years to seed children before taking my post, but time was not given." She grimaced, gripping his shoulder again for support. "Now, all that remain of the Wardens are children. The elders told me what they knew, and now I am the eldest."

Tyran ground the few teeth in his mouth and looked away. His mind wandered at the thought of the ancient civilization being run by children. He wondered what remained of his own people, the Stuhia, and whether they had fallen to ruin, too. He knew little about what happened after he left seeking Wolos in the north, save what Drast shared after reuniting. Their father was overrun by rebels, led by Maelili Kluk, and the power his family held in Lairhein was stripped.

By and by, the scene of carnage disappeared behind them as they trekked forward into the endless desolate terrain. Erzebeth floated along ahead of them, her thin green figure shimmering in the strange fog. Four separate times, they came across groups of Bukavac tramping along, from which Erzebeth directed them away without incident.

"The demons are drawn by Koldovstvo," Erzebeth explained while they walked. "The magic was gifted to the Stuhia from Marheena, and this is her world. The more you cast the magic here, the brighter the beacon becomes for the demons."

"The backstabbing skin-switcher speaks at last, sharing her incredible insights. Let us have a moment of silence for this momentous occasion." Drast cleared his throat, giving time for Erzebeth to snap back, but she said nothing. Tyran watched his brother adjust the bags before poking at the ghost again. "If I hear you correctly, you want me to struggle under the weight of these bags? Your little dragon scheme did not work in your favor, and now you hope to weaken us further before the next battle. Already we have given the precious stone to your inbred spawn, remaining weak and disastrously unattractive." Drast chuckled, looking at his wrinkled hands gripping the bags. "I assure you, we will not make it more than ten paces if I am not using Koldovstvo to play the role of pack mule. Unless the girl is capable of carrying her own gear again."

"I suspect whatever little energy is trickling through you is not enough to pinpoint our location," Erzebeth assured him, unruffled by his tone, "but if either of you were to display your power as you had with Zyem, we would surely not make it to the first Grumadki. Unless it is otherwise necessary, keep your feet on the ground and exercise restraint with your magic."

"I think she is a lying two-bit whore, Tyran. I do not think she can stop her tongue from fluttering in her mouth like one of her god's three-headed serpents," Drast said, clicking his tongue on the roof of his mouth. He revealed the remaining teeth in his mouth, intensely watching Erzebeth.

When she did not respond, he said, "I do not hear any argument."

"She is but a splinter of what she once was," Kam said, shuffling alongside Tyran. "You are not going to rile her up with your petty insults. She only cares about the journey ahead and seeing you fulfill your part."

"Who said anything about riling her up?" Drast sniggered with delight. "If she wishes to be an anvil, I will be the hammer. I am an expert at hammering. Right, Tyran?"

Tyran fluttered his eyes at the sound of his name. He may have been listening to their conversation, or he may have been sleeping and walking at the same time. He was not entirely sure, but Drast's wide eyes suggested he expected a clear response. Tyran had none to give.

As expected, Drast did not keep his mouth shut long enough for anyone to say anything. He turned his attention right back to Erzebeth. "Any other rules about which we should be aware? Or better yet, explain to us where we are going exactly. What is this Grumadki and where does it lead?"

Erzebeth answered like she was reading from the least interesting book ever written. "In the common tongue, the Grumadki is a shadow gate leading into an unhallowed place between space and time. The beings lurking there are darker and more dangerous than anything you will come across in the Netherworld." Erzebeth twisted around in the air to make eye contact with the brothers, all the while floating along backwards. "I wish I could tell you that a living being has survived the eternal madness and gloom of the shadow world, but the truth is no living being has ever entered a Grumadki."

"*So why are we?*" Tyran asked.

"Proof again that you are trying to kill us," Drast said.

Erzebeth said, "Wolos is held in the prison called *Heshayol*, beyond the *Tower of Eresh*, which are both leagues from where we stand." Tyran slipped against the frozen ground, nearly falling with Kam. He repeated the name of their destination in his head: *Heshayol.* Sounded like the least pleasant place in Thrice Nine Lands. Erzebeth pointed off into the distance. "Traveling the thousands of leagues between here and there would take us lifetime upon lifetime, and while time itself may not kill either of you while in the Netherworld, it will eat away at the rest of the world."

"The old-dark are keen on escaping their own prison in the Ash Tree," Kam added direly, "and once the old gods free themselves, they will destroy every living creature. Everything crafted in the world we know was not made by them. They hate it."

Tyran learned his religion from his father, spending hours at the desk reading and copying the ancient texts. He knew well enough that the modern world was built by the twelve gods of the pantheon. Each was said to have had a hand in its creation, while mortals gave some more regard than others. While exploring the nature of the Likhyi or even the gods may be interesting, he was more concerned with the immediate danger.

Drast seemed to have a similar thought. "Breaking free from the Ash Tree cannot be an easy task, even for the old-dark."

"No," Erzebeth agreed. "Already a means to be freed was roused and squelched. For now, the gods have given us the chance to change our fates by our own hand. However, without a doubt, another means to free the old-dark is underway, which is why we must be swift. One way or another, the balance you two offset must be restored. Therefore, journeying through the Grumadki is necessary, lest Aenar fall to dust waiting on you."

Erzebeth's words hung on the fog for the next several miles while they traipsed over the ice. Eventually they faded from Tyran's memory and he became caught up with viewing the rocks sticking at jagged angles through the crust of the earth, splintering in all directions. The difficult trek was to become more arduous.

Tyran noticed Drast steal a glance or two in his direction, as though he were checking on his well-being, but he said nothing. Tyran had a hard time looking at Drast, knowing his brother was but a reflection of Tyran's own frailty. His older brother did not look as though he should be capable of walking on his two spindly legs, and doing anything with his bruised, scrawny arms was a miracle. Despite his eccentric grin that was emboldened by his maddening years being imprisoned, Drast could be mistaken for one of the dead. Actually, the demons were likely in better condition than either of them.

Kam tugged at Tyran. "My leg has healed, Red. I can walk well enough on my own. Time for your brother to carry the stone for a while."

Tyran wanted to smile at the thought, glad to give Drast an opportunity to feel the Alatir Stone churn through his broken body.

He unhooked Kam's arm while she addressed Drast. "I suspect there is a great difference between a gash on my leg mending and you regaining a thousand years of life. Do not expect your youth to rush back at a moment's breath."

Drast dropped the bags with an exasperated sigh, specifically eyeing Kam's pack as though he expected her to immediately pick it up. "I was keen enough to recognize Tyran barely lost a wrinkle in the time he held the stone," Drast said wryly. "From all I know, this *trinket* is nothing more than a fancy rock."

Kam approached Drast, the cold air measured by the thick pattern of her breath fleeing from her lips. She held the Alatir Stone out to him. "Enjoy carrying your *fancy rock*, then."

"I am already giddy with—" As Drast removed it from her hand delicately, the words were stolen from him. He inhaled sharply as the glowing light burst from his mouth and eyes, outlining his body. "Nine Lands!"

Chapter VI

Dagmar is to blame, you know. None of this—madness—would have occurred if it were not for him.

"This is Father's fault, you know?" Drast reiterated, staring at Tyran across the fire burning between them. He leaned forward to feel the warmth, holding the Alatir Stone in his left palm, running his thumb along the smooth curvature of the gem. A shiver ran up his spine. The mystical artifact made him feel weightless. Whole.

Tyran squinted at Kam, who slept soundly between them, before refocusing his attention on Drast. The price of using Koldovstvo altered in the Netherworld, from stealing their life to draining their mental acuity. Or perhaps it had always done so, though no one had ever channeled so much as they had without dying from it. Then again, they were both quite old, so it was difficult to determine how much mental fatigue was due to age and how much was due to wielding Koldovstvo.

Drast was exhausted from battling Zyem and the Bukavac, but after being chained to a wall for over a thousand years, lying down to rest was farthest from his mind. His younger brother seemed equally disinclined, staring back at him with droopy eyes. Hours ago, Erzebeth disappeared, promising to return before they set off again.

He guessed she scouted ahead, but honestly cared little to know for certain.

You should care. You know she is the one who sent the army after you when you arrived. She is going to kill you here. It is all an elaborate plot.

Drast did not respond. He did not have time to get into it with the voice of Wolos. He finally had the chance to speak with Tyran without the ghostly skin-switcher eavesdropping, and he would not miss the chance.

"This is Father's fault," Drast repeated, hoping to entice Tyran to respond.

Tyran kept his mouth closed, working a chunk of bread around in his mouth. Drast patiently waited. During the past several days, the stone in his hand had restored some strength, but it did nothing to mend severed limbs or return lost teeth. As a result, when they ate, the effort was still a chore. However, he suspected they would not have to worry about eating for much longer. From his calculation, they only had enough food to last a week and nothing in the Netherworld was edible.

Whenever the Warden came to this realization, he would be ready to give her a piece of his mind. They would be starving soon enough.

Tyran scratched at his white beard, lightened only slightly from his time with the Alatir Stone; his beard now matched the thin strands dangling over his ears. Drast may have looked far worse than his brother, but he wanted to talk to Tyran.

This sudden thought reminded Drast how silence clung to Tyran when he did not hold the stone. He fumbled with the artifact and handed it over.

Tyran took the stone and finally spoke. "Placing blame on Father will not help us now."

Better than blaming yourselves.

"It may not change our situation," Drast said, "but it might lessen the toll on our minds. I see you beating yourself up. We were young when we defeated Wolos. We were following the will of our father.”

He had not seen his father since being imprisoned. He hated to admit that he tried to find him in Klukas after regaining consciousness following the battle against Wolos, but they were imprisoned and alone. They had done their father’s bidding, and Drast hoped they would be rescued. Klukas was unknown to most mortals, but the veiled world was a place any Stuhia could travel to while in their astral form, regardless of being bound under the Znaki symbol. Besides sneaking around unaware, the Stuhia could pinpoint any living being’s location through Klukas if they knew the individual personally. Yet his father had somehow been hidden from him. Of course, Erzebeth said Dagmar was dead now, which Drast believed; but his father must have done something to hide his existence for the years prior to his death. Likely more secrets hidden in the Varkolak.

Drast shivered and turned to look over his shoulder, almost expecting the demonic shape of his undead father to appear behind him. The fact that his father roamed the Netherworld terrified him. He would prefer never to see Dagmar again.

“Do not make excuses for us,” Tyran whispered after a while, as though he did not want to disrupt the flames dancing in front of them. Drast scooted closer to the heat, trying to remember what he had said to prompt such a response. He knew he’d said something about being young and doing what Dagmar commanded. Fortunately, Tyran clarified himself. “Many sons deny their fathers. They choose to lead their own lives without being obligated to bend the knee at their parent’s whim. And none who are young go so far as to slaughter a god. We were arrogant. Ignorant.”

Drast dipped his head at the blunt accusation, looking at his knuckles. Light red hair prickled up his hand and forearm. He may have taken too long a turn with the Alatir Stone. He was glad to have handed it back to Tyran.

His brother winced, clutching the white gem in his thick fist. The pale healing light illuminated his frame and brightened his eyes.

Drast scanned the desolate world around them. The sky continued to emit the purplish light, the fog never lifted, and the horizon was perpetually nonexistent. "I am not certain we have gained any wisdom in our old age," Drast said.

Tyran raised his eyebrows in surprise and then swiftly relaxed his face. "We are doing the right thing by being here, Drast. We are doing something noble."

"This is not noble. Noble is doing something good for the sake of good. This," he swung out his hand to the desolate, icy landscape, "is us taking a stab at redemption in hopes we do not become the demons we slaughter. We are not good guys, Tyran."

Decidedly not.

"You do not think we can change?" Tyran asked.

"What makes a man the man he becomes? What makes him become a different man?" Drast shrugged, tucking his nonexistent severed arm to his stomach. Even when he did not have the spectral arm, he could feel his fingertips. "I do not know the answers to these questions. Maybe some men can change. I think you might be able to change," his eyes drifted to Kam, "with the right prodding, under the right circumstances."

"We can become better men," Tyran pressed.

Drast hummed, his mind whirling with negativity. "Being a better man today does not erase what evil we wrought yesterday. We cannot evade consequence with a pretty smile and a kind gesture."

Tyran suddenly laughed, catching Drast off guard. "Why not? It has worked for you most of your life."

Drast was slow to return the smile. "True as that may be, my judgment has always been held in the hands of mortals, not under the watchful eye of the gods. I cannot outwit my fate."

"Mm. You are talking about Erzebeth's promise of us making it to Thrice Ten Kingdom? You think she is lying?"

Does a skin-switcher shit in the woods?

"I don't see why she wouldn't," Drast said, snickering, rocking back and forth. After a moment, and wiping a tear from his eye, he continued. "I have no reason to believe the gods would give a skin-switcher the authority to change our doom. You said it yourself, 'no one has ever killed a god.' No way the gods allow us into Thrice Ten Kingdom."

"Why did you come, then?" Tyran asked.

"It seemed the only way out of the prison." Drast shrugged. "I mean, we could have waited around to see if another ghost, maybe one of your former lovers, popped by to let us free, but the likelihood of that seemed to be, say, another thousand years or so in the making."

Tyran stared at him blankly.

He isn't buying it.

Haunting memories, ones he hoped time would help him forget, washed over Drast. The years since he and Tyran tramped through Valarun, heading to Anaerfell to slaughter Wolos, should have been forgotten. Yet the feelings still boiled his blood. He remembered leaving his father's side in Lairhein to find Tyran, who buried himself in a cave with their enemy. Erzebeth, the two-tongued Vucari, managed to discover Tyran's weakness for women and then seduced his mind with her vileness. At the time, Drast had no choice but to save his brother—though he was certain Tyran would see it as betrayal—using his own men against him. Only a few soft-spoken words allowed him to turn Tyran's generals against Erzebeth. While they failed to kill the Vucari, he was successful in setting Tyran and her at odds.

Erzebeth believed Tyran ordered the generals to end her life, which subsequently may have resulted in her imprisoning them. The punishment, no matter the guilt, was worth the alternative. He saved Tyran from Erzebeth.

Drast smiled, turning his gaze to the fire. "I couldn't

remember the last time you had spoken, or even looked up from that spot on the ground you were trying to bore through with your eyes. You needed out. For the first time in centuries, you looked awake."

"Do not do that." Tyran tensed. "Do not put your life on knife's edge because of me."

It is your duty, one of the few you haven't neglected over the years, to be an elder brother.

"You always used to talk about duty, but duty is something I have failed at." Drast rubbed the balding spot on his scalp. "No. If I die down here, I will have done it doing what I should have spent my life doing instead of following the whims of our father. Your responsibility—your duty—to me and to father is over and done with." He fixed his gaze on his brother. "Understood?"

"Mm."

"I consider that grunt the most sacred of oaths." Drast sighed, reaching for his bow lying next to him. "I think we have been in one place long enough. Probably time to keep moving. That way, right?"

Tyran looked over his shoulder, following Drast's gestured nod. "That is the way we have been going, if that is what you mean. Considering we have not changed direction in several days, we should be good." He reached for Kam, lightly shaking her shoulder to wake her. "Regardless, Erzebeth does not seem to have a problem finding us."

Kam stirred and sat up from the bedroll beside them, rubbing the sleep from her eyes. "Erzebeth has returned already?"

"No," Drast answered. "She can catch up."

The Warden nodded her head wearily, blinking several times in attempt to regain her senses. She slipped from under her blanket, adjusted her robes, and began to pack her belongings. Tyran used Koldovstvo to crush the fire he'd started hours ago.

Minutes later, the three of them were trudging over the

uneven ground, slipping and sliding in attempts to gain some ground before they needed rest again. After several hours, crags appeared in their limited scope of vision, barely discernable through the bluish fog. The time spent before reaching them seemed less than what Drast originally expected, but before he knew it, they were entering an arched pathway between the far-reaching mountains.

He peered skyward, unable to see the tip of the peaks from the new vantage point. However, he saw what appeared to be stone ruins built along the mountainside. Cut stone columns and broken walls were half hidden in the hanging mist. "I did not expect to see anything here besides flat land," he admitted out loud. "What do you make of that?"

"Demons surely did not build it," Tyran said. "What use would they have for it?"

Who was here before the demons?

"It looks ancient, like it does not belong here," Kam said.

"Older than Anaerfell," Tyran agreed, unwilling to stop walking to admire the structure. His brother appeared to have more energy; some of his muscle had resurfaced in his legs and torso. However, Kam continued to carry his shield on her back.

"Come to think of it, what is Heshayol, exactly?" Drast meandered down the mountain path. "Who would build a place to confine a god? Sounds absurd."

Absurdity is the flesh to the bones of eternity.

Tyran shook his head next to Drast as though the thought was fresh to him, too. "I suppose it will be nothing we might expect."

That sounds right.

Drast could not think of a response and simply dipped his chin. He allowed his mind to wander about what type of holding could withstand the power of a god and the being who would create it. The Netherworld was meant to be

Marheena's domain. She was the Frozen Witch; the Goddess of Sickness, Nightmares, and Hunger; the Goddess of Nature and Magic. Yet the gods were meant to have some unspoken pact between them, working together to keep the world spinning. What purpose would she have to build edifices in this domain of the dead? Why would she jail a god?

Who said she did?

His mind swirled. Men were not meant to understand the will of the gods.

After another hour, Kam addressed Drast, interrupting the steady beat of their footfalls. "I have always wondered, why did you two kill Wolos?"

Drast glanced over his shoulder, first speculating on how long it had taken her to build the courage to ask such a direct question.

Is she supposed to be talking?

He could feel the smile forming in the corner of his mouth. "Why are you speaking to me? Surely you have reached your allotted word count today?"

"You gave me permission to speak to you if you survived Babeyega," she said. "Do not blame me if your addled mind cannot remember."

Nine Lands! You did say that.

"Did I?" Drast scratched at his beard, looking to Tyran and hoping he could jog his memory. As expected, his brother said nothing. "I suppose I did."

"So, why did you kill Wolos? What would drive dragon-men to stand toe-to-toe with a god?" Kam pressed. Drast wondered if she was nervous, though she did not sound nervous. Yet she was a mere mortal—a skin-switcher—questioning those who had defeated a god.

Yeah. Why did you kill me?

"Our father told us to," Tyran responded with little emotion. He kept his eyes forward. "Do not think I avoid the blame. Our father pointed us down the path, but Drast and I made the choice to walk its length."

I am not a bad god, you know?

"The God of the Dead never helped us," Drast said. "Come to think of it, no god has done anything for any mortal, save Marheena, who gave us Koldovstvo."

"You call that a gift?" asked Kam.

"I would rather have Koldovstvo than be able to turn into a skunk, skin-switcher," Drast shot back.

Kam scowled. "No one turns into skunks."

You smell like one.

Drast giggled. "You should not say such things about your people. This is why no one likes you."

"What?" Kam's frown deepened. "Whether you like me or not, you need me. We do not need to be friends."

They like me enough to convince you to resurrect me.

"It is not like I have a choice," Drast said.

"Exactly. Have you listened to nothing Erzebeth has said?" Kam crossed her arms. "We are in this together, and Wolos needs to be reborn to lead the dead to their resting place."

Oh. That makes sense.

Drast turned away. "I am done talking to you."

Tyran cleared his throat. "I am almost thankful I will forget that exchange."

Drast smirked. "We could have danced around the truth for a few more miles. We need some fun while marching through this frozen hell."

Tyran gave Drast a sidelong glance and grunted. "The time for games has passed."

Has it?

"On the contrary," Drast retorted, "we have time for little else. By the gods, what does the skin-switcher need to know our reasoning for anyway?"

"Call it curiosity," Kam said. "The Vucari are scattered; the Wardens ever-dwindling in numbers. Chaos reigns over the other races of Aenar with war blanketing most civilized lands. People are suffering. The dead are wandering and killing innocents. And the old-dark—the Likhyi—struggle to free themselves from the Ash Tree. If they escape, our world will cease to exist. Our gods will be obliterated." She caught her breath. "I want to know why."

"So you claim," Drast mused, grinning at the skin-switcher. "Though I really do not care if you are telling the truth or not. We already decided to rescue your god. Besides, the *why* will not change any of those things."

Kam jerked Drast around, pulling him by the left shoulder. He spun, slipping on the ice and falling on his buttocks hard. Pain flooded up his spine from the impact. He opened his mouth to protest, but Kam soon stood over him, a hand resting on the axe-like weapon at her belt. He snapped his mouth shut to listen to her argument. "If we survive the Netherworld and Wolos is reborn, the *why* may keep others from making the same mistake. We need to know what arrogant thought—what narcissistic desire—drove the Kaligula brothers to madness!"

I would also like to know this.

"Shush," Drast breathed.

Tyran's answer was a murmur compared to her sudden frenzy. "Immortality. Our father wanted to live forever."

"Remove your hand from your weapon and step back, skin-switcher," Drast grimaced, the smile melting from his face. "Do not associate an old man with a merciful heart; I will turn you inside out where you stand."

Kam stumbled back, lifting her hands up. Her eyes flitted toward Tyran as though he might intervene while Drast used Koldovstvo to lift himself from the ground.

"She called us narcissistic, Tyran." Drast found his smile again. "The little girl thinks we suffer from loving ourselves too much."

"She's young," Tyran said.

Why would she think that?

Drast scoffed. "She's stupid."

"I am not! Though I would be a fool to place blame solely on your father for the hatred you each carry." Kam locked her jaw, her cheeks reddening.

"No matter whether our hatred was learned or passed down in the blood, it lives inside us," Tyran said. "You would do best not to remind us of our susceptibility to hate."

"Why's that, Red?" Kam dared to ask.

Drast inched closer to Kam as she dropped her hands to her sides. "You might remind us how much we *love* hating. I do not know about you, Tyran, but I get butterflies just thinking about it."

Tyran's long white beard rustled against his clothes as he spoke, disregarding Drast as usual. "Because when you spend your life being beaten down and then finally discover you are good at something, you do not want to let it go. Even when that *something* is hating, or scheming, or killing."

"You are monsters," Kam said.

Drast nodded as Tyran replied, "I suspect that is why Erzebeth decided to save us at Anaerfell. She required monsters to fight monsters, or Wolos would have no chance at life again."

Tyran grunted after he finished speaking as though he were agreeing with himself, and then continued into the mountains.

Drast stepped after him, gesturing for the Warden to follow. He put some joviality into his voice, causing her to stare back at him in bewilderment. "So, what kind of name is Kam, anyway?" he asked with a snort. "You cannot expect anyone to think you are a girl when you shave your head, hide your tits, and call yourself Kam."

She visibly swallowed, looking for a place to put her hands, and eventually tucked them on either side of her leather belt. Creases formed under each of her eyes as she processed his question. Admittedly, the discomfort and confusion painted on her face made her look cute, even for a

Vucari, but he stuck by what he had told Tyran before. He was not interested in sleeping with her, no matter how much he missed a good tussle or feared his bits would freeze in this forsaken land.

And it was getting colder.

"The name is Kamila," she finally said. "Kamila Artur. My duty is to Wolos and the Ash Tree. Having tits is irrelevant."

"Kamila, Kamila, Kamila," Drast repeated, tapping his chin. "Whoever made you think having tits is irrelevant—"

"Let's see whether you find having bits or not is irrelevant." She jerked the strange axe from her side hoop, catching it mid-air by the bone handle.

Oh, gods.

Drast jumped backward in shock as she flung the weapon over his shoulder at a cranny in the rock. Tyran shouted in equal surprise as a screeching cry, like an owl, rang against the cavern walls.

A twisted humanoid beast hurtled from the shadows to the ice. It thrashed and wailed, reaching clawed fingers at Drast, snapping its bladed teeth. The creature had the bone structure of a human with a head as pale and bald as Drast's, large pointed ears, and a smashed nose.

Kam was quicker than Drast or Tyran, sliding across the icy ground on her knees and ripping the axe free. In a single swing, she chopped through the creature's neck. Black-red blood squirted and sprayed across the ice.

Tyran scanned the rocks. "Where did it come from?"

Drast leaned closer. "What is it?"

The Warden stood. "This is a Strigoi. They can change their shape or even become invisible and are drawn to the blood of mortals. Erzebeth told me about them."

Drast kneeled to inspect the strange fiend, a shape-shifting demon like the Vucari. He spat.

"But you saw it," Tyran said.

"The Vucari can often see what Reds cannot," she

replied curtly. "I told you that you needed me to survive this place."

"By the gods!" Drast cried, springing to his feet. The Strigoi's clawed hands reached for the severed head, replacing the bloodied hunk of meat and bone on its fallen body. Skin and sinew stretched, stitching back together as the demon clambered to its feet.

Fire leaped from Drast's fingertips, lashing at the Strigoi's torso. The demon screeched, then sounded a gurgled roar, flashing its gore-covered teeth. The flames seared the flesh, but the demon healed as swiftly as the fire burned.

Do something!

Drast quickly transformed his arm into a maul and knocked the demon backwards into the rocks. The Strigoi rumbled and advanced.

That was a good idea.

Drast used Koldovstvo to withdraw several feet as the Strigoi lunged for him. The demon only succeeded in diving into Tyran's shield, which had been lifted from Kam's back and now hovered in the air with magic. Tyran matched the monster's tone, swinging his mace and smashing the Strigoi's head into his own shield. The skull caved, and the demon fell a second time.

"Wh—" Drast started, changing his arm into the semblance of a sword to defend himself. He hoped it cut as well as a real sword.

"I do not know," Kam hastily answered. She lifted an eyebrow at his magically-formed weapon, and then the Strigoi was rising again.

Tyran struck the Strigoi with his shield once more, holding it back against the rock of the mountain. The clawed hands raked the air at him.

Erzebeth suddenly appeared in front of Drast. "They will not die if you leave the skull intact. You must sever the head and cut it in two."

Drast staggered through the apparition of the skin-switcher and reached for the Strigoi with Koldovstvo. With a twist of his good hand, he pulled at the head of the beast while Tyran increased the pressure with the shield.

The spine cracked seconds before the head popped from the lanky torso, dousing the area with fresh blood. Drast lobbed the head at Kam. "Hack away."

The Warden did as she was told, hammering her axe downward against the demon until she split the skull at the bridge of the nose.

Look at that. The Vucari told you the truth once, unless the one now becomes two.

"You know, skin-switcher, you should consider telling us what enemies lie in wait and how to defeat them before you disappear for long periods of time," Drast huffed at Erzebeth. "Your precious god's life may depend on it."

"You have the Alatir Stone. A few scratches will not kill you," Erzebeth said. He glowered at her and her smugness. He was certain she would see them dead once Wolos was released from Heshayol. "I am glad to see you have closed the distance to the first Grumadki. It will not be long now."

Chapter VII

Drast's arrow zipped by Tyran's ear, sinking into the broad chest of the Bukavac with a *thwack*. Tyran leaped backwards with a grunt, trying to keep his feet sturdy on the slick ice. He hardly saw the Bukavac barreling toward him. When his back foot slipped, he embraced Koldovstvo, his skin tingling, and lifted himself into the air. He then advanced on the gurgling beast. With a swift swing, he pummeled the demon across the temple with his mace.

The Bukavac crumbled with an exasperated breath.

Tyran spun around, barking at Drast, "You nearly hit me!" His brother was already retreating farther down the diminishing path, the few white hairs sprouting from his scalp wafting with the rushed movement. The mountains on either side of them shrank over the past two days, promising another valley up ahead, where Erzebeth said the Grumadki awaited them. From the looks of it, little was left of the mountains.

"They went around the bend. We have to move," Drast said, seemingly oblivious to Tyran's complaint. Drast's forehead glistened with sweat beads, the blue-tinted fog whirling on either side of him. He fired another arrow beyond Tyran at the advancing Bukavac.

Tyran looked beyond Drast to where Kam and Erzebeth

vanished moments ago. "Why are you using your bow when you can fire the arrows with Koldovstvo?"

Without waiting for Drast's response, Tyran squared off with the enemy. He threw his mace through the air to hit another Bukavac advancing down the path. With a bit of magic, the weapon demolished the creature's face, leaving a bloodied clump of broken skin and bones. Koldovstvo powered the weapon back to Tyran's hand before the demon fell. He flexed his arm under the weight of his mace. The Alatir Stone restored some of his strength, but he was far from being spry again.

He squeezed the artifact in his shield hand.

When he twisted back around, Drast was staring at his weapon, his face painted with confusion. Then, with a slight shrug and a smile, Drast drew another arrow from his quiver with his spectral hand. He nocked it on the string. "Do not worry about me. I never miss my mark, save that one time when I shot one of my soldiers in the face…never mind that," he replied with a wild chuckle. He pointed at Tyran in the air. "Worry instead about this flying you keep doing. You are going to attract more of them."

Tyran frowned. "Three days ago, you could barely see your own feet."

A screech from beyond the clouds echoed into the mountain while a handful of Bukavac surfaced from the slope of the mountain.

"See? Because of you the Nithhoggr have come." Drast pointed to the sky with his bow. Tyran scowled at the sky, hardly hearing him. "We need to go. We cannot defeat them without Erzebeth." He mumbled to himself and then said, "I am telling you we are being strung along by the skin-switchers."

"Maybe," Tyran said absentmindedly, looking for an alternative reason for the greater demon's presence. "The legion must have grown since we counted this morning. Probably picked up some strays along the way." He peered at the serpent-shaped shadows turning through the clouds. The beasts were not difficult to miss, circling above them like vultures. Tyran could hear the faint vibration of their neck frills pulsating, along with a grating shriek echoing from their gullets.

The Nithhoggr had not appeared again since the first battle with the Bukavac. From what Drast said, Tyran was glad to have avoided them. While either he or Drast could rip the dark soul from the beasts with their magic, neither of them possessed the power to contend with the shade once it was free from the bodily form.

Tyran considered pulling the mountain down to block the Bukavac so they could focus on the Nithhoggr, but instead turned to chase after Drast. While the strategy may have been effective, he did not want to think what beasts beyond the Nithhoggr would be mustered by the excessive use of Koldovstvo. Erzebeth, whether she told the truth or not, promised that powerful spells attracted more demons.

"Erzebeth!" Drast sang out.

The echo touched Tyran's ears about the same time as an unclear object leaped at him with a throaty snarl from the shadows. He raised his shield in time to separate himself from the demon, although the momentum still slammed him into the adjacent wall of rock. Sharp nails clawed around the shield at his face and neck.

He yelled nothing intelligible, pushing his shield back against the demon, swiftly noticing the sharp ears on either side of the decaying bald head and snapping fangs of the Strigoi. The beast flailed backwards and leaped again, somehow reaching over his shield, the claws connecting with his neck. Tyran gasped, feeling the painful cut, and pushed the demon back again with his shield.

An arrow struck the Strigoi in the side, beneath the ribs, slowing it momentarily.

Tyran dropped his mace and clasped his palm over the cut to stay the bleeding. Yet no warm blood oozed over his fingertips. Despite the fading feeling of having his skin ripped open, his neck remained fully intact. He dropped his eyes to the white stone in his hand with amazement. The Alatir Stone kept him from harm, much like it had Zyem.

The Strigoi chaotically attacked again. Before the beast made it two steps, Tyran picked the demon up with Koldovstvo and chucked it toward the assailing Bukavac, knocking them both to the ground in a heap. The two rumbled, clawing over one another while attempting to stand.

Tyran pulled his mace from the ground to his hand, sweeping his vision to Drast. Another arrow snapped by him, piercing the Strigoi in the head.

The demon thrashed, reaching for the projectile sticking out from above his ear.

Tyran moved to Drast's side, pulling at his shoulder as he passed. The Nithhoggr screamed overhead again. "The Alatir Stone keeps us from physical harm."

Drast looked up to the Nithhoggr and shook his head. "I would not trust it to keep us safe from the shade of the Nithhoggr."

Tyran accepted his brother's quick reason and fled down the path toward the valley.

"The Strigoi is not dead," Drast called after him.

"I know!" Tyran shouted. He heard another twang of the bowstring, followed by Drast's footsteps echoing behind him.

The two of them skidded down the path, using their legs instead of Koldovstvo. The deeper they delved into the Netherworld, the thicker the hordes had become. Tyran remembered having little trouble during their first few days, but the last couple were a constant test to their fortitude. Tyran was beginning to understand how the Netherworld was overpopulated with the dead. They could scarcely turn a corner without discovering another roving army.

As they rounded the bend, the mountain path sprang

into the expected valley. Less than a hundred yards away, Kam had already transformed into the bies, fighting another cluster of Bukavac. Erzebeth floated ineptly nearby. Tyran gestured, saying, "I see them."

"By the gods, the small-breasted skin-switcher is going to get injured again. There are too many," Drast said. "I am not giving her the Alatir Stone again. I say if she gets injured, we kill her and be done with it."

"Help her, and send Erzebeth to me," Tyran said.

Drast looked back the way they had come at the demons trailing them. "Do not forget about the Strigoi."

Tyran nodded as Drast bounded forward with void magic.

Tyran whipped around at the sound of a Nithhoggr's wail approaching from above. He stepped into the valley, readying himself. The crowned head of the eyeless demon came at him like a battering ram, a toothy mouth opened wide to devour him whole. The webbed frill wildly quivered with anticipation for the kill.

Tyran dropped the mace into his belt loop and gripped the Alatir Stone in his fist behind his shield. He embraced Koldovstvo to help him hold the shield at the ready.

Erzebeth appeared beside him about the time he pulled at the Nithhoggr's essence with Koldovstvo, ripping the spirit from the being. The black wraith screeched, propelling itself at him while the husk of the serpent's body fell to nothingness.

The green light emitted by Erzebeth nearly blinded him, striking the shadow from existence.

When the light dimmed, he turned on the ghost of the woman. "You said Drast and I were meant to return Wolos from the dead. How do you imagine we will do that when you run ahead with your precious Warden?"

Erzebeth's voice was emotionless. "She holds equal importance, Red."

"How is that? I hold the Ojenek. I have the Alatir Stone.

Drast and I are dragon-men." The yell of another Nithhoggr resounded above him; the heavy footfalls of the Bukavac reaching the bend shook the ground beneath him.

The Strigoi suddenly clashed with Tyran from the shadows as its pale body wrapped itself around him, knocking him to the ground and slamming his shoulder blades against the ice-covered rock. He cried out, one of his arms trapped in the bindings of his shield, while the claws scraped down the wrinkled skin of his face in an attempt to rip him apart. The long nails raked down from his quivering eyeball to his hanging jaw. Viscid drool dripped from a swollen, forked tongue poking from between its fangs; the rotting pale skin was spotted with deep black spots of decay. Murky, discolored blood oozed from above the ear, where Drast's arrow remained stuck through the brain.

He squirmed at the sting of the claws, but the artifact made his skin as hard as stone.

Making a fist, he punched the Strigoi across the side of the head. His knuckles connected with the arrow, snapping it in two. He screamed despite the pain being fleeting. No blood flowed. The Strigoi rocked sideways with the impact, then swiftly rocketed its head back again with a hiss. Koldovstvo channeled through Tyran, prickling at his skin as he flung the demon off him.

"Time for us to go to the Grumadki, Red," Erzebeth said.

He lifted himself to his feet with magic to see the Strigoi already charging him a second time. He flung the beast back farther toward the Bukavac. In seconds, it was racing back at him again.

He could feel himself weakening from the use of Koldovstvo. His mind swirled.

He swayed. He knew the Alatir Stone gave him his voice and helped him recall moment to moment until wielding too much magic drained him.

"Stop calling me that. You know my name!" Tyran screamed

at Erzebeth. He could hardly believe they had shared gentle kisses and soft whispers a lifetime ago before he became her prisoner. Now, since reuniting, she refused to acknowledge him, like he was less than a memory.

"Kill the Nithhoggr. Kill the Bukavac. Kill the Strigoi. Save the Warden," she said in a dry tone. Her eyes flashed brightly, almost sardonically, still refusing to say his name.

"I was true to you until the very end and you betrayed me! I hope the guilt followed you to your grave." Tyran sneered with hatred. The Vucari looked back at him blankly, having no response.

The Nithhoggr screamed above him, growing ever closer.

With a snarl, Tyran pulled the Strigoi to him through time and space. The beast screeched in surprise as Tyran bashed the monster with his shield, sending it sprawling to the ground at his feet. His shoulder cracked under the impact, threatening to dislodge again. He ignored it.

Instead, he let loose his shield, flinging it downward vertically with Koldovstvo, decapitating the Strigoi's head from its shoulders. Gritting his teeth, he bounded forward, jerking his mace free again. With several steady swings, he flattened the skull into a pulp of bone fragments and bloodied tissue.

Tyran then turned on the many spiraling, bone-spiked demons racing at him from the skies. Forgetting his limitations on Koldovstvo and filled with sudden rage, Tyran tore the ethereal forms from the beasts before him. His own body shuddered under the influence of Koldovstvo, threatening to implode his physical form. If it were not for the Alatir Stone, he may have ripped himself apart. Yet he remained safe while the bestial bodies ruptured, the phantom demons floundering toward him until repelled with Erzebeth's energy blasts.

The Bukavac did not escape his wrath, their deaths intermingled with those of the Nithhoggr. He flung fire, wind, and lightning, holding the beasts at a distance, tearing them to shreds. Throughout the battle, his mind drifted to what he may have meant to Erzebeth years ago.

The two had first crossed paths on the shores of Rhian, her homeland, where he had initially taken her as his captive. His most loyal men warned him of his infatuation, but he refused to listen. He kept her alive even when pressed to lay her to rest. He could not say why he had grown to love Erzebeth; he suspected he was drawn to her for the same reason he hated her. He and she shared a similar quality, one that kept him alive. Stubbornness.

Drast counseled him of the threat she posed to them, being a Vucari and a Warden. He, too, wanted to have Erzebeth's skull crushed and be forgotten. In the end, Drast was right about her. If he had killed Erzebeth when given the chance, he and Drast would have died when they were meant to die, and they would have escaped this nightmare.

He would not be in the Netherworld slaying demons. He would not be risking his life to save another forsaken skin-switcher, and he certainly would not be having this conversation with himself.

Then again, if he were not here, the whole world would be doomed for eternity. Though maybe his first mistake was thinking it was not already.

Who was he? Who would he become?

A hand pulled at his shoulder, mad laughter echoing around him. "They are dead, Tyran. We killed them all." A moment later. "Tyran!"

The fire fizzled from his fingertips, dissipating into nothingness. A shadow fell over his eyes for a moment and the ground spun beneath him, suggesting how much magic he had cast. Too much. He struggled to keep his balance, refocusing his vision to see the dark stains of blood and the scattered dead.

Drast hit him on the shoulder as he twisted to see Kam slipping her robe around her naked figure.

He took a deep breath and let it out slowly.

Drast grumbled. "If Koldovstvo pulls the demons to us, I suspect we have drawn every horde within a hundred miles to our location. Our deaths may be nigh. We can soon bring this tale to a close, eh?"

Tyran backed away from Erzebeth, confusion washing over him. *Where are we? What are we doing here?*

"Come," Erzebeth said. "You must get to the Grumadki."

"The what?"

No one answered him. For the next half hour, he followed Drast into the valley.

He began to remember his purpose in the Netherworld when the wooden crossbeams of the Grumadki were identified looming in the distance, even through the speckled fog, a testament to the ancient builders. Each stilted piece of timber, thick as Tyran's torso, was angled, stretching nearly fifty feet into the air. One of the crossbeams had a wide notch carved in its side to fit the second beam, creating a triangular opening underneath. As they drew near, Tyran could see nothing special about the ingress or the wood. Nothing shimmered. Nothing stirred. Besides the indentation in the wood, the Grumadki looked to be two limbless trees that fell against one another.

As they neared, Kam slung her pack onto her arm. "We can eat the remainder of our food while we wait."

Drast stopped next to Tyran, looking around the wasteland. A smile spread over his face, and he spoke with more force than necessary. "You mean we are out of food? Where do you plan to get more?"

"There is no more," Kam answered.

Erzebeth hung behind the Warden. "You will feel the hunger pains, but you will not die from starvation."

"We are expected to be hungry for the rest of our journey?" Drast chortled, slapping his leg. "This is rich. Absolutely rich! By the gods, why did we not ration what little we had better?"

"The food would have spoiled the moment we entered the Grumadki," Kam replied irritably as though she may have told them as much already. "Please give Drast the Alatir Stone for a while."

Drast raised his hand at Tyran, gesturing for him to keep the stone. "And how long until we reach Heshayol?"

"If the remaining Grumadki are intact like this one," Erzebeth replied hesitantly, "about two months."

Tyran reached out his hand to receive the bread and dried meat from Kam. "And if not?"

Erzebeth replied, "Much longer."

Her words lingered for some time while Kam, Drast, and Tyran chewed their few tidbits, blankly staring over the wasteland.

When Tyran finished, he reached inside his pocket to retrieve Ojenek. The smooth bluish gem had a slight glow inside, like a twinkling star behind a thin layer of clouds. He could not say how long he sat on the cold ground, looking back and forth between Ojenek in his right hand and the Alatir Stone in his left. His mind flitted from thought to thought, unable to quite ascertain what he exactly thought. Old memories blended with daydreams of the future; his past transgressions greyed away to hopeful possibilities. Whether his old mind was fickle or the very nature of the Netherworld impacted his thinking, Tyran could not say.

During the years at Anaerfell, Tyran made lists of questions he wanted answers to, whether about the order of the universe, the will of the gods, or the purpose of his own eternal suffering. Now he struggled to recall those existential questions that haunted him. He speculated Erzebeth, in her death, may have the answers he sought if he could remember what he wanted to ask, yet he doubted she would freely tell him anything. Based on her attitude toward him so far, she clearly cared nothing for him. Drast may very well be right that they were nothing but pawns in her scheme to rescue her god.

The realization of how little he meant to a woman he once loved did not rock him as much as it might have in his younger years. The reality of the situation was bleak. She was dead. He would be soon enough. He could not be angry at her for refusing him the same which he kept from others his entire life. And still he could feel the anger swelling in his chest. She did not give him time, consideration, or love.

Tyran squeezed the two trinkets in his hands. "Erzebeth," he almost choked, "where did these artifacts come from? How were they created?"

Drast jerked next to Tyran as though the sudden sound had startled him. "You said that, right?"

"I did," Tyran replied.

Drast nodded, pulling at his beard and eyeing Tyran suspiciously before tilting his eyes to the ghost. Kam, who already repacked the bags multiple times, reorganized the packs again in preparation for travel.

Erzebeth's emerald eyes flashed with amusement. "The Stuhia created them during the ageless days when they were fascinated with blending their newfound magic with common objects."

Tyran remembered his father speaking about this during his adolescence. "Before it was outlawed."

"Yes," Erzebeth said. "I doubt anyone living or dead knows how many artifacts were made or where they are all located."

"Why would the Stuhia create Ojenek? I cannot see why anyone would consider making a key to free a god at Heshayol." Tyran turned his gaze from Erzebeth to the cold stone in his palm. "Surely we would not have even known about Heshayol?"

"I suspect not," Erzebeth agreed. "While the Stuhia and Vucari would regularly meet with the gods at *Iriy*, the City of the Gods, in the early ages, they would not have known the workings of the Netherworld. Though such a thing hardly matters. Almost all the trinkets made by the Stuhian people had multiple functions, most of which were hidden from even the craftsmen.”

Tyran’s face must have reflected his confusion, because she continued, “Although the Stuhians could wield Marheena’s magic, they did not wholly understand the nature of Koldovstvo. Some may have discovered that fastening Koldovstvo to an armband or blade gave them greater strength in battle, never understanding the magical item might curse their bloodline, poison their mind, or even lure the enemy to them.”

“Like the demons are drawn to Koldovstvo here in the Netherworld,” Drast said.

“Yes,” Erzebeth said. “Not every artifact held negative properties, nor did all artifacts have great benefits. Your people experimented for a long while, resulting in blights, madness, and even death. Eventually your overseeing councils banned further creation, finally understanding Marheena’s magic runs deep in this world and is more ancient than even she.”

“You mean Koldovstvo is as old as the old-dark?” Tyran asked.

“Older still,” Erzebeth said.

Tyran replayed the lectures he heard from his father as a child, remembering little regarding the history before the old-dark. “What is older than the Likhyi?”

“Kowin,” Kam spoke with hesitation. Erzebeth turned to the Warden, her face laced with concern. “Kowin is older than everything.”

“Yes,” Erzebeth agreed.

Drast eyed Tyran, puzzled, then asked Erzebeth, “And what is Kowin?”

“Kowin the Deathless is more than a god…he is Koldovstvo. His power is so great, he is kept from the plane of mortals, restricted to Thrice Ten Kingdom under the watchful eye of Svarog and Svathevit,” Erzebeth started, struggling to identify the entity. Tyran knew the names of the gods she mentioned. Svarog was the Grandfather of the Gods, sitting at the pinnacle of the pantheon, the ruler of Thrice Ten Kingdom. Svathevit the Red was the God of War, who had four heads to remain ever vigilant.

"What do you mean he *is* Koldovstvo?" Tyran cleared his throat, trying to conceptualize her words. "Does he have access to all magic?"

Erzebeth rocked her head, considering his question. "Yes, but more than that. The old-dark, as you might know, are each empowered with one of the eight cruxes of Koldovstvo."

Tyran hummed to himself. He did not need an explanation on the cruxes. He was a Stuhia and well versed. Koldovstvo was broken apart between elemental magic—fire, sky, stone, and sea—and entropic magic—void, primal, profane, and sacred. All Stuhia could wield elemental magic and a singular entropic magic based on their bloodline. The Kaligulas held sway over the void magic, whereas other bloodlines may incite emotions, cause rot to the body or mind, or mend wounds and invigorate allies in battle with holy blessings. The Likhyi, on the other hand, were each an essence of Koldovstvo, wielding any given magic to perfection.

Drast's elevated voice jerked Tyran from his digressive thoughts. "What do you mean Kowin is all of the Likhyi together?"

Tyran must have missed the answer to his question.

"Just as I said," Erzebeth said. "Kowin controls every part of Koldovstvo. While slight rudiments of the magic run through your blood, he is the original source of Koldovstvo. His power is limitless."

"We should be lucky Svarog holds him, then," Drast said.

Erzebeth raised her hand to silence Kam, who was already shaking her head. "The tether holding Kowin has been loosened so he might keep the old-dark imprisoned. He roams Aenar combating the growing strength of the Likhyi, returning them to the Ash Tree again and again. But the roots have been severed, the waters run dry, the bark is splitting, and the limbs are wilting. If Wolos is not soon reborn, the Likhyi will find the means to escape and they will reshape the world."

Tyran grunted.

Drast said, "I do not understand. Kowin has access to unlimited power. Why does he not command the world? It sounds as though he could destroy the Likhyi and the gods."

"Do you only think of dominance?" Kam blurted.

"No, Kam. Drast is correct," Erzebeth said. "Kowin desires the very thing, but Svarog holds his soul, coercing him to do the will of the gods. Yet we should remember the gods simply want to restore the balance lost with Wolos's death. If he is not renewed, Svarog would certainly give Kowin his freedom."

"Excellent." Drast grinned. "So why are we still sitting here? For wanting Wolos freed so badly, we certainly spend a lot of time sitting and telling stories."

"Because I cannot enter the Grumadki, nor could I tell you how to traverse the shadow world beyond," Erzebeth said, gazing through Tyran and Drast at the gate behind them with irritation. "Only Kowin can escort you through. And so, we must wait for him to arrive."

Chapter VIII

Drast marveled at his breath, fading inches from his lips, and then sucked in another lungful of cold air. Another battle had been won.

He lost count of how many days they stood guard over the two towering sticks behind him: the Grumadki. The Netherworld seemed to grow colder with each passing moment. He squatted, tilting his head to stare at the demons they just killed, lying dead around him. "I am a bit fuzzy on how demons become demons."

Kam grabbed her robe from the ground, pulling it over her shoulders. She stepped over one of the bloodied demons at her feet. Drast lost count of how many legions they had defeated over the past several days, waiting on Kowin. "Death is a prerequisite. Would you like to find out?"

"No one asked for your opinion, *Small-tits*." Drast snipped. "I was asking the glowing skin-switcher, who somehow avoided becoming one."

Kam looked at her chest, then back at Drast. "What did you call me?"

Erzebeth's vacant expression turned towards him, the Grumadki visible through her translucent form. "Are you asking what should happen or what is happening?"

Both.

"Both." Drast blinked, ignoring Kam's twisted face.

"All mortals are given a charge in life—" Erzebeth started.

"I know this part," Drast interrupted. "Jump forward."

"All mortals are given a charge in life." Erzebeth narrowed her gaze, starting back from the beginning.

Too bad she is already dead.

"I would kill you if I could," Drast muttered.

"And," she went on, "if they live their life as they are meant to, Wolos will lead the mortal to Thrice Ten Kingdom to rejoice with the gods. However, if the mortal does not finish what he or she was born to accomplish, they will be twisted by the death magic of Marheena and left to roam the Netherworld."

"Well done," Drast said, fumbling with the Alatir Stone in his bow hand. "You have told me what every living being on Aenar already knows. My question was how, not why."

"Marheena has access to all strands of Koldovstvo but uses profane magic to twist the souls into demons. If you are asking me what mortal becomes what demon and why, I would not be able to tell you," Erzebeth said. "But whether we are talking about the Bukavac, the Nithhoggr, or any other creature, they were all once living."

Tyran strode forward, wiping fresh blood from his cheek with the back of his hand, dropping his mace into his loop. Drast threw the Alatir Stone at Tyran. He caught the gem and said, "That does not explain why you are like you are. How did you escape the fate of all other mortals? Did you meet your charge?"

"I am a Warden," Erzebeth said.

Tyran tossed his shield to the ground. "Which means what? You do not follow the same rules?"

"Which means she is bound to protect the Ash Tree, even after death," Kam said, stepping in front of Erzebeth. Her robe was pulled fully over her naked body.

"Shut up, *Small-tits,*" Drast said.

Kam eyed Drast over, locking her brown eyes on his spectral hand. "I will speak when I wish…*Lefty*."

I think she just insulted you.

"Lefty?"

"Yes, *Lefty*!"

A pretty good insult too.

His eyes flicked to his good hand, Kam's chest, and back up. He smiled. "We are of an accord, *Small-tits*."

Tyran, oblivious to their side conversation, took a hard tone, facing off with Erzebeth. "So you are blessed by the gods while the rest of us are doomed?"

"I gave up my life for Wolos. A husband. A daughter. A future outside of anything beyond service to the Horned God," Erzebeth said. "I will forever live a hollow death, without rest or solace."

"Why would you do something so stupid?" Drast asked, seeing his brother step backward, swayed by the Vucari's dull words. He inched forward, sliding by Kam. The voice in his head whispered menacingly, and Drast repeated the words to the best of his ability.

She is lying.

"You are lying."

She would not give up her life for a god. The gods curse mortals.

"No way you would give up your life up for Wolos. The *gods* turn mortals into demons!"

Why?

"Why?"

Why?

"Why?"

Why?

"Why!"

"Drast!" Tyran blocked his brother's view of the ghostly Vucari with his wide frame.

Drast blinked. He could not see why his brother had raised his voice. "Yeah, Tyran?"

Erzebeth interrupted them, gliding around the two

brothers, her eyes fixated on Drast until she stood between them and a startled Kam. "The pantheon cannot destroy the souls of mortals, nor can they have them forever roam Aenar aimlessly. The demons, a creation of Marheena, serve as vessels for those souls that cannot reach Thrice Ten Kingdom. Every soul yearns for paradise, hoping to break free of their torment. Since the first death, Marheena has bound them to the Netherworld in their ghastly forms or, at least, she did until the two of you broke the cycle."

"I suppose the gods believe suffering is necessary and not every being is worthy of the Kingdom." Tyran grimaced. "I think what my brother is getting at is that the gods' superiority to mortals is evident by them twisting men into monsters."

"The gods are superior to mortals," Kam snapped, turning her nose up. "Why can you not accept that? Thinking anything more is arrogant."

Erzebeth would have done well to have some inflection in her tone, but she spoke with the enthusiasm of a barren desert. "The progression of life and death has little to do with power but, instead, has everything to do with order."

"And what is the purpose of this so-called *order*?" Tyran asked.

"That is a question to which I have no answer," Erzebeth said.

Even in death, the religious do not have the answers.

"Convenient," Drast muttered.

A roar of Bukavac stamping beyond the fog resounded.

Tyran reached for his shield as Kam began to disrobe. "I am glad they give fair warning before advancing."

Drast faced the clamor in the distance. "I have a right mind to head through the Grumadki without Kowin. Nothing in there can be worse than what is out here."

You would be surprised.

Kam threw her weapon, the axe spinning head over haft and sinking into the chest of an unseen Strigoi to the left of

Drast. The demon gurgled, its clawed feet falling out from underneath it. Drast stepped away as Kam rushed forward, her naked flesh visible for the world to see. She stepped on the stomach of the monster and tore her axe free, then hacked at the demon.

The Strigoi raised its hand to block the first swing, only to have its fingers lobbed off. The beast screeched, flailing back. Kam silenced the Strigoi, sinking the blade into its throat. Blood sprayed over Kam's legs and feet.

Drast raised an eyebrow as the naked Vucari continued her assault, severing the head and splitting the skull in two. "I will be dreaming about this tonight."

"Nine Lands, Drast." Tyran shook his head. "Keep something to yourself. We do not need to hear every thought you have."

If he only knew.

"If you only knew."

More battle roars sounded in the distance, followed by a high-pitched shriek Drast could not place.

He reached for his quiver, only to remember he had run out of arrows some time ago. With a shrug, he lifted his bow and aimed it at the advancing Bukavac. A magical arrow crackled over the curved wood, nestled gently against the string. He did not need to draw the string to fire, but he did anyway.

Drast shot the magical arrow at the first Bukavac surfacing through the mist, striking it in the stomach. The creature snarled, throwing back its horned head, and rushed forward. More of the ice demons followed.

Kam matched the tone of the beast, twisting into the form of the bies. Her spine cracked and lengthened, skin darkening with muscle swelling beneath her skin. Dark hair sprung through the length of her body as her narrow feet warped into hardened hooves, similar to those of the Bukavac. Drast turned away about the time the horns extended from her skull, raising his weapon to shoot again.

Watching her pretty face change into the semblance of a glorified bull nearly sickened him.

Having a snout for a nose is better than having no nose at all.

"But why cows? You command dragons."

Drast sensed Tyran shift next to him, probably staring at him with confusion. He did not really care. His question was important.

How long would your people last if your enemy could switch into dragons?

Drast wrinkled his brow, remembering the thousands of Vucari who they had waged war against every summer. "Cows are fine."

"Drast!" Tyran said. "Fire already!"

The demons were on them, more than Drast could count in a passing glance. Tyran's mace cracked the skull of the Bukavac he shot moments ago, knocking it back. Kam rushed at another, her fist striking the icy-blue beast across the jaw.

Erzebeth hung in the air uselessly like an arbitrary cloud.

Drast leaped back, shooting arrow after arrow. The bolts of energy rained down on the enemy. The demons dropped one after another on the opposite side of his bow.

The shriek he'd heard before the battle resounded again, drawing his attention to a pale, wispy female whizzing through the mist between the Bukavac. She was nearly translucent, eddying to and fro through the giant monsters as though the tides of battle fed her will to exist. He thought he could see thin coils of energy twining around her wraithlike figure.

Her thin black lips, hollowed nose, and dark-encircled eyes were lifeless. Long strands of black hair whirled behind her naked body as she approached Tyran on the battlefield.

His brother bashed another Bukavac back with his shield, unaware of the dead woman at his rear.

Drast fired. To his surprise, the magical arrow went through her body, harmlessly sinking into the fog on the opposite side.

"Tyran!" Drast's heart thumped in his chest.

His younger brother turned around in time for the woman to touch his chest. He choked, eyes widening under his bushy eyebrows, and fainted. His body went rigid, falling backwards to the ground, landing on his back with a hard thud. His head cracked against the ground; the Alatir Stone bouncing free from his shield hand.

"No!" Drast released another arrow at the woman to no avail. The projectile disappeared like the first one. Leaping over a dead body, Drast hooked his bow on his shoulder, and embraced Koldovstvo. The *thing* slowly assailed Tyran. Lines of fire, shards of ice, bolts of lightning all formed in the space between Drast and the demon, and one by one, the elemental energy passed through the creature without impact.

The pale woman ignored Drast, straddling Tyran's chest. She leaned forward, her bare breasts pressed against Tyran; she then touched him on the forehead with a clawed fingertip.

He is going to die.

"No!" Drast dodged a Bukavac's blade, then ignited the beast on fire with Koldovstvo.

The demon over Tyran widened her mouth beyond what was physically feasible and shrieked. Any other time, the cry would have caused Drast to cringe, but he fought against the knee-buckling sound.

He would not let Tyran die.

Leaping the distance with magic, Drast reached Tyran's side. His brother convulsed under the demon's touch.

"The Nocnica is draining his life," Erzebeth said, flashing into existence on the opposite side of the ethereal creature.

Drast reached for the Nocnica, his hand touching nothingness and sinking through the entity like his weapon or magic.

"You must—" Erzebeth started.

"If Tyran dies, I will kill you!" Drast screamed over the top of her. He tensed his jaw, refusing to let the impulsive smile slip through. "Again."

She is not listening.

Erzebeth's lips moved but Drast refused to hear what she said.

"I hate you, Erzebeth. I hate you. I hate you," Drast cried out, drowning in his panic. "You brought us down here and he is dying!"

She hears nothing. Only herself.

"Drast, if you want to save your brother—" she tried again.

He ignored her detached expression as the Nocnica twisted her neck and screamed in his face. The toothless, elongated mouth caused him to stumble back, the sound causing his head to ache. He clasped his temples, falling to his knees. He could hear the Warden roaring in the distance, continuing to fight against the attacking Bukavac.

She might kill you, too.

Erzebeth drifted closer, her ghostly form bursting with a green light. She was seemingly unaffected by the Nocnica's continuous blood-curdling cry. "Get Ojenek to save your brother. Hit the demon with the stone."

He blinked, nodding numbly. He tried to pull the stone to his hand with Koldovstvo. Nothing happened.

"I told you before. You cannot use magic to manipulate the stone," Erzebeth said.

Drast dropped his left hand, inching it over the frozen terrain until finally reaching Tyran's pocket, where he knew his brother kept the blue-colored stone. Jamming his hand into the fabric, his fingers touched the smoothness of the artifact.

He wavered on his knees, his head aching from the Nocnica's endless shrieking. He could feel blood dribbling from his nose.

With his own eternal cry, ringing in his head tenfold by the voice of Wolos, Drast jerked his hand free and swung at the Nocnica with Ojenek enclosed in his fist. He collided with the specter delivering a solid blow, striking her in the cheek and open mouth. A white light pierced through a crack in the skin where blood should have surfaced, causing the demon to screech all the louder. The crack then split across the body like broken glass, splintering over the demon's skin until she finally powdered into a thousand pieces.

The demon disappeared, leaving Drast with the muffled sound of Kam's fist smashing into a final Bukavac near the Grumadki.

Tyran's eyelids fluttered beneath him.

"Are you alright?" Drast asked.

His brother looked back at him, his eyes glazed over. He raised his hand to his head, and then grunted. Drast pushed Ojenek into his brother's hand. "Keep this close."

Drast stood up and turned around to the sound of a slow clap. "I thought the two of you would be dead by now."

"Kowin," Erzebeth acknowledged. Drast eyed the dark-haired man standing beneath the apex of the Grumadki. He scarcely noticed the Warden changing back into her human form, collecting her robe and axe.

Kowin crossed his arms, staring at Erzebeth smugly. His long black hair hung perfectly over his red-colored breastplate.

The so-called god has arrived. Is he more favorable than I?

"Look for yourself." Drast reached for Tyran, helping him to his feet while eyeing the two longswords at Kowin's belt. He turned his focus to Kowin. "We have been waiting for you. What took you so long?"

Kowin gave a half-smile. "Follow me."

Tyran grunted behind Drast as expected, scooping up his shield and mace.

Drast reached for the Alatir Stone, clutching it in his left hand. "No. I have a lot of questions in need of answering."

"I am not answering your questions. I am in a hurry, and you will be dead soon enough," Kowin said, motioning for them to follow.

I think I am the better conversationalist.

"I have questions." Drast grinned.

Kowin ignored him, twisting around and walking through the Grumadki.

Kam looked to the dead Vucari with hesitation.

"Go with him," Erzebeth said. "I will meet you on the other side. But do not trust him."

Chapter IX

The shadow world dissolved. Tyran flailed from the darkness, falling onto his hands and knees a half second before fully slipping and landing spread-eagle on the frozen soil. The ice-cold air of the Netherworld stung at his skin.

His senses were muddled. The tips of his fingers burned; the taste and smell of mold clung to his tongue. The disarrayed cries of those he could only believe were Drast and Kam were deafened, sounding a lifetime away, and his eyesight was jarred with dashes of color smudging across his vision.

The ground shook beneath him.

"Gods!" Drast wheezed from somewhere close. "What is—"

A hacking, strangled cough tore through Tyran, forcing him to spew thick gobs of mucus and spit. He lurched to the side to keep from convulsing into the pool of disgusting liquid he had spewed in front of his face. As he rotated over to his back, he attempted to hold back another violent itch crawling up his throat. His body jerked under the strain, and soon he entered another coughing fit.

"It will pass," Kowin rasped near Tyran's feet. His tone was taunting, nearly gleeful at the sight of their suffering. Tyran bobbled his head, trying to glower at the figure looming over him. His memory was peppered, recollecting little of what happened beyond the gate of the Grumadki. Kowin leaned closer, scowling. "The three of you should be dead. No mortal has ever survived the shadow plane. No matter. The demons are thicker in the heart of the Netherworld. You will never make it to the next Grumadki."

Tyran shivered, clenching his jaw with frustration. The horrors of the shadow world were already forgotten, like a morning mist. Yet Kowin's tone was unmistakable; he was not a friend.

"You—you must—see us through," Tyran said, forcing the words as his eyes adjusted to the obscure plane of the Netherworld. The bluish fog wafted over the land, swirling against itself in strange patterns. Admittedly, the frozen wasteland was not as vibrant in color as Aenar, but more light existed here than through the Grumadki.

The brightness nearly burned his eyes.

"What is wrong with you?" Drast coughed, forcing the words. "By the gods, you are meant to help us."

Kowin grunted in satisfaction, speaking his mind as his boots crunched against the ground. "My obligation to help see Wolos freed grows less attractive by the day. If ever I find the means to free myself from Svarog's hold, I will stop Wolos from being reborn."

Tyran pushed himself up on his elbow to gaze at the so-called god. He looked as human as Tyran with his piercing sapphire eyes and stringy hair. His crimson breastplate was as bright as fresh blood, and while he had not yet used the swords at his side, Tyran did not doubt his faculty with them. "Wolos would do better to stay dead," Kowin said, speaking more to himself than Tyran.

Tyran searched for a response, but his head hurt too much to think.

Drast attempted to stand to Tyran's left and rapidly fell back to his knees. Kam, beyond Drast, choked uncontrollably in the fold of her arm. She lay flat and useless on her back.

Tyran eyed the Grumadki behind Kowin, almost identical to the one they had entered, hoping to find Erzebeth waiting for their arrival. She would probably have a better understanding of Kowin's threats, but she was nowhere to be found.

Kowin stooped to Tyran's side, his breath sticky against his cheek. "At best, you might make it to the Tower of Eresh, but you will not escape its phantasms for five hundred years at minimum. If you think the shadow world was frightening, wait until you step foot in the Tower. What you discover within will leave you horrified and loathing yourself."

"Is that supposed to make sense to me?" Tyran blinked at Kowin, who appeared in a disarrayed blur of colors. *"Have we spoken of the Tower of Eresh? Why are we going there?"*

Tyran's questions were answered with silence.

Drast finally rose to his feet, straightening his back with a groan. His tone was soft, the underpinnings of a laugh making its way up from his chest. "You know little of what we have endured, Kowin."

"Nor do I care." Kowin rested his hand on the hilt of his curved blade, twisting away from Tyran. "I suspect that by the time you reach the next Grumadki, I will have come closer to escaping the restraints of the niggling gods. Aenar needs to be cleansed."

"And then what of us?" Drast challenged.

"What of you?" Kowin laughed. "Once my soul is safe from the hands of gods and mortals alike, I will return to kill you and your brother. I will not allow some damaged creations of the pantheon to wander the Nine Lands, ever-infamous for being *god-killers*."

"Wolos underestimated us, too. Try not to withhold your shock when we kill you first, Kowin." Drast's face burst into a smile, sliding his bow from his shoulder and cupping the grip in his left hand. His spectral hand was already reaching for an arrow in his quiver.

In less than a breath, Kowin zipped from where he stood to stand behind Drast. Tyran embraced Koldovstvo, throwing himself onto his feet when Kowin grabbed Drast by the scruff of the neck and snarled at them. "You are mistaken to threaten me, mortal. I am deathless."

Kowin vanished.

Drast hurtled himself away with Koldovstvo, landing at Tyran's side. He whirled around with his weapon drawn toward the Grumadki, where Kowin had stood a moment before. He fumed. "Where did he go?"

"Back to Aenar, I am guessing," Tyran mumbled, realizing his fingers were curled so tightly they hurt. He took a deep breath, unballing his fists. He could not say he or Drast were ready to fight another god.

"I agree." Drast said to no one in particular, slinging his bow back over his shoulder. "He should never have been released."

"Erzebeth said it was necessary." Kam struggled to her feet, turning from him and Drast to examine the flat terrain surrounding them. Tyran noticed her hair was longer, with a tuft of dark hair sprouting from her head. Something strange happened while they were in the shadow plane. Had his mind wandered again?

Kam adjusted her grey robes. "Worrying about Kowin will not help us at present. He will return when we reach the next Grumadki. Until then, we should press for the Tower of Eresh."

"So we are going to the Tower of Eresh? What is this place and why did Kowin know about it before us?" Tyran ground the few teeth in his mouth. He could not say that Kam had not told him once already, or even more than once, but the Warden was naïve to think they could forget Kowin's threats so easily. Tyran would not forget! He swore it to himself. He would remember Kowin was dangerous. If they did not cover ground swiftly, Kowin would be anything but an ally

when they crossed paths again.

Despite his chest shaking with suppressed mirth, the sour look Drast gave Tyran suggested his thoughts were not far from the same truth.

"How many more Grumadki must Kowin lead us through?" Drast arched his thick eyebrows. Tyran took a step back as though he was only now seeing Drast for the first time. The frilled white beard and nearly bald scalp had been replaced by scattered grey hair and a thick matching beard.

"I do not remember you looking like this in a very long time."

"I have no idea," Kam said, answering Drast's question.

Drast visibly tensed, his mustache smashing against the clump of grey hairs beneath his bottom lip. "You must be crazy if you think we are going to overlook the fact that he not only wants us to fail, but that he also wants us dead."

"I must remind you that we need him to pass through the Grumadki. No one else knows the way. The old-dark are breaking away from the Ash Tree. We have to get to Heshayol, or we will all die," Kam said.

"We are supposed to be dead anyway." Tyran clenched his jaw, reflecting on his lessons about self-preservation. He'd learned from the best—his father, who taught him to always strike before being struck. The phrase "kill or be killed" was not hard to understand. Yet he could understand why they must leave Kowin alive.

Kam looked at Drast and then rubbed the top of her head. "How long were we in the shadow plane?"

"It felt like minutes," Drast replied, lifting his arm to examine the lack of wrinkles on his hands. He then pulled the Alatir Stone from his pocket. "I held the stone most of the way through, save when we were exiting again. I—"

"I have been waiting for nearly six weeks." Erzebeth suddenly spoke from behind Tyran.

Tyran spun around to see the floating ghost staring back at him. *"How long have you been here?"*

"Where have you been?" Kam asked.

"While time passes differently there than it does here, you should not have taken this long. Kowin obviously was not in a hurry to bring you back to the Netherworld. In the past month, the old-dark's power has grown, negatively swaying the races of Aenar. Governments are faltering; civilizations are crumbling. The people are turning on one another. Wars are breaking out from Maharia to Haemus Mons," Erzebeth said plainly. Tyran winced, unfamiliar with how great the world may have become during his captivity. The Vucari looked past him. "Where is he?"

"Aenar," Kam said.

The ground rumbled slightly under Tyran's feet, almost like an earthquake.

Drast chuckled, saying nothing of the shaking earth. He shook his finger at Erzebeth. "He is biding his time. The bastard thinks he can reclaim his soul from Svarog and somehow keep us from setting Wolos free. Did you know about this?"

Erzebeth's color dimmed, drifting away from them. "I told you we could not trust him."

"Trust him?" Drast's grin widened. "Our problems are a bit deeper than meager trust. He wants to kill us, skin-switcher! And not just Tyran and me, but all of us!" Drast squared off with the dead Vucari.

Tyran cleared his throat, raising his voice in the hopes that it would be audible. *"You mean to tell me he could actually stop us from reaching Heshayol?"*

Kam stumbled closer to Erzebeth with quick footsteps as though she would chase her to the end of the earth for a clearer explanation. "Is he not duty-bound to help us while Svarog wills it of him?"

Erzebeth shimmered as though she might disappear; Tyran thought she might possibly want to track Kowin down to lecture him about his commitment to the will of the gods. The Vucari hung her head. "While he is obligated to aid us, he can resist the driving force. At least for a while. Like a pitcher can hold only so much water before it overflows, Kowin will inevitably reach his limit," Erzebeth tried to explain. "He is commanded to lead us through the Grumadki and the gates of Heshayol. But if he manages to struggle against the gods long enough to find a means to his own release—if he breaks away from Svarog—he will be able to act however he chooses."

"I lost you after *obligated*," Drast cracked, folding his beard into his fist. "I say we put an arrow through his skull and let bygones be bygones."

"An arrow will not harm him," Erzebeth said. "Our only chance is to release Wolos before Kowin is able to free himself. If we are successful, the gods should return Kowin to Thrice Ten Kingdom."

"Should?" Drast stared at Erzebeth in disbelief, rocking his head back and forth, his mirth increasing despite his furrowed brow. "I have so many hateful words dancing on the tip of my tongue, I cannot decide in which order to speak them." He slammed the Alatir Stone into Tyran's chest with a strained smile, almost knocking him down with the sudden force. Tyran accepted the stone, feeling the rush of energy spill over his body. Drast kept his attention on the glowing Vucari. "Point us in the right direction, eh? I mean, if time is *so* valuable, we should start moving. I doubt Kowin is standing around, prattling on."

The ground tremored again. With the Alatir Stone in his grasp, his mind cleared. The muscles in his jaw ached as though he may have been holding his face too tight. The words came from his mouth in a scratchy whisper. "What is that?" Tyran scanned the bluish fog on the horizon and the purplish sky above them. He could not see anything moving in the distance.

"We have reached the depths of the Netherworld now," Erzebeth said. "The war march of greater legions shakes the ground for miles in all directions. They pursue hidden paths to the surface, hungry for the flesh of mortals. Our road to the Tower of Eresh will not be easy.”

“Mm,” Tyran mumbled, eyeing his shield strapped on Kam’s back. “Best give me that.” The girl pulled the steel guard from her back and handed it to him. He fastened it to his arm, using Koldovstvo to help manage the weight, and then exchanged the Alatir Stone to his shield hand so he could wield his mace when needed.

Drast grinned at his side, likely laughing at Tyran’s habit to use the ineffective familiar armaments, even though his own hand hovered over an empty side quiver.

“Something is approaching in the distance,” Kam said.

Tyran lifted his chin to see the shadow of a man approaching through the fog. While the ground wobbled, he could see that no fiends followed the single entity traipsing forward in the shadows.

Drast jerked his bow to position, readying a magical arrow over the curved handle.

“Wait,” Tyran said. He squinted against the poor light, making out wavy red hair and a thick, unruly beard. The discolored skin was nearly rotting but, even in death, the man stomping toward them was unmistakable. “It is our father.”

Chapter X

Drast's heart palpitated in his chest, heavy and inconsistent. His head spun, the advancing figure of his father a blur. Perspiration dotted his skin despite the cold. The sheen of sweat made the icy air bite more deeply. He reached out blindly with his nub, pressing it against Tyran's arm, unable to summon the will to create his spectral hand. "Am I mad or dying, brother?"

Tyran twisted his mouth in disgust, watching Dagmar Kaligula advance toward the Grumadki. "You are not dying."

You are not mad, either.

"That is good." Drast nodded numbly, unsure if he could trust his brother's judgment. If his father were an illusion, he had no doubt Tyran would be affected by the spell. He hurriedly searched for another means to guarantee his eyes were not failing him. Gritting his teeth, he inched closer to Kam, reached around her with his working hand, and clasped onto her breast. "They may be small, but they will do in a pinch."

He squeezed.

Kam swatted his hand away, turned, and backhanded him. "What in the name of Wolos do you think you are doing?"

Drast staggered back from the blow, unable to keep the grin from his lips. "I needed someone to knock some sense into me."

"Ask next time." Kam pulled away, the vein in her neck pulsating. She adjusted her robe and snapped, "I would be more than happy to oblige."

That is kind.

"It's just not the same." He spat blood. "I just wanted to make sure you still had your vigor within you, *Small-tits*."

"I assure you, *Lefty*, that will not be a problem," she responded dryly.

"My sons!" Dagmar's voice resounded off the barren stone rising jaggedly about them as he passed beneath an arch created by the crumbled ruins of what appeared to have once been a great statue. The remains of an extended arm, broken at the wrist, leaned against the head with its jagged crown to form an opening nearly thirty feet high.

"Forget Kowin. *Father* is the one not to be trusted," Tyran growled.

Drast was acutely aware of both Erzebeth and Kam turning their heads slowly to fix his brother with the same flat gaze that he knew was on his own face. He doubted any of them would be making the mistake of trusting his father.

"My brave, loyal sons," Dagmar intoned, the smoothness of his voice rattling like a once whole death shroud now shredded and torn by time and decay. "I knew you would come back for me eventually and rescue me from this undeath."

"Father." Tyran stood stiffly, no emotion filtering through his stony countenance.

Why won't anyone stay dead?

Drast nodded. "Right?"

Dagmar closed the distance, coming within half a dozen paces and placing a hand on his chest. "Yes, it is I, your father. I have wandered the Netherworld aimlessly for a thousand years, praying that one day I would be rescued by the nobility and persistence of my sons."

I am dead, but not. Erzebeth is dead, but not. And now your father. It seems like someone should get a handle on this.

"I think that was your job, was it not?" Drast smirked.

Dagmar's face darkened. Whereas once upon a time his wrath caused his face to infuse with crimson, it now flushed with blackness carried through throbbing ebony veins in his forehead and neck as he looked upon his eldest son.

Drast, somewhat unaware of the sudden turn or the cause, met his father's gaze and blinked in surprise at the sudden display of anger. "What did I say?"

Dagmar's lips peeled back momentarily, revealing half-rotten teeth and brackish gums; long-nailed fingers clenched into fists.

Kam stepped back, her fingers gripping the haft of her axe, ready for whatever might come of the tension. "Would you strike your own son?"

"Time has not been kind to us, Father," Tyran said, his speech quick. "Best not to read too closely into the words of your son."

Drast looked back and forth between Tyran and their father, not entirely certain what had just transpired. Muttering, he said, "You know, if you did not just show up unannounced, talking my ear off, we would not get in these straits. I cannot be expected to do what I must if I cannot follow what is going on around me."

The flush of his father's face slowly eased, as it was his turn to look back and forth between Tyran and Drast, his gaze lingering on the former. "I suppose that is true. You are weary, I am sure, my sons. It is not easy being in this place, especially for the living. You are brave to have ventured hence for the well-being of your father."

Well, if I am a god, and a dead one at that, you should at least give me a little respect. I have the wisdom of the ages and you might learn something if you paid attention to me rather than the nonsense going on around you.

"Don't you think you are asking a little much?" Drast said, looking hard at a stone not thirty feet away, not sure what his father had said. "I will do my best, but I am only one man."

That is all I ask.

"Of course," Dagmar smiled. "So long as you are willing to try, I can show you the way."

Drast jerked back to his father in surprise. "What in the Nine Lands are you talking about?"

Tyran cleared his throat, crossing his now thick arms over his chest. "I think you just agreed to help Father in some way."

Drast vigorously shook his head. "I do not think so." He pointed a finger at Dagmar, wishing he could remove the smile from his face. "Where were you when we were bound in Anaerfell for the last thousand years?"

Their undead, unctuous father spread his hands. "Seeking a way to help you, my son. I knew you were bound, obviously, but what could I do alone against the hordes of Vucari filth that inhabited the place?" He shook his head. "Nothing, my noble son. I was as helpless as you were, aged as I was from escaping Lairhein after the populace rose against us, incited by the mendacities of the Kluks."

He does seem to enjoy the sound of his own voice, does he not? Reminds me of someone else I know.

Drast laughed aloud. "Mendacities? They had no need when the truth was sufficient. The evil we wrought upon our own people paled only when compared to the evil we wrought upon the Vucari." He looked to Kam and Erzebeth. "Do you two have anything to add? I would be eager to hear your thoughts."

"I have enough issues with my own father, I am in no hurry to take up the one you have with yours," Kam muttered sardonically.

Erzebeth's eerie voice crept among them. "During the time of the conflict between the Stuhia and the Vucari—"

"Do not pretend," Tyran interrupted, cutting off whatever the ghostly Vucari would have said, "that the Vucari had any more than a single Warden looking after us."

"That you could see!" Dagmar raised a withered finger triumphantly. "Why would they show the entirety of their numbers to you?"

Kam snorted. "I was alone."

"Only one or two Wardens tended to you during your *stay* at Anaerfell," Erzebeth added, her voice drifting among them like a passing breeze.

"More lies!" Dagmar snarled, stepping closer and twisting his finger at her. "Skin-switchers cannot be trusted, my sons. We were at war with them long enough for you to know that—long before any dreams *we* had of immortality. Do not be taken by her beneficence, trying to tear asunder the eternal bond between a father and his sons."

All along? A millennium passed. Surely he could have found the time, especially after you did what he asked of you.

"An excellent point."

"Thank you, my loyal son." Dagmar reached out to touch his shoulder.

"Not you." Drast snorted, pulling away. "You had more than a thousand years to free us from our prison. To give us a reprieve from the pain, hunger, torment, and madness." He gestured to his father's face. "You found a way to conquer age, to reverse its effects, rotten as you may be now. Why did you not return to us to set us free?"

Dagmar sighed, turning to walk away as he spoke. "Ah, my son. If only it were so simple. The path I chose led me far from you, and as way leads unto way, time escaped my notice. For the gifts I received, payment was due, and in the course of that payment I found myself bound in a prison myself." He turned around. "Look at my mottled flesh, decaying and rank with rot. I found my way to deathlessness, becoming a man who even the gods themselves cannot kill, but I am eternally bound to wander the Netherworld without means to escape," he cocked his head, "until now."

Do not engage him.

Drast nodded silently to himself, but Tyran said, "Then you have everything you have ever sought. You have our congratulations and farewell." He began to walk away, brushing past their father. "Come, my brother, we have a task."

Finally! I was sick of standing here anyway.

"Do you even have legs?"

That! Well, that is an excellent question.

Tyran looked at Drast with confusion painted on his features. "Yes—and I intend to use them."

They had not walked more than a dozen paces before Dagmar was beside them, his lips pinched in obvious frustration. For a time he said nothing, merely walking beside them as they began to trudge up the incline toward the dismembered pieces of the statue.

"I understand, Tyran, the hardship I have caused you and your brother. I had hoped that time would help to heal the rift between us, but it seems that the rift has only grown wider." He shook his head solemnly. "Let me travel among you and repair what has been broken. If time is not enough, I can make amends as best I am able."

They crested the rise as Dagmar spoke, passing beneath the arm and jagged crowned head to reveal a swelling throng of demons. Bukavac milled about, gnashing their teeth, while eyeless Nithhoggr continuously turned in a widening gyre. Nocnica swarmed like a black fog among the masses, blurring the presence of other demons: Witiko, Dreka, Skyrz, and others of which Drast had no knowledge.

Tyran grunted, stumbling to a halt.

That is a big horde.

"I've seen bigger," Drast muttered with a half-grin, though his mouth went dry.

Dagmar chuckled. "A legion you will not have to face, so long as I march at your side. I am here for you, my sons. I can protect you in this place." He shrugged. "And perhaps, in return, you will speak with me and give me a chance to make amends."

"That is so kind of you, Father," Drast began, a smile forming on his lips that he could not withhold. "I have always dreamed of having familial hugs in which we wept upon each other's shoulders and told each other our hopes and dreams."

Dagmar turned his gaze toward his son, the black flush again rising up his neck into his cheeks.

"Admittedly," Drast lifted his stump, momentarily forgetting no hand was attached, "I did not envision such heartwarming moments with quite the smell of death coming from you. Though if I must be honest, I did think you would be dead before it ever occurred."

The flush had reached his father's forehead and he growled through bared teeth. "Drast—"

Drast caught sight of his stump and laughed. "And I suppose hugging has become somewhat more difficult now than it used to be, you know." He fixed his gaze to his father's. "I seemed to have lost part of myself in the pursuit of one family member's obsession." He waved his stump. "I don't suppose you could get that back for me? I have not quite gotten used to pleasuring myself with the left, if you understand my meaning." He paused, waiting for a response that did not come. He continued, "Although I suppose I could have figured it out if I had not been chained to wall for the last thousand years."

Kam snickered.

Dagmar turned to face the young Vucari. "Your mockery has no place here, skin-switcher. Keep your teeth shut or we will see how you manage after being flayed alive!"

Drast shook his head. "I do not think so, Father. She does have her uses, and flaying would not be in our best interest." He shrugged. "Besides, I have grown to enjoy Small-tits."

Oh really?

He giggled, his breath escaping him for several moments while Dagmar glared in anger, Tyran frowned in confusion, Kam blushed, and Erzebeth fluttered expressionless.

"I mean," he sputtered, "they'll do in a pinch." With a loud guffaw, he fell to his knees, holding his side with his good arm.

Chapter XI

Tyran's tears froze before they could descend from the corners of his eyes, but his anger heated his ears.

Knotting his fists in an attempt to stop trembling, he trudged half-heartedly behind Erzebeth and Kam with blurred vision, his feet dragging so much that the layered frost adhered to his boots. His shield arm ached from holding the Alatir Stone so tightly that he could feel the strain pass his elbow. He did his best to ignore it and trudged forward.

He did not try to rub his tears away, no matter how distorted the ranks of demons became on either side. The ice-strong Bukavac stamped to the left and right; the eyeless Nithhoggr soared above. Unnamed devils and demons multiplied, joining the horde, encircling them and stretching in all directions. He did not care.

"You and your brother have made a lasting testament to our capacity for sovereignty, one which will never be forgotten. The Kaligula name has become eternal," Dagmar spoke to Drast in a fervent whisper behind Tyran. "It is only a matter of time before the world trembles at the sound of our name, bending the knee with absolute devotion. How can any god be revered when we have claimed the name of *god-killers?*"

Dagmar laughed.

Tyran listened for Drast to echo the laughter and was not surprised when it came. His brother could not contain himself, whether he agreed with their father or not.

Dagmar had kept the scores of demons docile, as he said he would with his newfound power, allegedly claiming that when he stabbed himself with the magically forged dagger, *kaelandur*, he was emboldened with greatness. Tyran could not dissect the truth from his father's rambling explanation. He only knew his father apparently used the magical weapon to *kill* himself. Given Dagmar's obsession with eternal life, Tyran could not believe he would willingly take his own life unless cornered. Though despite *killing* himself, his father maintained he was not fully dead, not like the other demons, anyway.

Dagmar continued to fill Drast's ears with his self-aggrandizing words. Tyran hoped his brother was wise enough to see through it, if not ignore him altogether. "Just think about how the dragons lost their influence, their *magic*, over mortals when the Stuhia slaughtered so many of their kind. As a people, we showed our dominance over the winged serpents. We were not *given* the name 'dragon-men'. We took it!" The words were a hiss between Dagmar's teeth. "Now we have claimed the name 'god-killers'! We bettered those who created us, Drast. Can you imagine the power within our grasp?"

Dagmar laughed again. Drast hooted even louder. Madly.

Tyran's heart pounded. He told himself that his father's power over the demons was all that kept him *alive*—that is, kept him from Tyran's wrath. He may not remember much, but the hate Tyran felt for his father stayed. Every day, chained to the wall at Anaerfell, he promised himself that he would kill his father.

Now with the opportunity available, however, he could not say whether he could murder Dagmar or, better yet, if

Drast would agree to see it done; but Tyran's gut urged him to do it. The last moments at Anaerfell—after Drast felled Wolos and was thought to be on his deathbed—Tyran met Dagmar in Klukas. The moment between them gave testament to his father's truest nature.

Dagmar, who believed Wolos had survived, scorned his sons for failing him, promising to find immortality without them. While time may have eased the spiteful words, Tyran's fury still raged at the memory. He could not erase the satisfied smirk Dagmar wore when thinking his sons were dying and he would drink from the Waters of Life, living forever.

Dagmar deserved death. A painful, long death, but Tyran was not blinded to his own weaknesses. He mentally struggled to remember moment to moment, and he was physically outmatched by his father and the demon armies. Nine Lands, he could even claim the mission ahead held greater importance than his desire for revenge. No matter the excuse, when push came to shove, Tyran knew he might not have the will to take the light from his father's eyes.

"Ah, son. You two have done well, indeed. I would have never imagined you could have survived at Anaerfell, but you persevered." His father yammered on behind him, singing praises and apologies, keeping a smile so firmly planted on his face, he could rival Drast. "By the gods, your imprisonment broke my heart."

Drast mumbled something unintelligible. Tyran was certain Drast was not even speaking to his father, but having a quiet conversation with himself. Dagmar did not seem to take notice, caught up in his own oration.

He walked faster his legs to escape his father's voice. His knees cracked with the effort. Nevertheless, he did not stop until he reached Kam and Erzebeth.

The undead Vucari addressed him the moment he reached her periphery. "Regardless of the copper dagger being gone, your father is tainted by the magic of kaelandur.

He will always be pushed to tear down the Ash Tree and release the old-dark to destroy the world." Erzebeth kept her chin forward, speaking under her breath, while Kam stared at him, her brown eyes burning into him from the opposite side of Erzebeth's ethereal form.

Erzebeth went on, "He is already waning. He has been down here less than a year, but in his mind, it has been a thousand years or more. The time is wearing on him, drawing him back to Aenar. Whether we bring Wolos back or not, Dagmar will always desire to find a way to release the Likhyi."

"He cannot want them released," Tyran retorted, not bothering to turn around to see if he had been heard. The rambling tone of his father had not lessened in the least.

Erzebeth dimmed in color. "It does not matter what he wants. Remember, Kowin does not have any interest in assisting us, yet the gods sway him. The power forcing your father is stronger still, invoked by the curse of kaelandur. The magic will eventually force his hand against those he loves, against himself."

"You mistake him. He loves no one *but* himself." Tyran looked away, catching sight of demons on either side of them again. He could not see an end to the monsters. And while some gnashed their teeth or growled, none lifted a hand against them. He tried to change the direction of the conversation. "You said he was dead."

Erzebeth glanced at Dagmar and Drast over her shoulder, considering his words. No doubt, she inspected Dagmar's blood-red eyes and rotting, pale skin. The cold of the Netherworld did not steal away the stench of death and decay, not from his father or the dead armies. "He is hardly alive," she said.

Tyran hissed under his breath, hearing the derision in Erzebeth's words. He did not want to talk with Erzebeth about whether Dagmar lived or died. Those discussions were meant for him and Drast. "You think we should kill him, then? You see him as a threat."

"He is a threat, Tyran. Not only is his magic limitless like yours in the Netherworld, but also in Aenar. Moreover, he cannot be killed in Aenar. By the magic of kaelandur, he can be killed only here," Erzebeth said with a grimace. "Do not act stupid. You know the difference between an ally and an enemy."

He locked his jaw to keep his tongue from rattling. He thought Erzebeth was an ally at one time, until she locked him away at Anaerfell. Even now, she pretended to be on his side when she only served her own self-interest. Everything inside of him may have screamed to end his father, but his desire to see it done practically vanished with Erzebeth's prompting. He did not doubt what she said—Dagmar may always be a threat to the Ash Tree—but she likely kept a greater truth sealed from him.

He sucked the frigid air through his nostrils, noticing Kam, who had not averted her gaze except to assure her feet stayed on the path ahead. He wondered what the two skin-switchers talked about when he and Drast were not in earshot. While he could not remember most of their trek, he understood they had traveled a great distance across the Netherworld already.

"If he is so dangerous, why have you not killed him?" Tyran asked.

Her face was expressionless, scanning ahead. "I do not have the power." Before he could say more, Erzebeth quickly added, "And neither does the Warden."

Kam did not argue with Erzebeth, her face as solemn as the ghost's. Tyran did not know how much Kam knew previously or what knowledge a Warden might be privy to during their tutorship. He only knew procuring knowledge from the skin-switcher was like squeezing water from a damp rag, and every tidbit of information Erzebeth finally chose to share was more alarming than the last.

Tyran snapped, "If she is so weak, why did she come

here to begin with?"

"I am not weak," Kam said. Her teeth flashed with amusement. "Unless you only measure strength by the hair on your chest."

He wrestled against the urge to clash against her childish behavior; she and Erzebeth were the ones advising him to kill. He would not be derailed from his question. "Why are you here, then?"

Despite Erzebeth's unmistakable look of warning, Kam's tongue loosened. "I am here to do what you and Drast cannot."

Tyran paused, searching for a response. "What are you talking about?"

Kam stepped around Erzebeth, if not partially through her, and glared at Tyran. She barely reached his chest, chin jutted upward with the sudden air of a full-grown woman who was used to speaking her mind and being heard. "I am here to sacrifice myself so my god may live," she said candidly. "Once Wolos is freed from Heshayol, he can only be resurrected if a living being offers up their life. It is the only way the dead can cross the Kalinov Bridge and rediscover life. Sacrifice." She lifted her finger as though she might stab him through the chest with it, and then pointed back in the direction from which they had come.

Tyran's mouth twisted oddly. The strain of the muscles in his face hurt as he tried to contemplate the enormity of what she shared. "Why did you say nothing?" he finally managed.

"What would it matter? You can barely remember one day to the next, and your brother is caught up in a world separate from reality. You likely will not remember half this conversation come tomorrow," she said. "Besides, in the brief moments you behave sanely, I have seen enough to understand where you place your loyalties. You think only of yourselves. Neither of you would willingly die to see Wolos return."

He was not certain if she was right, but her words struck deep enough to sicken him. "Why not? Our lives are already at risk by being here. We are already practically sacrificing ourselves."

"A great difference lies between the threat of your life and the definite end to it," Erzebeth said. "The abyss between the two is ever-reaching. I would not risk the fate of the world on the vanity of the Kaligulas."

"Though," Kam said with a click of her tongue, "if I were to fall between here and Heshayol, one of you would have to lose your life to succeed, or all would be for nothing. You said once that you were duty-bound, yes? Which do you hold to a higher standard: life or duty?"

Dagmar and Drast stepped up on either side of Tyran before he could respond. Kam's mouth snapped shut. She backed away slowly, fixated on Dagmar's cruel grin.

"Unwise to threaten my boy, Vucari scum," Dagmar said grimly.

His hand folded around Tyran's shoulder, squeezing it slightly as he did when he was a boy. Dagmar took a deep breath through his nose, as loud as a gale whipping through a hollow in Tyran's ear. "I have no love for your unholy quest to bring back a god we rightly killed. To think you have the nerve to steal away the glory of our family name disgusts me to the core. My sons are not your puppets to torment," he sneered. "What do you say, boys? Should we watch the Nithhoggr rip the little one to pieces before we return to the Kalinov Bridge?"

Drast chuckled as though Dagmar was telling a joke. "We already decided we are not killing the Warden."

Dagmar's face twisted with aggravation before slipping into a half-smile.

Drast hummed to himself, bouncing his head to some unheard voice. He met Tyran's eye before speaking to their father again, his question booming over the din of the demon hordes. "Tell us, why would we hurry back to the bridge, Father?"

Dagmar's chest swelled and he lifted his nose, looking down upon them. He seemed to have been waiting for this moment. "Ah. Well, either of you may transfer your life source to yours truly. I have spent more years down here than I can bear, and the thirst for life is wet on my lips. Clearly fate would bring you here so I may return to the world of the living."

"What?" Tyran pulled away from Dagmar. He wondered how time passed in the minds of the dead.

His father maintained a look of innocence. "Let our enemy live if you want, but why follow them any farther? The girl already said she was going to kill herself. So, let her. She does not need an audience." His father raised his hands, reaching for Drast, who instinctively stepped back as though he might be hit. "Sons, I have always loved you, taught you all the necessary skills to endure a dangerous world. Look at what you have accomplished; look what you have survived because of me. I gave you life. I made you strong. Can you not find it in your hearts to return to me what I have given you?"

Tyran was in shock. His father could not possibly believe half the nonsense he was saying. Either his transcendence to death caused him to go mad, or he was lying through his decaying teeth. Tyran swallowed, his voice quivering more than he would have liked, a shadow of what he wished it to be. "I will see Kam to the end of her journey to free Wolos."

"Oh. I will, too," Drast said, a grin slipping across his face, dipping his gray beard to his chest.

Dagmar folded his arms and smiled again. "Of course, I understand. She would never make it to Heshayol beyond the demons without you. How could she? You are Kaligulas; no other mortal could manage this place." Dagmar nodded to himself while Tyran gawked in confusion. Drast's facial expression was not far from his own. "We will lead her to the chambers as you promised, and I will keep the horde from crushing down upon you. I would do anything for my dear sons."

Chapter XII

Erzebeth led them forward across the wasteland.

Days passed into weeks while they marched through the tangled demons dispersed over the frozen tundra. The creatures' distorted faces, bloodied and marred, became more regular than the speckles of color seen in the frost beneath Drast's feet. He went to sleep listening to their growling and raspy undertones, and woke to their looming faces. The monsters stumbled around them and flew above them, ever-increasing in their numbers.

Drast and Tyran had done their best to speak to each other in private, but Dagmar was never far away from them, looming and insistent. Despite Tyran holding Ojenek, he said he never heard anything intelligible coming from the beasts, suggesting the monsters spoke no audible language. Any sense of order or interaction among them was at the direction of Dagmar and in silence.

At one point, he and Tyran considered using Koldovstvo to hurry themselves along and escape Dagmar, but there was no guarantee their father could not follow with his horde, given his access to Koldovstvo. Besides, if ever their father stopped singing their praises and decided to turn the monsters against them, they could be overrun. The mental fortitude to fight against such great numbers would be impossible, even with the Alatir Stone in their possession. Drast was certain they would now lose a battle amid the legions surrounding them.

They had no choice but to walk and walk.

And walk.

"You have time. You have time. You have all the time in the world," Dagmar whispered to himself. Their father repeated some variation of the sentence off and on for a couple of days now, staring furiously at Kam and Erzebeth.

Time passes differently for him. Each day plodding behind you could be a year for him.

"He always said he wanted to live forever." Drast stepped away from his father. Dagmar did not even glance in his direction, but his scowl noticeably deepened.

Most people want to live forever. No one wants to die.

"I would not mind dying," Drast replied.

Kam said something next to him that he missed, and instead he focused on Wolos's voice.

Wait until you are dead before passing judgment.

Realizing he was making the same mistake in thinking as his father, Drast nodded. "That's fair."

Kam's boyish tenor resounded over his shoulder again, causing him to turn around. "We covet life while doing little to nothing with what we already have. Life is a privilege, and we think we are entitled to more."

"What are you talking about?" Drast squinted at her.

Her gaze darted between each of his eyes. "I thought we were having a…never mind."

At least if Small-tits is talking, we know she isn't dead yet.

"A silver lining," Drast murmured.

Scratching his head, he fell back into step with the rest of the party. The voice in his head teased at his fears, wondering whether Dagmar would attempt to slaughter the Warden when they rested. Drast could imagine Dagmar thinking he could then sway Tyran and him to return to the Kalinov Bridge if Kam permanently disappeared.

In recent nights, Drast discovered Dagmar lingering over them with feigned patience while they slept. Luckily, Erzebeth—like Dagmar—did not need rest and would remain vigilant in watching over them, even though she claimed several times she needed to seek out Kowin. Drast was not sure whose presence he felt more uncomfortable with, but he was somewhat glad he had not yet woken to find Kam's body mutilated or missing.

"You have time," Dagmar repeated from the far back.

Apparently, he has time.

"If you are eager for us to be done, Dagmar Kaligula, direct the dead away from here. Clear our path," Erzebeth said. She turned to watch Dagmar with suspicion, as though she expected him to set the dead upon them at any given moment.

Drast nodded. "Yes, yes."

Kam chimed in. "By all means, and then take your leave with them. You and your rambling are neither wanted nor needed here."

Dagmar sneered at them before catching Tyran's eye, and then swiftly relaxed his expression. "I would be a fool to leave my boys alone with a backstabbing skin-switcher and her minion. Did I not recently hear that you, Erzebeth, are the one who locked them away at Anaerfell?"

Drast grinned at the accusation, recognizing his father's attempt to turn them against each other. His father was an intelligent man, eking out the most damning information and then throwing it against those whom he intended to delegitimize. Of course, plenty of details had come out during the past few days, and Dagmar would not let the knowledge go to waste.

Dagmar continued, "You refused to let them reunite with their family? I can only imagine what twisted betrayal you have waiting for them at the end of this little march." Dagmar nodded at Tyran as though they had made a secret pact.

Did they?

Drast shook his head. "I do not think so."

Dagmar frowned at him. "Well, I will stay right here beside my sons with my army. I will be waiting for you to show your true colors, and then you will watch your little princess," he pointed to Kam, "be ripped apart and feasted upon."

"You are as insane as your sons." Kam stomped along, folding her arms under her breasts. "Finding pleasure in the pain of anyone, even your enemy, is sickening."

"Pain is necessary in life and especially in war," Dagmar snarled. "Might as well find some joy in what cannot be avoided."

By that logic, you should find joy every time you get kicked in the bits.

Drast cackled, "I hate getting kicked in the bits!"

He could feel eyes on him for several moments. Realizing the absurdity of the situation, he doubled over, tears in his eyes.

"I would never have guessed," Kam said dryly before turning back to Dagmar. "The Vucari and Reds have not been at war for over a thousand years."

"But you have kept my sons as prisoners of that war for a thousand years? You cannot say that the war is ended and then keep my sons from their home. Do not take me for a fool." Dagmar sneered.

That is a fair point.

Drast echoed the voice.

"Your sons committed a crime against all of creation, not only against the Vucari people," Erzebeth said. "They were imprisoned as criminals, not as warriors. The war is ended."

Dagmar snorted. "Just because your people scattered from your northern homes and then forsook each other does not change the reality of the situation. You skin-switchers fled to the south in search of the Ash Tree, and those who were not gobbled up by the centaurs went mad in the Dyndaer," Dagmar said, picking up his pace to near Kam. His voice began to rise in volume, booming across the empty expanse of barren rock. "Your people no longer fight us because we won the war! We killed your god and watched your weak civilization diminish to near nothingness."

His words seemed to have struck a chord, Kam's jaw quivering with rage, her teeth grinding together.

"Leave her alone," Tyran said, his voice grating and the Alatir Stone gripped in his hand.

Drast followed his brother's lead, his heart hammering in his chest. "The skin-switchers responsible for that war are a thousand years dead."

"Have my sons grown soft?" Dagmar turned from Kam, clenching a fist at his side. "Do you remember nothing of the honor and legacy I taught you? All that I have done to make you into the men you are, and you stand before me in defense of this filthy skin-switcher?"

"It is you who know nothing of honor and legacy," Kam said firmly, drawing Dagmar's attention again. "It was I and my ancestors before me who kept your sons alive while you wandered Aenar pursuing your own interests instead of those of your sons. We kept them alive, where you would have let them die. My forebears dedicated their lives and the lives of their children to keeping your sons safe." She drew herself up as best she could, despite her smallness. "Learn from my people what it means to have legacy and honor, Dagmar Kaligula."

I suppose you two probably would have died in the snow that day.

"As a general rule, I prefer not dying," Drast said.

Did you not just say you wanted to die?

"I changed my mind."

"She dedicated her life to tend to her enemy," Tyran murmured musingly.

"Bah!" Dagmar spat. "You are both fools if you believe her drivel. It had nothing to do with you and everything to do with her dead god. Of course she kept you alive. I knew she would, as would all those who came before her. Do not let her muddy your memory of the pain that came before it. You were her prisoners!”

What did your father do to help?

“And you did nothing to save us!” Drast shouted. “Of the two, she and her kind kept us breathing and you did nothing. You could have saved us from that prison at any point in the past millennium, but you are a selfish, self-absorbed man who did nothing but save your own skin!”

Dagmar gagged. “I cannot believe what I am hearing. Have you two forgotten your heritage? Those skin-switchers broke you.”

Tyran scoffed. “No, they kept us alive after you sent us to die. The Wardens have given us a chance at redemption.”

Dagmar scoffed, narrowing his eyes at Tyran. “You do not redeem glory.”

“One man’s glory is another man’s agony,” Tyran said and spat, droplets catching in his beard and mustache. “Consider for a moment that *your glory* was never *ours*.”

His father stepped back, eyeing him and Drast. His mouth fell open, his jaw crooked with disbelief. He finally set his attention on Drast. “You feel this way too? You think I steered you poorly?”

Not to put too fine a point on it, but you did lose an arm and end up imprisoned for a thousand years based on his steering.

Drast tightened his lips, first looking to Tyran and then their father. His nostrils flared with frustration, evidence that he had no interest in having this conversation. When he finally opened his mouth, laughter spilled out. He could not say why. It bubbled up from deep within his belly and he could do nothing to hold it back as it overflowed his lips.

Kam’s brown eyes flashed with fury. “Killing Wolos has only brought suffering.”

Dagmar lifted his hand, spanning over the many demons at his command. “Death is suffering. These poor souls have been twisted at the hands of the gods because they did not do what the gods wanted them to do. Why should we be held victim to the whims of gods?"

"Why not?" Erzebeth asked, dipping down by Tyran's side. "They breathed life into you. Why can they not take it away?"

Because it is your *life?*

"Is it?" Drast chortled.

Dagmar's voice deepened, almost snarling in response to the ghostly Vucari. "Why should they give us life and then dictate how we live it? Do we not have autonomy? You think we are simple-minded slaves to the gods?" The Nithhoggr screeched above Dagmar as if they heard his calling, swooping closer to the lot of them on the ground. "No intelligent god would create a man to be free-thinking and then threaten him to be obedient or suffer. The gods must be pawns in a greater scheme."

Who says the gods are intelligent?

Drast tensed at the accusations, the Nithhoggr circling above them. The Bukavac rumbled nearby, several turning their heads.

Erzebeth stared at Dagmar, her pale green eyes illuminating eerily. "You are right. The gods are as much spokes in a spinning wheel as we are. They did not design the wheel."

"Who did?" Tyran stepped between them.

"Is it not clear? Kowin," Erzebeth said. "Kowin descended on Aenar from the cosmos, a being of order, and beheld the madness wrought by the immortal Likhyi." Turning from Dagmar, Erzebeth moved to continue toward their destination. "Being more powerful than all of the old-dark combined, he trapped them in the Ash Tree, creating law from chaos. He then formed the pantheon to preserve the balance, to manage the ebb and flow of existence, and to assure the old-dark forever remained trapped in their prison." As they followed and she spoke, the Nithhoggr subsequently lifted back to the skies and the Bukavac dropped back, ignoring them once more.

Drast searched his memory, wondering if he knew the answer. When nothing came to light, he asked, "If he is all-powerful, why would he need the pantheon? Why could he not just manage the cycles and elements himself?"

"The same reason you build a ship instead of swimming across the sea or cut down a tree with an axe instead of a jagged rock," Erzebeth said. "It takes less time and energy to create a tool."

"He was the clockmaker, while the pantheon was his clock," Kam said.

Tyran looked at them with the same dumbfounded expression that Drast knew must be on his own face.

"Exactly," Erzebeth said. "Yet as the clockmaker, he was beyond the function of the clock. He held too much power and was a threat to his own creation. Therefore, his creation—the pantheon—trapped him to keep the clock eternally working." The Vucari caught Tyran's eye. "When you killed Wolos, you broke the clock, giving clearance for chaos to reign once more. The gods are simply trying to reset the system by any means possible, whether Wolos is reborn or Kowin destroys it all and rebuilds the clock."

"If he chooses to rebuild the clock…" Kam's voice drifted off. She shook her head despondently.

Erzebeth asked, "Do you now understand?"

Drast raised his bushy eyebrows with a wild grin. "I might, skin-switcher, if you could stop playing your games for one moment and tell me one thing." He folded his arms across his chest. "What in the Nine Lands is a clock?"

Chapter XIII

"We are going to Heshayol to see Wolos reborn. The Tower of Eresh and then to Heshayol. This is my duty. My duty. My duty," Tyran repeated. He did not fully understand what either of the places truly were, but he made the effort to remind himself of their task every morning and several times throughout the day in the hopes of not forgetting.

The traveling was easy—or should have been—if it were not for the company. Tyran lost track of the days some time ago. He supposed the exact time was unimportant if they continued moving their feet whenever awake. Ice-capped mountains came and went, valleys dipped and disappeared, and the demons were constantly watching over them. Each day, he and Drast continued to exchange the Alatir Stone as they traveled along, feeling their vigor restored, their physical bodies nearing what may have been during middle age. Their wrinkles lessened and their hair lengthened, gaining little color in the grey. More importantly, with each passing day, Tyran discovered two things: one, his memory strengthened, and two, the rot in his brother's mind was not being cured by the Alatir Stone.

He wondered when, during their long imprisonment, Drast began to slip from reality and what he may have done to prevent it.

Even now, his brother ambled behind him and Erzebeth, in the company of Dagmar and Kam, caught up in his frenzied laughter. Oftentimes, Drast fought to hold back the laughter—almost as though it pained him—but in moments like these, he stared wide-eyed at the demons around them, chortling without restraint.

Tyran looked at the shining white artifact in his shield hand and asked the burning question to their seemingly all-knowing guide. "Erzebeth, what is wrong with Drast? Why is the stone not healing his mind?"

The Vucari looked at the Alatir Stone in his open palm. Her ethereal features gave away nothing of her thoughts, and he was left only with her lifeless words. "Drast's affliction is as permanent as his missing appendage. He cannot be cured of it."

"Why not?"

She looked away from him. "His prolonged captivity has broken his mind. Where your sickness derived from time eating away at your senses, his illness primarily developed from suffering."

Tyran clenched his jaw at the thought. Even though they were both free from Anaerfell, she suggested Drast would always be trapped. Tyran's throat threatened to swell and restrict his voice, but he forced his tongue. "You mean to say that you did this to him."

"I did nothing." She waved off his suggestion of her culpability so quickly—and simply—Tyran almost overlooked how unbelievably heartless she sounded in her indifference.

He grimaced. Erzebeth doing nothing did not save her from being guilty of the circumstance in which she placed him and Drast. She could deny causing Drast's madness all she wanted, but she undeniably had a hand in laying the groundwork that inflicted his insanity. Tyran knew this to be true. His own life was a testament to how treating others could impact them for years to come. Every action, meticulously planned or not, spirited an inevitable reaction.

In reflection, he wondered how many choices the gods gave him and how many were invariably caused by the influence of others.

His wonderment stayed with him for several hours until he forgot his frustration with Erzebeth. His long strides cut away the miles, easily matched by his father and brother. Kam, who kept the pace in the early days of their adventure, now struggled to keep up with their grueling pace.

After a while, they came upon many oversized stone archways. The large grey stones were stacked, chiseled with faded images hidden under thick layers of silvery ice. The archways were twice as wide as Tyran and four times as tall, forming a perfect semi-circle beneath the purplish sky, wide enough for the five of them to walk shoulder to shoulder.

Tilting his head back, he scratched the grey hairs on his chin. The archways tickled at a memory of seeing strange ruins in the mountains upon entering the Netherworld. He could not recall the full details of the event, but he remembered questioning their existence in this forsaken realm. He restricted his thoughts to himself while they passed under a dozen or more arches, bypassing the multitudes of demons stretching in all directions around them.

At one point, he caught sight of Erzebeth in his periphery and had a sudden tremor in his stomach. He swiftly blamed the ache on hunger, which had intensified over the past several days. He was no stranger to having no food and little sleep. He spent countless hours at Anaerfell with nothing but his tongue to chew on, feeding on haunting visions of what once was or what could have been. Still, he grabbed his belly—as though it were to blame—when the unwelcomed image flashed across his memory of pressing his lips against Erzebeth's in the ice-covered mountains of Valarun. He mentally fought to push it aside until his head ached. He did not love Erzebeth. She was dead; he knew he soon would be too.

He searched for an excuse for the intrusive memory. His body was exhausted. There could be no other explanation for the discomforting visions.

"Are you okay?" Erzebeth asked.

"Mm." Tyran almost jumped at her sudden interest. He must have groaned louder than he thought. He quickly sought something to redirect himself from speaking his thoughts, noticing another looming archway in the distance. "What use do demons have for these? Who built them? This is Marheena's realm, is it not? Was it her?"

"No, she did not build this," Erzebeth answered, her tone lacking the emotion he thought to have heard a moment before. "The Netherworld was not always a resting place for the dead. This world once was as vivacious as Aenar before wasting away. Once upon a time, the land was filled with its own people and culture, with civilizations more advanced than anything we have ever known."

Tyran clicked his tongue. "What would cause a world to become *this*?"

Erzebeth replied, "I do not know, but if the old-dark are released, I suspect Aenar will become a reflection of this hell. If Kowin frees himself from the gods, we can only guess how he might further shape the Netherworld or Aenar."

"Wait. Kowin made this?" Tyran asked, following Erzebeth as she navigated them through the dead. His shoulder brushed against a Bukavac's arm. The beast rumbled but made no move, remaining passive under Dagmar's control.

He averted his eyes from the frozen demon.

"He did not make this world or cause it to crumble; he simply reshaped whatever ruin it became and bound it to Aenar. He created the Grumadki, the Kalinov Bridge, and the Tower of Eresh. He built Heshayol. As I said before, we could not traverse the Netherworld without him," Erzebeth said.

Tyran blinked, feeling like he was seeing the Netherworld again for the first time. "How many beings like Kowin exist across Nine Lands?"

"Even I cannot know the answer to that question, but I suspect infinite possibilities," Erzebeth mumbled.

"The Kaligula name was supposed to be a name of power. Authority." Dagmar interrupted them from an uncomfortably close distance, causing Tyran to stop and spin around. He saw Dagmar was not addressing him or anyone specifically, but rather talking openly to himself. Kam halted in the far rear, also surprised by the outburst. Even Drast, who remained at Dagmar's shoulder, cocked his head at their father. Dagmar hung his head almost as though he forgot they were in his company; his eyes looked watery. "We have nothing now. The three of us are all stuck here in the Netherworld. Our titles have been stripped. Our name has been cursed. We have no future. No hope. Nothing."

Tyran held his breath. In his entire life, he never saw his father cry, and now he looked to be on the brink of tears. The mass of demons began to shift, responding to Dagmar's apparent despair. A low moan filled the air.

Dagmar clenched his hands into fists, pulling them to his chest as though he were cradling himself, his face still pointed at the frosted ground beneath his feet. He wailed, his strong voice carrying an undercurrent of frustration and sadness, "This is all my fault, boys. I wanted something great for our family. I wanted you to have the life my father was too afraid to give me. I wanted a legacy we could pass on for generations, and look at us now…empty-handed."

"What—what is this?" Kam faltered, her brow furrowing at Dagmar first, then looking at Tyran and Drast. "Is this just another scheme to win over your sons? We have made our decision. We are freeing Wolos."

"No," Dagmar babbled, spouting water from his lips and inciting salty tears to flood down his cheeks. His death-white skin may have paled. "I…I…"

Drast became rigid, taking a couple steps closer to Tyran, distancing himself from Dagmar. "I think death broke him."

A series of discordant howls resonated from innumerable Bukavac and Dreka, lifting their muzzles as one. Above, the Nithhoggr shrieked, sending chills up Tyran's spine.

"Oh, gods!" Dagmar collapsed to his knees in a fit, his chin lifting as he reached for Drast and Tyran. "I am broken! My soul is cracked beyond repair. Can you not see it, boys? I was the Arkhon of Lairhein. The Stuhians, the city, everything was ours to rule for eternity. *Ours!* But it was all taken by those devilish Kluks. When I thought you were dead, I abandoned the city. I let those Kluks have the city. I could have returned and crushed them." He shook his head despondently. "Instead, I found the acclaimed *Kadari* and helped protect the Ash Tree."

"Who?" Kam wrinkled her nose. "The Wardens protect the Ash Tree."

Dagmar fought to keep the sneer from his face. "The Vucari have been missing from the world. The *Kadari* have guarded the Ash Tree for over a thousand years, while converting nations to follow their religion of the Lightbringer. Nearly every kingdom now recognizes them as the guardians of Aenar."

Kam scowled, but Dagmar did not give her a chance to respond.

"I rose to power among their number and forged a new path to restore the Kaligula name to history." Dagmar now sobbed, placing his face in his shaking hands. His body convulsed as he heaved, forcing the words from his tongue. Tyran could only watch, horrified at his father's absolute breakdown. "Beyond the grave, the Kluks came for us again, robbing our name from history, stealing our righteous glory."

"Nine Lands, what is he talking about?" Kam murmured

from her position in the small circle that had formed around Dagmar.

Tyran could only shake his head. Drast, on the other hand, giggled, finding unparalleled humor in Dagmar's grief. His lips vibrated through the spurts of laughter so loud, he almost drowned out Dagmar.

"I had no choice but to accept this fate I have been given." Dagmar's lamentations increased, ignoring Drast. "My soul burns for the Ash Tree's eradication, even if I must march to its location and rip it apart with my bare hands. Limb from limb. Bark from trunk. Until my fingernails bleed. I have no love to see the *thing* die. The tree gave me life for so many years, and yet I have no choice." Dagmar curled forward, averting his eyes from Tyran and Drast. His head nearly touched his knees. "The gods have cursed me. I cannot fight this dark desire they have inscribed on my heart. I deserve death."

Bukavac and Witiko jostled among them as Dagmar wailed despondently, gnashing their teeth and tearing at the ground with their claws.

Erzebeth lingered behind Tyran, looking down on Dagmar in his pitiful state. "He does deserve death."

"I do," Dagmar echoed.

Drast's face reddened, nostrils flaring, despite his maddened mirth. "You would like for us to kill him, eh?" He rushed several steps closer to Erzebeth. Tyran instinctually wrapped an arm across his brother's chest, holding him back from the Vucari. "Do you not think I see what you and Small-tits are planning? No doubt you want one less Kaligula around so no one can disrupt your little plans." Drast swung out at Erzebeth, missing wildly over Tyran's shoulder. "I know you want us all dead. Do not think I have forgotten who you are or what you did. I will not be caught unawares. I know you. I know you!"

"Drast," Tyran grunted with surprise as his brother's might pressed against his flexed arm. Drast's strength was returning. He caught Dagmar from the corner of his eye, still crying, staring at his own hands in disbelief. "Control yourself, brother."

"Give him the stone," Kam said, keeping her distance from them all, "and maybe he can regain his sense. He has not proven to be reasonable otherwise."

Tyran squinted at the Vucari, frowning. "You want him to hold the Alatir Stone when he is like this? Are you equally mad? He would be unstoppable."

"He cannot hurt Erzebeth," Kam said.

"And what about you?" Tyran hissed, swelling his chest at the Warden. Drast's words rang true for him. He wanted Dagmar dead for good, but not at the suggestion of the skin-switchers. "You are weak and pathetic. Any of us could cut you down with a simple thought."

The color washed from Kam's face. The Warden evidently needed a reminder of who he and Drast were and what they were capable of.

A light flashed in Drast's eyes upon hearing him, his mouth opening in sudden excitement. He twisted his head slowly, chewing on his inner lip in contemplation before speaking aloud. "Oh, I would kill her, Tyran. Prettily. I do not need a magical rock to take the *little princess's* life. I like girls as much as the next man, but do we really need her?"

"No, Drast! Stop this!" Tyran bellowed, unsure if his jaw had locked up in his distress. He wrapped his brother up in his arms. He tried to speak again, seeing Kam retreat into the throng of demons behind her. She was already loosening her weapon, a hand on her robes in case she had to turn into the bies. The beasts around her growled in unison but did not attack her.

"Her death will accomplish nothing, much like my miserable life." Dagmar continued to sob.

"By the gods," Tyran muttered, holding tight to Drast.

"Drast Kaligula!" Erzebeth shouted, her green light bursting around her, illuminating the immediate area. "We are not your enemy! Unless you plan to sacrifice yourself or Tyran, you will leave the Warden alone!"

Tyran kept his grip but stumbled forward, almost knocking Drast over. His older brother grabbed his arm with his good hand to help keep their balance. As they rooted their feet against the ice, Drast vacantly looked at Tyran and grinned. His brother's words were inside somewhere, fighting to be free again.

"No one touches Tyran." His words were barely audible through his mirth. He jerked out of Tyran's grasp, the grin stretching to his cheekbones. "They do not care about us. We have no more allies, Tyran."

Dagmar slurred behind them, looking at Drast and Tyran hurtfully. "This is my fault. Gods, I understand. A brave man would have accepted his death. I should be dead!"

Erzebeth dimmed, speaking to Tyran as Drast dropped to Dagmar's side to offer a hand. "Your father would be better off dead, young Red. Either kill him or keep walking. Regardless, we must reach the Tower of Eresh."

"Speak of his death again, skin-switcher, and we will see how testing the patience of a Kaligula serves you." Drast smiled.

Tyran swallowed. His brother settled the argument with a threat, freeing Tyran from making a choice. He was admittedly somewhat relieved. While he hated his father and even preferred his father be dead, as the days passed, the idea of personally slaying Dagmar became more difficult to fathom. Then again, he did not want to see the Vucari cut Dagmar down either, no matter how much he begged for release.

"Does Kaligula even mean anything anymore? We should set off for the Ash Tree. We should tear it down so we can all end this charade," Dagmar muttered.

Erzebeth remained stone-faced, motioning for Kam to follow. The Warden swung wide in her path to reunite with

Erzebeth, hanging close to her as though she could protect her from the wrath of the Kaligulas. Erzebeth said, "Know that whatever you do not come to terms with prior, you will face in the Tower of Eresh."

Tyran eyed Drast, gripping the Alatir Stone behind his shield. It was time he handed the artifact over, but he suspected Drast could wait a while longer. As for his father, he continued to sob on the ground, slowly reaching for Drast's outstretched hand. Without the gesture, Tyran wondered if he would have moved any time soon.

He took a breath, the fog in his mind clearing with the understanding that no one would be exchanging blows. He hurried to stay close to Erzebeth and Kam. "Out with it. What will we find in the Tower of Eresh?" he asked.

"Answer him, Kam," Erzebeth instructed.

Kam readjusted her robe, assuring her strange bone-handled axe was affixed to her belt. She looked off in the distance as though she were reciting from some ancient textbook. She was surprisingly calm considering how close she came to fighting Drast moments ago. "The Tower is a place of misery, where you will face the transgressions of your mortal life. We are taught the gods gave each of us a charge—one task or set of tasks to accomplish during our lifetime. Sometimes we choose to stray from the path and cause harm to those who we cross in the world. No one can tell you what you will come across in the Tower. The experience is different for all, but you can expect to face the hurts you inflicted on mortals, outside of your charge, tenfold."

Tyran's throat tightened. "You mean to say if I was meant to kill a man, I would suffer nothing for his death in the Tower, but if I murdered without divine purpose, I will be chastised for each case."

"Yes," Erzebeth said with certainty. "But while our minds may jump to murder, you will find every defilement toward another is punishable."

"Insults, theft, torture, rape..." Kam said, checking over her shoulder cautiously between sentences. "These devices, which we mortals label as evil, are not vile in themselves; in fact, they are tools used to shape the world around us. They provide motivation, teach lessons, or even redirect some back to their charge in life. However, when someone deviates—let us say, murders a being outside of their fate—they upset the stitching of reality, and they will pay the penalty for their wrongdoing."

Tyran looked over his shoulder at the sound of footsteps to see Drast and Dagmar closing the distance. Dagmar moved slowly, his head hanging and words dribbling from his lips with little energy. Drast did not seem to be paying much attention, mumbling to himself and eyeing the demons on either side.

What the two suggested was terrifying. He could not fathom, nor remember, the number of men, women, or even children he harmed during his life. His mind flooded with a handful of memories from beheading disobedient soldiers to raping his fiancé to crushing a Vucari village—men, women, and children included—beneath a mountain.

"And how do you know if what you did was right or wrong?" Tyran asked. "Seems like a setup to have no measure as to whether you should kill a man or not in the moment."

"Such is the nature of our lives. The Tower will be your pendulum," Erzebeth said.

"And what if you were supposed to kill a man but did not?" Tyran scowled.

"You mean, if you did not complete the charge given in your life?" Erzebeth clarified. "You already know. You would be refused entrance into Thrice Ten Kingdom and become a demon, forever cursed by Marheena's death magic."

"Nothing matters," Dagmar moaned. "Taste death, my sons, and you will understand. The Netherworld, Thrice Ten

Kingdom, our *charge* in the world only enslaves us in life and death to the whim of the immortals. We cannot escape."

"Shut up," Tyran growled.

Drast crowed with delight at Tyran's outburst before speaking to Erzebeth. "Why can we not go around the Tower?"

His question surprised Tyran, suggesting he may have been listening all along.

"The tower is a gateway to the next Grumadki," she replied. "There is no other way to reach it. Much like the nexus of Babeyega, you will be walking on a narrow bridge into a void between this world and the shadow plane. Because you are mortal, you cannot reach the platform without taking this hidden road."

"But you can go there with us?" Tyran asked.

"No," Erzebeth replied. "I will find Kowin to meet you beyond the Tower at the Grumadki."

"Do not go, my sons. The path is ahead is futile. I have been there many times. Come back with me to the Kalinov Bridge," Dagmar cried. "Do not leave me here alone. The Tower will swallow you, possibly for eternity!"

Tyran looked at her suspiciously. "Can we escape the Tower of Eresh?"

Drast rumbled next to him with suppressed laughter.

"I hope so," she replied.

Tyran spent the next hour or so in torment, listening to the howling of his father as he reiterated his many sudden sorrows and begged them not to enter the forsaken Tower of Eresh. Admittedly, Dagmar's behavior was unnerving since they found him in the Netherworld, but the change in demeanor was more than Tyran could stomach. He had passed the Alatir Stone over to Drast some time ago with little interest in having it returned until they survived the Tower.

He was concerned he would not have the nerve to enter the Tower knowing what might await him inside, but by the time the black spiral came into view, Tyran was ready to flee through the doors into the Tower to escape Dagmar. He could already feel the underpinnings of a headache surfacing.

He narrowly saw the Tower of Eresh in the thick blue fog, but they unexpectedly found themselves standing at its base with the arched doorway sitting inches from their noses. The misty opening at the bottom of the black pillars, as dark as lava rock, was like staring across thin smoke wafting over a fire pit. He considered the white-grey haze, seeing nothing more but a reflection of himself. He then turned his attention to see how far up the fortification stretched, but his sight was blocked after ten feet by the familiar mist of the Netherworld.

"Do not get trapped by the illusions inside," Erzebeth warned. "I will direct Kowin to meet you at the next Grumadki, and I hope he will guide you swiftly through its shadowed pathways. But remember, every moment you waste in here is an opportunity for him to gain his freedom. You do not want to exit and find him waiting for you, freed from Svarog's hold."

"He did promise us he would be waiting on the other side," Drast said. "Do tell him that I will be sorely disappointed if I do not see him waiting with open arms."

"Please, do not go inside," Dagmar said. "Nothing good can come from it, I promise you."

Kam stepped up, saying, "We do not have any time to waste." She stepped through the shimmering door.

"Please!" Dagmar wailed.

Drast lifted his shoulders apologetically at Dagmar. "I am sorry, Father. I will not be bested by Small-tits." He paraded through after her, laughing with every step.

Tyran shadowed Drast, hearing his father scream his name in desperation as the world behind him swept away.

Chapter XIV

Drast blinked against the fading white light that flashed upon entering the doorway to the Tower of Eresh. The voice of Wolos evaporated entirely, leaving him in a disturbing silence he had all but forgotten. Drast, however, could not reflect on the sudden change. In a few short breaths, the thought of the Tower, along with the Netherworld and the last thousand years, faded like a dream upon waking, leaving him confused.

He hurried to call out for Tyran before the bright light completely vanished. His voice echoed into an abyss. His frame lurched forward with the sound, forcing him into a body and mind that were not his own.

His lips and tongue felt woolen, thick and unmanageable with no moisture to produce words or sound. Before him stood a young version of himself that seemed out of place and foreign. From where he stood, the other Drast looked tall and imposing with a gleam in his eye that he could not recall. He attempted to situate himself, but only could count the four walls on each side and take note of the bolted door behind his younger self.

"Come," the younger Drast said, "your eyes have followed me like the tide follows the moon. Do not act coy now."

Words that were not his own spilled from his lips in a torrent, his voice shaky and feminine, stirring half a memory from what seemed a dozen lifetimes ago. "Were the tide afraid the moon would reach down to assault it, your words could not be truer."

The other Drast chuckled warmly, the glint in his eye growing fiercer. "Yet the tide sees the moon, water striving to conquer land, attempting to follow it into the sky." His grin widened, breaking from the word play. "No, girl, do not think yourself unwilling or unwanting. Like the sea, you have gone beyond your boundaries to seek me out."

"But—"

The younger Drast stepped closer so that the two of them were touching. "Come, Kura, you know you have been waiting for this."

He blinked, suddenly remembering the details. He was in his room, except it was not *his* room, it was the room of the other Drast, who promptly held him down and rubbed his manhood against him. It was not a pleasant feeling. He was looking through the eyes of Kura, the busty maid in Lairhein who helped care for his father's home. She was loyal even when the traitor, Maelili Kluk, gathered a mob to assault their estate.

Drast gritted his teeth, not knowing when the younger version of himself found time to remove his belt or his britches. His fists clenched, holding his breath, incapable of lifting a hand to fend off his younger self despite the overwhelming desire. He squirmed in vain.

Forced to his feet by the other Drast, he avoided making eye contact with himself and therefore was forced to look at his own chest. The confines of his old room were visible in his periphery, smelling like vomit mostly from his drunken stupors and frequent failings of spewing into the chamber pot.

Unexpectedly, his back slammed against the wall. He could not escape his assailant. His persistence, his hunger for flesh, looked odd from Kura's point of view—foreign, like finding one's possessions in a stranger's home. A shiver quaked through his flesh as the younger Drast placed his hand upon her, running his finger gently over the shoulder toward his chest. Her chest. The boundary between himself and Kura seemed to melt away until each sensation was shared so completely he could not separate the two. Her thoughts raced through his head.

Panic. Fear. Disgust.

"Kura," the young Drast murmured lustfully, one hand on the breast and the other reaching behind her to pull her close. The hand on her chest suddenly snaked behind her head to force their lips together. A cold sweat covered her skin in horror, stomach churning as bile welled in her throat, unable to pull away from him.

He tasted like alcohol and bile.

Squirming, he tried to push away from the kiss, from the closeness, but the wall left him no room and the other Drast mistook the movement for complacency, if not compliance, as if he were trying to grind against him.

"Please!" he heard Kura gasp from trembling lips, unable to say more.

The other Drast growled like an animal, pulling at her skirts, trying to displace her undergarments as best he could. Drast felt Kura grinding her teeth so greatly they might shatter. She pressed her thighs together, trying to slow his progress, but inevitably failed against his strength and forcefulness.

Finally he ripped at her bodice, failing to fully expose her but not seeming to care. Drast worked his hands, trying to hold together the torn cloth, and his younger self took the opportunity to spin her around and push her face against the wall, bending her forward. Trying to keep from cracking her head against the wooden panels, Drast smacked his hands into the walls, only to have Kura's skirts thrown up.

Before Drast could react, his younger self was inside and

he felt Kura's stomach sink like a stone, numbness filling her, radiating out so that her flesh lacked all feeling. Her muscles became flaccid. Her knees failed so Drast thought he might fall to the rich carpets covering the ground—now seemingly colorless and harsh—but his other self held Kura's body upright.

"I—knew—I—would—make—you—weak—at—the—knees!" he grunted rhythmically.

"Drast!"

Dagmar Kaligula's voice echoed down the hallway.

The young Drast could not finish what he started.

A wave of relief surged through Kura, fusing into Drast's own senses. Her visceral reactions of dread and nausea still overwhelmed his wits, leaving in his mouth a foul taste of self-repugnance that he could not rid himself of, no matter how much he tried to swallow it.

Her mind's eye faded away, leaving Drast alone in the blackness of the Tower of Eresh, though the tears on his cheeks and the numbness of his flesh were still present. He tried to keep himself from retching on the stone, hugging his abdomen with his one good arm even as the blackness flashed white again.

"Gods," he whispered.

Drast's blood pounded, his feet struggling to find purchase in the sand, running as fast as he could. Racing thoughts of fear and a fingernail's grip on hope fueled his aching limbs onward, his chest straining to pull in the thick, foggy air.

His skirts tangled in his feet and the sand tripped him up every few feet. He could not manage a rapid pace, yet he would not slow down and he refused to look back.

Who was he? Whose eyes did he see through now?

Suddenly he screamed with a feminine voice and fell to the ground with an arrow embedded in his thigh, pinning his skirts to his leg. It was his own arrow. He recognized the longer curved vanes that helped to ensure his arrows always flew straight and true, a technique none in Lairhein had replicated.

Drast's mind raced backward in time, stretching to the life he lived in Lairhein. The beach, the fog, the arrow to the leg of a woman running down the beach.

Elena Kluk.

His eyes—her eyes—finally found their way back to see his other self lowering his bow. Struggling to stand, he gasped at the pain before limping forward, a thick vein of panic pulsing through him. Her heart pounded, keeping her from thinking clearly. Irrationally, Drast hoped that his younger self would not follow.

After a few lumbering, agonizing steps, Elena turned around, struggling to keep herself upright. Her hands lifted on either side of her breasts; she hoped to protect herself with her magic. The air around the other Drast congealed like blood so that he seemed to move through slowed time, feet sinking in the sand and striding at a snail's pace. The air restricted the younger Drast's movement.

He could feel her power with Koldovstvo, or at least the power she thought she had. Even as she cast her magic, the aging effects of Koldovstvo were readily felt, draining her life away with each moment in a way that Drast had not felt since before he had performed the ritual with his father and Tyran.

Despite the other Drast being slowed, he remained bound for only a few moments, and then he pushed through her magic like a parent pushing away a child. The other Drast rid her of sight and sound.

The steady, rising panic of Elena became his own. While she aimed to disable or kill the younger Drast, her actions with Koldovstvo were only half executed. Her mind was peppered with irrationality and thoughtlessness. What she could think echoed in his head, while he had no way to communicate back to her.

Don't let him hurt me. Please, gods, mercy. Can he show mercy?

Just let him kill me. I'd rather die that feel any more pain. Please don't let him rape me. Oh, gods, please not that!

And then sight and sound was suddenly restored to her, but the other Drast stood before her, blurred even from a few feet away.

Her voice, unnerved and aged, rattled. He could tell she did not recognize herself, speaking in a muffled tone. "How do you have such power? What are you?"

"I am Stuhia as they were meant to be." The other Drast tilted his head cockily, though she could not make out his expression. "You weak, sniveling Kluks have drained the Stuhia of their glory and authority. Under the Kaligula name, honor will be restored and the Vucari will tremble under the heel of our boots."

Tears further distorted her vision, blinding Drast. He could make out only the vaguest humanoid shape through Elena's eyes before she dropped her gaze. Her shoulders shuddered in absolute despair. She thought of her home, her friends, her family, and herself.

What had the Stuhia done to deserve the evil of such men? Could they have done anything to stop the Kaligulas, or was this always what would come?

Hope was taken from her.

Aloud, she said, "I will go. I will flee and cause no more trouble for your family. I am an old woman now. I can do nothing but live out my few remaining days." She tried to find the other Drast's eyes but saw only the shape of him. "Please, let me leave Lairhein and find my kin."

The shape moved slightly. "Unfortunately, my father was quite specific in how I am to deal with Kluks."

Elena shuddered, raising her hands to cradle her head, full-throated sobs wracking her decrepit frame.

"I will make it quick," the other Drast whispered.

A sharp pain in her neck.

Darkness.

Light.

Drast tasted the venom of a dragon's poisoned blood, felt it burning in his veins and bursting through his lungs, stealing his ability to speak. Retching, he realized he was in Skell's mind, one of his disobedient soldiers who tried to gain the power of the three-headed dragon on the cart behind him instead of tossing it over the cliff at Drast's command. Despite himself, Drast felt a small modicum of hope when he saw his younger self approaching in his hazy vision, knowing the pain would soon end. For the second time, he felt his neck snap.

Darkness.

Light.

The alehouse in Lairhein blurred. Muddled, drunken confusion overcame him. He was Peter Kluk, staring across the table at himself, hearing quick words spill from his lips while barely understanding any of it. The discomfort of too much drink coupled with heavy coins resting in his gullet caused him to groan. The game had been lost.

He screamed through Peter's teeth as the coins burst through his stomach, ripped through the fatty flesh. The sound echoed around him, lasting longer than he remembered. His shredded abdomen left him clinging to the fringes of life in tears that wracked his body, only worsening the pain, until he finally bled out on the filthy floor of the tavern, surrounded by people too afraid to help him.

They all feared the Kaligulas.

Darkness.

Light.

Maelili Kluk held back her bright red hair, tears stinging the corners of her eyes. Drast forced her to decide between her own life and the life of her brother only hours ago. Now she retched in the woods at her decision, overwhelmed with the burning hatred and bile that filled her. She relived her decision through nightmares, night after night, for nearly a century until she finally died.

Drast watched every dream in horror, Maelili's misery

reborn inside of him.

Darkness.

Light.

His father screamed his name to an empty house, left alone to discover he had been betrayed by Drast, his worthless son. The people of Lairhein laid the full of their wrath at Dagmar's feet. No fury felt fuller than that of Maelili, who matched his strength blow for blow with rage until he was decrepit from the long years added by Koldovstvo and he fled from Lairhein, hobbling alone into the wilds to live as a beast.

Darkness.

Drast bawled for mercy.

Light.

His younger self snatched a hot poker from the hearth and turned to look at him. He gripped at the floorboards uselessly, immediately realizing he was looking at himself through Tyran's eyes. He could see the trepidation dancing in his eyes, yet the nervousness and fear manifested itself into a smile pulling at the corners of his mouth. The desire to pull away, to flee from the glowing rod of iron, tugged at his muscles, but Tyran remained unmoving.

"Burn him." His father's voice was harsh. He pulled his eyes toward Dagmar, standing with his arms crossed.

He eyed the poker and addressed the younger Drast, speaking as Tyran, low and emotionless. "Do it."

He could feel his brother's defenses rising against the coming pain. Tyran retreated inside his head, pulling Drast with him, so that he nearly stood outside of his body. He watched the other Drast advance with the poker and press it forcefully against his arm. He grunted against the pain, but did not scream or yell.

In his head, Tyran was safe. He did not withdraw. Did not flinch. Drast did not know what to make of his brother's disassociation. How could he not feel this pain? Was he truly numbed to the violence inflicted upon him?

Tyran's thoughts began to overcome his own. A slow reverie of quiet moments filled his mind.

Tyran ran as a young boy in a field, shirtless and laughing, a dog nipping at his heels. They ran forever, never slowing and never tiring. The sun was always bright, and the grass was always soft.

Walking through the trees with only the moon to light his steps, Maelili at his side, smiling at him with bright green eyes and saying nothing. Her arm around his waist and his around her shoulder so that they could barely walk, but they refused to sacrifice each other for either haste or stability.

The steady crash of the waves on the shore played music for him. Tyran lay with Isolde watching the sun rise. Neither spoke. It was the simple silence of comfort and warmth that only two people in love could possess. He gently stroked her hair and she hugged his chest, watching the sun bleed the darkness away.

Tyran and Drast walked alone through the streets of Lairhein. Tyran was silent, chin up to feel the sun on his face. Drast walked with a grin and swagger. The people of Lairhein smiled at them with neither a harsh word nor a wary look. It was a memory that Drast himself possessed, not long before they went to meet their father and he sent Tyran away to the Shade.

Time and again memories flashed through Tyran's mind, pulling him away from the burning and the pain. They were always quiet, always immune to the harsh reality of the world and never touched on any pain or despair that might have followed.

Finally, Tyran blinked away the memories to look upon the other Drast, teeth gritted in what could still be described as a smile. His younger self sweated more from the heat of the poker than did Tyran. Dagmar watching with his arms folded across his chest and a light in his eyes that Tyran's mind did not seem to register.

"...yes, Tyran?" their father finished.

He grunted, not hearing what was said.

"Good. Then you will kill her. Tonight. I want to hear nothing more from you or this girl, or any other." Dagmar's voice sounded relieved, almost as if he had fought and won another battle. "We do not have time for such petty concerns." He waved a hand. "Go, Tyran. Drast, you will stay and speak with me a while longer."

Darkness.

Drast grabbed his face with his one good hand. He could not dredge up so many happy memories even if he tried.

Did my brother really block out all the bad, or was it just for the moment?

Gods, he could feel how happy his brother was in those brief moments.

Was the memory of Tyran and me walking the streets still one of the happy ones or did I ruin that after what I did to Isolde?

More light.

An icy landscape, white on white along with the odd flurry of snow blurring his vision. Night had come, but Drast could see unusually well. Almost as well as he could see in the daylight.

"Do you see anything?" a man's voice said; the voice was familiar and had a Stuhian accent.

His eyes would not move. Whoever he embodied stayed focused on the landscape, not bothering to turn toward the man.

"Nothing." His voice was feminine, and one he was all too familiar with after recent days. Erzebeth.

Drast struggled to be free from the skin-switcher.

What did I do to Erzebeth? Why am I in her head?

After a moment, she said, "Why are you out here and away from the camp, Drem? You cannot see in the dark any better than your men. Return to the young Red and the warmth of your fires." Drast gulped, knowing she spoke of Tyran. They were marching towards Anaerfell.

Her eyes finally turned to the Voivode.

Drem's lips were pursed. "I follow orders." His voice was firm and clipped.

Panic washed over Drast. He had given the orders Drem spoke of—he remembered that well enough. A little speech about setting an example for the men, which meant that Kormish should be coming along soon.

They failed in killing her, though.

Why am I in her head?

Erzebeth jerked around, the sound of crunching snow catching her attention. He caught sight of Kormish trudging slowly up the snow embankment, the camp hidden behind him in the folds of the mountains called Valarun.

He avoided Erzebeth, focusing on Drem instead. "A word, Drem."

Drem's eyes flickered to Erzebeth before nodding with a grunt. The two Voivodes clumped a dozen or so paces off into the snow, then put their heads together and whispered.

Erzebeth's eyes had initially followed their movements, but soon she focused ahead, watching them from the corner of her eye. Her thoughts began to race.

Both of his Voivodes. Two. Why both? Makes no sense. The Red has made his threats, sure, but only threats. He has defended me. He must think I am a liability. He must think I will betray him. Stop it! You do not know why he is here. He could just be delivering orders, relaying scout information. But why Kormish? Why not any nameless, faceless troop? Anyone could do that. No, it must be. They can only be here for one purpose.

Slowly, a quaking filled her chest and a sheen of sweat covered her skin, cold and fearful. Her senses heightened.

Kormish and Drem finished speaking and stomped back towards her. Kormish did not turn back, and from her periphery, she could see his eyes fixed on her. His hand eased the sword at his belt.

Drast felt as though she might explode. Her teeth ground together, nostrils flared, and eyes began to water, as though it took all her effort not to burst into tears. Her chest ached, as if someone pulled her beating heart from it.

Kormish angled away from Drem as if to pass behind her to join her on her other side, but her keen ears caught the sound of his sword rasping from his sheath. Before the weapon was halfway out, she turned, her right arm covered in fur with a heavy bear's paw that swept across Kormish's chest, ripping through cloth and flesh, then crushing bone. The impact seemed to be enough to stop his heart fully—the man fell, unmoving.

A bestial snarl came from Drast—through Erzebeth—and she clawed through the snow, the darkness protecting her from the other Voivode. Drast could hear Drem stomping after her with a curse on his teeth. She moved with quick feet, leaping and tumbling through snow drifts and snow banks as sharp flashes and cracks of lightning followed her. Clouds began to gather above and the little light given off by the night sky had long vanished into blackness.

Drast's heart thudded in tune with Erzebeth's, echoing in his eardrums. She was angry. Scared. Hurt.

Another bolt struck, this time hitting her hip and sending her spinning, the pain eliciting a sharp cry, but she barely paused, twisting and rolling in the snow like a wild animal to come to her feet.

"Die, you Vucari whore! You killed him!"

A second bolt attempted to catch her in the dark but veered off wildly, cracking against the cliff face.

"Stop this, Drem!" she yelled frantically, staying low in the snow, out of sight.

Drem was visible ahead, but he seemed to have lost her in the dark and snow, loosing another bolt and striking nothing.

Leaping from cover with a roar akin to a charging bear, she barreled into his chest, knocking him down. Raising a paw to end his pursuit, a bright light suddenly erupted around her, blinding her. Confused but unaware of the source, she swung her paw, only to encounter a barrier of nothingness that prevented her from striking home.

"Stop her, Tyran!" Drast recognized his voice, though Erzebeth remained blinded by the light and could not see him.

"You did this!" she cried, slashing against the nothingness. Drast could feel the hole in her chest growing. Her jaw clenched against the tears welling up inside. "You sent your best to kill me, Tyran Kaligula. It was not good enough!"

She began to move away slowly, keeping her face toward them, shivering in the cold.

Tyran's voice sounded as hard and emotionless as it always did. "I did not tell anyone to harm you, Erzebeth." The light he cast started to fade. "I would never hurt you. I promise you that."

"Kill her, Tyran," Drast heard himself say. "She tried to kill Drem, she will kill us!"

She fell back into the darkness and snow, the light fading completely. With a mouth full of bile, she spat. "Rabid dogs!"

And into the dark and cold she ran, heedless of direction, full-throated sobs filling her—filling the night.

Darkness.

Light.

Memory after memory flooded through him. Memories that were not his own of heinous acts committed against any who crossed him. He relived hundreds of lives through those he killed, betrayed, and harmed. He heard the thousands of lies he told, ruining people's lives and the lives of their children. In the end, he lay broken and sweating on the cold stone floor of the Tower, hugging himself and weeping for what he had wrought.

Chapter XV

A white light pierced Tyran's eyes, bright as direct sunlight, from a wide stone passageway ahead. The color blinded him from seeing inside the Tower. Lifting his hand to reduce the intensity, he stumbled forward only a couple steps before the light flashed and shattered like broken glass. A moment later, he found himself beneath a clouded sky, staring at the colorless crown of towering mountains.

"The Shade Fells? How have I come here?"

The din of men rallying echoed around him. He gasped, twisting his head to and fro to gaze at the many faces he once led into battle. He could hardly remember their names, not that he ever knew many of them. Their war-like screams echoed in his head, ricocheting inside his skull like it was a hollowed cavern. These men must be long dead by now; they belonged in graves, silenced. Yet they stood in defiance, shouting at him with their weapons raised, glaring at him with unmistakable bloodlust.

He tried to move away from the forty or so soldiers in his immediate vicinity but found his hands were bound, his arms stretched around a rock several feet taller than him. He pulled back helplessly, unable to keep his nose from being smashed against the red stone. His arms ached from how tightly they had been pulled around the boulder. The cold rock pressed against his bare chest.

"I bring you to the Shade to seize glory." The deep tone of his youth echoed behind him, booming over the roar of the army. "Together, we conquered the darkness; we defeated the serpent. You have allowed fear to seize you. I cannot allow softness to exist in the heart of any soldier among my men, especially my Voivodes." The crunch of footsteps against the sand sounded behind him. "How will you answer for your crime against your Ser and your Serder, Voivode Meran?"

His heartbeat thudded in his ears. He was familiar with his tyrannical tone, one that he used often with his soldiers to strike fear in their hearts. No enemy should be more terrifying than the general.

He could not understand why he was hearing his own voice.

"Silence will not lessen your punishment." Movement from Tyran's left pulled his attention. From the corner of his eye, he saw a reflection of his younger self looking back at him. His blue eyes were sharp, the red beard lining his jawline glistening with sweat. His younger form looked as solid and stern as the rock he was now tied against.

Tyran sucked in a breath of air. *"Where am I? What is this?"*

His younger self growled. "Three pathfinders were found with their necks cut. Tell me, what was wrong with the path we already scouted? Why did you send them to their deaths, Voivode?"

"You have made a mistake," Tyran shouted at the man who dared mock him. *"I am not Voivode Meran. He is my man, and he is dead! I am Ser Tyran Kaligula. Release me from these bindings, you fool."*

The other Tyran scowled. "Have it your way. Be silent. For your family's sake, let us hope you can endure your lashings."

"*I—I spoke…*" Tyran stuttered.

"Today we will see whether you will first abandon fear or life, Voivode." He watched in horror as the man, pulled the familiar mace with the iron ball fastened to the end from his belt. He tapped it against Tyran's cheek before turning around, displaying his old shield, still crafted from yew and hardened bull's hide. As he stepped out of view, Tyran realized he could no longer feel the weight of his own weapons on his belt. "I will not call the healers when we are done."

"*Who are you? What are you—*"

His words were lost when the mace slammed into his side, cracking the lowest rib. He crushed his nose into the red stone, nearly breaking it, and then the second blow hit, tearing into the flesh beneath his right shoulder blade.

"*Gods!*" he screamed, twisting his head with a sudden force and smashing his face against the boulder. The soldiers around him yelled in fury, likely angry about the three dead pathfinders. Among their number, he saw the most loyal of his Voivodes, the man who always followed his orders. He screamed for help.

"*Drem! Help me!*"

The Voivode stood, flinching, watching the solid end whack against him again and again. He could see his blood flinging across the dusty ground behind him. He could taste it in his nostrils. Slobber, tears, and coppery blood.

"*Stop. Please. Gods. Stop.*"

The other Tyran struck him again and again, roaring at him about his uselessness. His failure. Three…four…five times.

Blackness welcomed him back into the Tower of Eresh, the scene of the Shade Fells vanishing. Tyran crumbled to the rock beneath his feet and wept. While the injuries were gone from his flesh, the pain continued to stab along his back and sides. He could not stand. He could scarcely breathe.

"What happened?" he moaned, searching in the pitch for an answer. He could see nothing. No hallways. No stairs. He was surrounded by absolute darkness.

His mind replayed the callous beating he had received, a reflection of the flogging he gave Voivode Meran years ago when Tyran retrieved a dragon from the Shade Fells for his father. The incident was not uncommon for him. He regularly disciplined his soldiers and his four Voivodes when they acted against his orders or in accordance with their own free will. He was their Ser. He held absolute power, especially when they ventured beyond the gates of Lairhein.

Meran survived his punishment, dying months later during the battle against the Vucari and Torn'ash in 45 CE. Tyran wondered how long he wished for death after the beating or wanted Tyran to be beaten in equal measure.

The floor beneath Tyran's feet fell away, and he suddenly slammed against the coarse dirt of the courtyard. He cried out, rolling over onto his back. Sunrays pelted him in the face. He swiftly got to his feet, feeling the weight of a practice sword—more of a stick—in his hand.

"Nine Lands. Where am I now?" The sound of footsteps stomping across the earth drew his attention. He lifted his weapon in time to parry the weapon swinging down at his skull.

Clack!

He twirled his weapon to the left. The right. Over his head. *Clack. Clack. Clack!*

Striding to the side, he took a moment to examine his attacker, who was none other than a very young version of himself…at about eight years old.

"By the gods, no!"

He stared into his own blue eyes, already losing much innocence at this age. Freckles danced across bridge of his nose, his red curls bouncing over his ears as he advanced with the stick again. He sucked in a breath. If he was facing himself, he could be no one other than Drast, a couple years older than himself.

He kept an eye on his younger self while scanning the courtyard of the Kaligula estate, seeing Dagmar glowering from a distance, instructing their every move.

His fists were clenched at his sides. His shouts echoed off the bloodstone walls. "Do not retreat! Find the weakness in your enemy's form and strike hard. No battle should last more than a few swings. Death or victory! No mercy!" His father's face was hot with anger rather than the sweltering heat. "Come on, Tyran! Crack your brother over the skull. Stop skulking about like a Kluk."

He watched through Drast's eyes as his younger self raced forward to deliver the blow only to slip on the sand and fall to his back with a thud. Tyran forgot how young and innocent he once was.

Drast halted his own advancement, a sour taste filling his mouth. He swallowed, then whispered, "Get up, Tyran."

"Nine Lands, Drast!" Dagmar fumed, stomping across the courtyard unaware of the faint words. Their father screamed the length of his walk until he was shouting in his son's face. "Your enemy has collapsed, and you are standing there like a dainty woman! Tell me, are you a warrior or a whore? Do I need to dress you in a skirt and send you to the market?"

Drast froze under his father's shadow. Tyran had the impulse to meet his father's eye, but Drast kept his chin down. The practice sword shook in his brother's hand, looking through the crack of space between Dagmar's arm and body. Tyran's younger self cowered in fear on the ground. His childish eyes met Drast's for a moment with terrified uncertainty. Drast darted his eyes away.

"Answer me!"

"I am a warrior," Drast whispered unevenly. "I am a warrior."

Dagmar grabbed him by the shoulder, lifting him several feet off the ground and slamming him back down again. He barely had the chance to get his feet fortified under him to run alongside the furious footsteps of his father. Dagmar practically dragged him to where the young Tyran lay frozen.

"Your enemy has fallen, Drast. Strike him!" Dagmar commanded.

Tears touched the corners of Drast's eyes, his father keenly watching him. Tyran could feel his brother's throat tighten; his limbs shook.

He recalled the horror of the memory, but he never imagined how the even affected Drast. His own thoughts of his brother's agony were washed away as Drast's thoughts raced though his mind like they were his own.

Please, Father, do not make me do this.

Drast closed his eyes as though the action might make him smaller. Despite the sun beating down on him and the sweat beads forming on his brow, Drast's fingers were cold.

"Strike him!" Dagmar boomed.

Drast's flinched at his father's shout. *I am so stupid.* His hand trembled, loosening his grip on the practice sword. "I will take Tyran's punishment."

Pain seared in the back of his skull as Dagmar hit Drast in the back of the head. "Do not make me tell you again."

He will hate me.

Drast looked to Tyran through the blurred vision. The courtyard seemed to spin from his brother's perspective.

The young Tyran nodded at him, sitting upright on his elbows. "It is okay."

With trepidation, Drast finally lifted the stick and brought it down across young Tyran's head. *Crack!* Blood surfaced through the red hair, the young Tyran falling to the dirt with a groan. Drast gritted his teeth, the sorrow catching in his chest.

"Harder, Drast," Dagmar hissed. "I have seen chamber maids stroke a cock with more vigor."

Drast's emotions ripped through Tyran as he hit the young version of himself harder. Tyran realized he personally found the strength to block out the torment, but his brother felt everything.

Blood splattered across the dirt, a gash splitting above younger Tyran's eye. Drast was unable to speak a word, waiting to hear what more his father might say.

"Good," Dagmar said, crossing his arms. "And now so you may learn the price of compassion—Tyran, stand to your feet and strike your brother down. You will not stop until I say."

For what felt like hours, Drast was battered with the practice sword, leaving him bruised, bloodied, and lying on the warm sands of the Kaligula courtyard. At no point did Drast detach from the pain or think of anything more. Every strike and sting was experienced fully, his brother's thoughts bent on how much he deserved the punishment.

The scars of that beating never left Tyran, reminding him to leave mercy to the hearts of women. Their father said the emotion did not belong on the field of battle. Yet Tyran never contemplated how the moment shaped his brother.

How else had his numbness kept him from understanding the grief inside his brother? Had Drast's anguish been what finally broke him at Anaerfell?

Tyran writhed against the stone of the Tower, uncertain if he had traveled more than a few steps from the door. He yearned to escape the visions of the Tower, clawing for something to help him escape. He would leave the same way he entered. He would let Wolos remain dead and the world burn, so long as he could be freed from this horrible place. He swallowed the thick air, reaching helplessly into the dark.

"Stop this!" He could hear no echo, despite his desperate plea.

His stomach rumbled. His ribs cut at the insides of his gut, threatening to burst through the thin layer of his skin. His body might as well have been crushed under a mountain of boulders given the constant pain coursing through him from head to foot.

He lost track of the many past experiences playing through his mind's eye, inflicting the physical and emotional scars he left in the wake of his life. Not only did he live through the pain of the soldiers he slaughtered for their ignorance, but also that of their wives and children. He relived the devastation of the Vucari village of Charreni, which he crushed under a mountain, but as the women, men, and children. One by one, until he thought his chest itself would be crushed under the insurmountable grief.

He could not say how much time passed. His skull was crushed. He was burned. He could taste the blood of his enemies on the edge of his tongue, their every thought and feeling being recreated through him.

In every instance, he was left on the opposite end of his wrathful hand, and no matter how many times he begged his old self to stop, he wrought death and war without restraint.

Suddenly he was back in Lairhein, the breath of winter crisp on the afternoon wind whipping over the Neabou Sea and through the lively marketplace. From the corner of his eye, he caught a glimpse of loose locks of bright red hair whipping in the wind. With an exasperated breath, he watched his fingers twirl the thin strands. He would the hair anywhere.

"Maelili Kluk. Why would I be Maelili Kluk?"

The Kluk family was the Kaligula family's sworn enemy, but Tyran did not remember hurting them. While he schemed to help his father steal the crown from them, he did not kill them. He went against Dagmar, saving Maelili from what should have been an inescapable fate. Any deaths delivered to the Kluks were Drast's handiwork.

He searched his mind for an explanation as to why he was seeing life through Maelili's eyes.

"I saved her!" Tyran cried, twisting around and catching a reflection of himself in a nearby shop window. Maelili's green eyes and perfect smile stared back at him.

She was beautiful.

An image of himself, barely sixteen years old, appeared over Maelili's shoulder. The coldness in his eyes and firmness of his chin were unmistakable. Maelili must have been clueless as to what Tyran saw so clearly; he could feel her heart race in excitement at the sight of him. She spun on her heel, reaching for his hand.

"We need to talk," he said, grabbing her hand and pulling her toward the alleyway. The distant look in his eye was inimitable. He did not even try to make eye contact with her.

Through Maelili, Tyran allowed himself to be pulled between the shops, laden with barrels and wooden crates, hidden away from the hustle and bustle of the city street. The sense of excitement in his chest did not lessen. Maelili... *loved him.*

"We cannot continue *whatever* this is any longer," his younger self said, spinning Maelili around. Even at close distance, he did not look at her eyes. Instead, his gaze was fastened on her lips or somewhere beyond her shoulder.

Maelili's mind raced in confusion, causing Tyran to feel dizzy. He almost forgot how he and the Kluk girl had ducked in the shadows, exploring their curiosities together, hidden from the watchful eyes of their families.

"You are a stupid girl with stupid fantasies," his younger self went on. He let go of Maelili, already preparing himself to leave her in the alleyway. "My family will eventually prove to Lairhein how unfit your father is to rule as Arkhon, which will undoubtedly shine light on your shared incompetence."

Tyran could feel Maelili's heart breaking, short heaves of breath working their way from her lungs and through her lips. She tried to reason with him. "Tyran."

"Run along and play in your fantasy world, Maelili, but keep my name far from your lips." He walked away, turning his back on Maelili.

A scream resounded in his head, ripping him from Lairhein and to the grove beyond the city walls. His chest seared with Maelili's heartache, and yet he knew he was no longer in her flesh. The blood-curdling cry tore through the air again, conjoined with the frantic sobs and moans of a woman suffering unbearably.

Tyran's eyes were shut, squeezed so tight he could see nothing but spots in the forced darkness. Physical pain tore through him from his groin to his belly, where *something* forced itself inside of him. Repeatedly. Forcibly. Hatefully.

"No. No. No. Not this," Tyran begged, hoping to forever forget the injustice he wrought on his betrothed, Isolde, before Drast slit her throat. Dagmar ordered him to steal her life, and when he could not, he robbed her of her virginity in the hopes that she would flee from him and Lairhein forever. Drast was sent to see the original command was done.

"I am sorry. I am so sorry."

He thought he might vomit, his skin burning with such heat that sweat dripped down his neck and back, despite lying on the cool earth. The screams continued as he resisted—or better said, Isolde thrashed—to fight against his unbreakable grip. He was far too strong for the red-blonde girl, whom he promised the world and gave nothing.

Daring to open his eyes, Tyran saw the vile expression of himself staring back—cold as death—so close he could feel the sticky breath against his cheek. He was ruthless, ripping into Isolde's flesh without limits. Her torn skirts and dress half-raised over her head to hide most of her face were minor to the stabbing agony trailing down her thighs. Not to mention the blood that pulsated from whatever he tore in his rage.

Trapped beneath the lace, through Isolde's watered eyes, he observed his emotionless self destroying the woman beneath him. He gasped, choking, feeling every violating thrust. And inside Isolde, the unconditional love she once held for him dissipated into absolute numbness. Eventually she stopped fighting, hopelessly turning her head and weeping into her strained arm.

Tyran never felt so dead inside.
Eternally dead.

Chapter XVI

"Stop! I will not go!"

"Let her be! She has another purpose."

Drast stumbled forward in a haze, the sound of Kam and Erzebeth's voices tugging him along, out of the darkness of the Tower of Eresh.

"She is for whatever purpose I deem, spirit," his father's voice responded.

This is not going to end well. Best push aside your misery if you wish to live. You cannot kill us!

Drast blinked at the return of the voice. It had been gone during his time in the Tower. He had been so focused on the experience that he had not even noticed the absence. He did not understand what power the Tower of Eresh would have over his mind to silence the voice of Wolos.

Passing through a stone archway, Drast entered a grotto brightly lit by a sourceless white glow. His feet were heavy with despair, the lingering impact of the Tower gripping at his heart and mind. He found the strength to lift his head, ignoring the loud rumbles of his stomach. The pain in his gut almost took him to his knees.

He froze, a shiver running up his spine. Dagmar held Kam by the scruff of the neck while Tyran and Erzebeth faced off against him. Kam writhed against his touch, trying to break herself free.

"You will not take her, Father," Tyran said in a low, raw voice. He grasped his stomach, suggesting the intensity of his own hunger pangs. Yet his pale face and strained eyes stole Drast's attention.

He could only imagine he looked the same after his experience in the Tower. His mouth felt full of wool and it took a moment for him to generate the saliva necessary to speak. "What is going on?" he managed.

"I am taking my life back!" Dagmar snarled, unwilling to take his eyes from Tyran and Erzebeth. "This chit will give me that much back—only fair considering your failure to kill Wolos."

I am not dead! I am not dead!

"I know!" Drast snapped, feeling frayed from his recent trauma. The yelling almost brought him to tears.

"Then why did you ask?" Dagmar growled, tightening his grip on Kam. He moved as though he might walk around Tyran.

"We did not fail," Tyran said through gritted teeth, giving Drast a sideways look. He sidestepped to block Dagmar from advancing. "If we had failed we would not be roaming the underworld now trying to bring him back to life."

"If you had done it right, death would not exist!" Dagmar shook Kam. "And now, for me, it will stay at bay at least a while longer."

If Dagmar takes her, he is sentencing you to death. You need the skin-switcher. If she is gone, someone must take her place.

"If you take her, Father, one of your sons must die," Drast said. "A sacrifice must be given to return Wolos to life and to fix what is now broken."

"Good!" Dagmar sneered at Drast. "If your brother has any sense, he will make certain it is you. And when you lie dead, he can join me."

Drast fumbled for a response, feeling his throat tighten

up. He bit his inner cheek, hearing a ringing in his head.

"I said," Tyran growled, "you will not take her!" Kam was suddenly free from Dagmar, flying back across the grotto, propelled by Tyran's use of Koldovstvo. The young Warden slammed into the uneven rocks, groaning in half-shock and pain.

Their father tumbled and rolled until he slid to a halt at the far edge of the cavern. He snarled, rising to his feet with his own limitless magic. His voice gained power, echoing through the hollow. "You would raise your hand against your father in protection of a filthy skin-switcher!"

Kam immediately began disrobing, her visage already transforming into the fearsome countenance of the great bull-creature.

I would raise something for the skin-switcher.

Drast giggled. "But her tits are so small!"

Dagmar, Tyran, and Kam turned to look at him. He eyed Kam's bestial form and gulped, then moved in a similar fashion as the others, but to look over his shoulder at the Tower of Eresh.

He considered returning to the nightmares.

Erzebeth spoke in the lull. "She is more important than your petty battle with mortality. Remember that you are mortal. Remember you must die."

"I must do nothing!" Dagmar's roar filled the cavern, drawing Drast's attention again. "Give her to me or face the full weight of the Netherworld thrown against you!"

Kam snarled, baring sharp fangs behind bovine lips. Her massive hands curled into fists and uncurled to revealed black claws, ready to tear their father apart.

Your father's fury will kill everyone. To find peace, he must be quelled. He cannot take the skin-switcher.

"Brother," Drast addressed Tyran with hesitation. He did not like what the voice proposed, but how could he argue with the voice of Wolos? "I do not think she wants to go."

Tyran grunted and nodded without shifting his gaze from Dagmar. "Kam will do her duty and we will do ours."

"Then you will be torn apart by demons." He hissed. "I will take the last one breathing to free myself from this hell!"

With a throaty cry, he raised his hand at the wall of the enclosed cavern and, using Koldovstvo, heaved it inward. Large chunks of stone flew toward them along with smaller stones and a cloud of dust. Drast's magical appendage leapt into being as he and Tyran raised their hands to halt the projectiles mid-flight, protecting themselves and Kam from the danger.

The debris hung suspended for a moment before dropping harmlessly to the ground. Flaring his nostrils, Drast used a gust of air to clear away the dust, only to see a swarm of demons pouring through the crevice.

Do not let us die. By the gods, stay alive.

Drast tilted his head as though he could make the voice fall out of his ear so he could focus on finding a strategy. Gathering himself, he embraced his magic, feeling the warmth run through his veins, and powered himself into the air. Seeing no other alternative, he promptly pulled at the strewn stones and rocks with Koldovstvo and pummeled the legion of hellions spewing from the gaping maw.

"We must keep them from filling the cave!" he cried.

Beneath him, Kam had already charged into the throng, her fangs and claws going to work against the mass of demon flesh. The full of her wrath—at being taken for nothing more than a pawn—was apparent in the reckless approach with which she dispatched the devilish creatures.

"Drast!" Tyran sounded strained, standing below him.

Casting his eyes down and back, Drast saw Dagmar attempting to crush him with the rubble. Rocks several times larger than Drast floated at his back, wavering in the empty space. Tyran fought to keep him from becoming paste, holding more than a dozen large stones at bay against the power of their father.

Drast reached into his pocket and pulled out the Alatir Stone. He forgot he had taken the artifact into the Tower of Eresh while Tyran held Ojenek.

Gripping the stone, Drast zipped through the air, out of the path of the stones. He used Koldovstvo to pick up half a dozen of his own and threw them at his father, who was forced to relinquish his concentration on the stones aimed for Drast and fly out of the way. The numerous projectiles flew about the grotto crashing into the walls and ceiling, sending stalactites careening down.

Your father seems intent on killing you.

"He is always that way," Drast breathed. "I wonder if he is serious this time."

Drast lobbed falling rocks at their father, who now tore through the grotto, spewing fire at Tyran from his outstretched hands.

"Help Kam!" Erzebeth's reedy voice was barely discernable over the roar of demons and the crash of stone.

Everyone is so demanding.

Drast snorted with irritation, trying to find the Warden in the milling throng of demons. Even as he located her, surrounded and struggling against overwhelming numbers, the sound of screaming Nithhoggr pulled at his attention.

I told you this was not going to go well. Everyone wants you dead; even fate wants you dead.

"I know!" Drast snapped.

Pulling his bow, he used his magical arm to begin drawing and loosing magical arrows at the demons surrounding Kam, using Koldovstvo to split them and twist them to take out as many of the creatures as he could.

Why even use the bow? Your magic alone would likely be more effective.

"Shut it! I cannot think," Drast muttered, shouldering his bow. Summoning dozens of magical arrows about him, he waved a hand to send them into the horde below, eliciting a multitude of roars and cries from Kam's attackers.

He hoped he did not strike her by accident.

The swarm of large Nithhoggr burst through the growing entryway, sharp sickles clenched in their fists and wings tucked. Rows of bladed teeth flashed in the ashy light pouring from the gap. Drast hurriedly reached out with Koldovstvo to tear them asunder. Erzebeth stayed close, focused on protecting Kam; a bright pulse of green light tore apart the screeching souls breaking free of the Nithhoggr's shells. One after another the two worked to eliminate the threat.

What little smugness he felt at having dealt with the Nithhoggr dissipated when a boulder struck him in the right shoulder. He dropped his bow to the ground and careened through the air, the stone threatening to crush him against the cavern wall. With only the surface of the rock visible, he called on stone magic to break the rock apart, transforming it into sand; the momentum still sent him crashing into a wall.

The air was knocked from his lungs despite holding the Alatir Stone. He tumbled for a dozen or more feet before he caught himself, but the overuse of magic was starting to make him dizzy. Shaking his head to gain clarity, he caught sight of another boulder and another beyond, racing toward him. He used the same tactic against the oncoming boulders.

The sand stung his face, nearly blinding him to all else in the grotto. He rubbed at his eyes and coughed. "Erzebeth, where is Tyran?"

"He has fallen to a Nocnica, so Dagmar has turned his attacks on you. But Kam is being overwhelmed. More demons are flooding in. You must keep her safe." She recited the events in her range of vision emotionlessly.

She probably called the Nocnica on him, knowing his bad luck with them.

Drast shouted at her. "You did this! You planned all of this, skin-switcher!" He choked, overwhelmed with sudden emotion. "You want your revenge against Tyran, but I ordered his Voivodes to kill you. Save him! Hate me!"

The ghost stared at him blankly, unmoving.

Her plan is already coming to fruition. You will both die here.

"Gods." His jaw quivered with realization, thick fear rising in his gullet. How long had his brother been bound by Nocnica? Ojenek was in Tyran's pocket, which meant that Drast would have to get around their father and riffle through his pockets to find it. He could not pull the stone to him with magic.

She planned this so well. You have no hope of surviving. Tyran is as good as dead.

"He cannot die." Blinking away the sand, Drast could see his brother on the ground almost thirty paces from him with the Nocnica on his chest. The demon screamed in his face, stealing his essence.

Kam roared in the opposite direction, defending the opening to her limited ability. She once more disappeared in the horde of endless demons.

If she dies, we all die.

Filling his lungs, Drast thundered, propelling himself to where he could see demons focusing their attacks. Kam would be trapped somewhere within the mass of snarling beasts. Without much aim, he launched fire at his father from his magical hand while, with somewhat more accuracy, doing the same at the demons surrounding Kam. Even if she was burned a bit, she might survive.

As demons fell, Kam's horned head and shaggy mane became visible. He closed the distance and encased Kam in a bubble of solid wind. Then with a guttural roar, Drast erupted the earth around her in a spray that sent the demons sailing away in all directions. The gruff, harsh sounds emitting from the beasts were ear-splitting, but Kam could move around the battlefield again.

He released the Warden onto solid ground and twisted in the air to continue the onslaught against his father. Dagmar met his gaze with measured hatred.

Drast curled his lip, letting scenes from the Tower play

through his mind. Because of his father's commands, Tyran may forever hate him, even if his brother never could say the words. Flame flew from Drast's hands and he tore stalactites from the ceiling to launch them like great spears.

His father met the fire with wind, sending the inferno into a million wavering tendrils while deflecting the hunks of rock into the demons below. Dagmar moved like water, halting Drast's attacks with ease. With a simple gesture, he constructed whips of air summoned from nothingness and bound Drast in place.

Koldovstvo flooded through Drast, giving him sway to diffuse the magic almost as quickly as it had come to life. He blinked to keep himself conscious, feeling the drain on his mind.

Stay awake or we will die!

Drast bobbed his head, knowing the voice spoke the truth. He raised his hand to attack again, but his father had used void magic to propel himself away. Drast turned in time to see Dagmar reappear behind him, shooting an engulfing flame.

Drast cried out, trying to redirect the flames. He clutched onto the Alatir Stone, feeling the scorching sensation across his flesh. His body felt as though it were covered in fiery welts and blistered skin.

Use the Warden.

"Kam cannot fight my father!" Drast wailed, seeing his father's guise nearing on the opposite side of the blaze.

Use the dead one.

"I thought she was the enemy," Drast said. He twisted his neck to look for the skin-switcher. He saw Tyran first, still motionless with the Nocnica on his chest. His brother looked as pale as death.

He could not help him while he was trying to hold back Dagmar.

Despair ripped at his senses. Gritting his teeth, he screamed, "Erzebeth! By the gods, I am sorry! I need time, you worthless skin-switcher."

She wafted by as he dodged a tendril of flame. "I have no physicality. I cannot fight anything but the Nithhoggr."

Drast loosed a great gust of wind toward his father, glad to see him tumble away for a moment. "You will have no spirituality if you do not find a way to help! Do you want Wolos reborn or not?"

She blinked her translucent eyelids blankly before floating away, a streak of flame passing through her to reach Drast.

He flew backwards, trying to move beyond the reach of the fire, but struck against the wall of the Tower of Eresh. He was not certain how he moved back to the edifice again. At the last moment, he encased himself in a protective bubble of magic, hiding his eyes from Erzebeth.

A sudden bright green light erupted a distance away in front of Dagmar, who shouted an unrepeatable curse. Drast blinked several times, and then lowered his shield. He flew to Tyran as fast as his magic would carry him.

The thin black lips of the Nocnica were stretched wide in an endless scream beneath her hollowed nose. The wisps of the wraithlike figure danced behind her with more vigor than her lifeless black eyes.

Trying to ignore the naked demon sitting on his brother's chest, he dug through Tyran's pockets to find Ojenek.

Best to die by your father's hand than that of the Nocnica.

"Stop talking to me!"

As his hand clasped the stone, Erzebeth's voice was in his ear. "I can do no more."

Drast looked up to see his father barreling forward, a score of flaming stones hurtling at him and Tyran. Holding his breath, he shoved the Alatir Stone into Tyran's relaxed palm with his ethereal hand and then pulled Ojenek free with his good hand. Rupturing the cave floor, he formed a thick casing of rock to guard against the flaming stones, then confronted the Nocnica. Standing upright, he punched the demon as he had before with Ojenek secured in his fist. The wraith screeched and fell away; the sound of fiery rocks cracking against the wall rumbled, but they did not break through.

He used Koldovstvo to fight against the strength of his father, who aimed to tear through the wall. The rock wall swayed like a wave around them for only a moment before stopping completely.

He is going after Kam if she is not dead already. She better not be dead.

"I know." Drast shook with exhaustion. He could not wait patiently for his brother to wake. He slapped him hard across the face.

"Ahh!" Tyran's eyes shot open.

"We have to help Kam!" Drast snapped, slapping him again for good measure.

Not waiting for a response, Drast burst through the stone capsule and found his father moving toward the hole in the cavern. As expected, Kam was roped with strands of Koldovstvo and being dragged behind him. The demons followed Dagmar's will, ignoring the two and marching toward Drast and Tyran.

You are losing.

"You are really not helpful for being a god." Drast spat, springing a tendril of air to pull his father back. In the same motion, he spotted his fallen bow and jerked the weapon back to his hand. A spectral arrow aligned over the base before he fastened his grip on the handle.

Dagmar struggled to fight against the tendril of air, glowering at Drast from a distance.

Foremost, who said I was a god? And second, gods are never helpful.

Drast grinned, his first arrow going wide. The stress of the battle and the overuse of magic made him feel ill, and all he could do was smile.

Dagmar pulled free from the magic, rushing around the grotto again with void magic, leaving Kam to collapse to the ground in her bies form. She landed on her back, scrambling to regain balance on her oversized hooves. The milling mass of demons originally coming at Drast snarled, turning to attack the skin-switcher.

Before Drast could move to aid her, a stone crashed into his back, sending him down with her. Between his feet he saw Tyran rushing to Kam's aid, slinging lightning from his hands like stones from a sling. Righting himself, Drast spun to face Dagmar, who had a mixture of annoyance and mild amusement etched on his features.

We may have gained the upper hand. Though he does not think he can lose.

"He never did," Drast murmured.

Using void magic, he reappeared to his father's left, careful to ensure he was visible in his periphery, then to his right, then in front, then right, then left, and everywhere in-between in rapid succession before placing himself out of sight above his father. He loosed a magical arrow straight down at his father, who still turned, trying to find his son. The arrow embedded itself in Dagmar's left shoulder, eliciting a cry of pain.

He jumped with void magic again, but Drast was quick to follow suit, finding a safe place at the far side of the cavern, where he had a clear view of his father's stopping point. As expected, Dagmar appeared behind where Drast would have been a moment earlier.

Drast fired another magical arrow that struck his father in the leg. Dagmar snarled with fury, following the trajectory of the arrow to find him.

Flying forward, Dagmar attacked. He unleashed a torrent of fire, binding tendrils of wind, and a mass of stones that seemed to come from every direction at once. Drast desperately tried to move away but found himself, once again, bound. With a snort, he broke the bonds and zipped away, using a great net of air tendrils to pull his father to the cave floor. Dagmar, however, found the means to escape the trap too, having an endless supply of Koldovstvo.

Drast could feel the mental exhaustion tightening his eyes along with a dull throb at the base of his skull. He could not keep this up, and he supposed that his father was not quite so affected by the strain, given that he was not entirely living.

He fell to a knee, almost too light-headed to continue. He ground his teeth, uncertain how he could win. With limitless magic, he and his father could escape from any bindings or violence that either could possibly inflect on one another.

"You cannot win, boy!" Dagmar snarled, walking in the shadow of the battle between the demons and Kam. Drast skimmed the area for Tyran but did not see him among the fighters. The battle cries and roars of the demons had tapered considerably. He saw that the hole in the cavern was sealed with malformed rock. The rest of the demons were tossed out dead or being handled by Kam, for whom the odds were much better. His father's words resounded in the grotto. "You were never strong enough to face me. You are too weak."

"You are my father," Drast returned, meeting Dagmar's gaze. "I never wanted to fight you."

"Bah, sniveling whelp. If you will not let me have the skin-switcher, then it must be you or your brother who brings me back from this place." He flashed his black-stained gums, motioning broadly with his arms. "And I know who is the easier quarry."

I think he means you.

Drast could not help but snicker. "Yes, I believe he does."

With a twitch, Drast sent a stone crashing into Dagmar, slamming him against the wall. He recovered before falling, but his arm hung loosely at his side. Broken. He did not groan with pain. He only deepened his frown and glowered at Drast.

Another rock, larger than the first, crashed into Dagmar's chest. Drast heard the bones snap and fracture within his father's frame. Dagmar fought to speak while Drast searched for the source of the attack.

He located Tyran stepping out from behind the archway leading to the Tower of Eresh.

Black blood spewed from Dagmar's lips with an exasperated moan. He fell over onto the boulder. Heaving, he tried to push himself back up with his working arm.

Tyran appeared beside Drast, sneering. "You will not find either of us to be easy prey, Father. I will not let you kill him or me. If it must be so, we will die taking you from this world."

"You should know I let you rot in Anaerfell, despite my desire to kill you!" Dagmar sneered, spitting blood. "You left me—your father—in Lairhein to face the Kluks alone. You deserved to suffer!" Dagmar yelled disparagingly.

Screaming over his father's final words, Drast stood and used Koldovstvo to slam his father's head downward against the boulder again and again. Three times. Four.

Blood gushed from an open wound splitting over Dagmar's brow.

Drast then tossed the boulder to the side with his magic and jerked his unconscious father to him. He hit the man across the jaw before letting him fall.

Impressive display of anger. Keep it up and you might become your father.

Tyran grabbed his shoulder.

The emerald light of Erzebeth's ghost-like form illuminated the area as she floated behind them. Kam, too, appeared, next to her, pale and naked. Their next task would be to dig her robe from the rubble.

"The demons are defeated," Erzebeth said.

Drast shook uncontrollably. Their father lay at their feet,

still alive for all that Drast could tell, but certainly not moving any time soon. His body was broken. His brains were spilling from his skull.

He stepped back when Dagmar sputtered, "Killed by my...own sons. What tragedy is this?" He wheezed. "What dark design played by cruel gods?"

Seems like a great deal of work on the part of gods.

"The gods do not care about you," Drast muttered breathlessly. He gripped onto Tyran to hold himself up, knowing he could lose consciousness at any moment. Tyran pushed the Alatir Stone back into his hand.

A slow clap sounded from somewhere deeper in the tunneled cavern. Kowin strode from the shadows. "Well fought, mortals. It is time for the next Grumadki."

"Only one loose end to tie up first," Kam said, crossing her arms.

Drast smiled weakly. "Look, Dagmar. Kowin is a god and does not care about you."

He turned to Tyran, who, he found, was watching him.

"It is time to end him." Tyran grunted.

Drast nodded, licking his lips. He looked back to his father. He needed Tyran to move first, to say something more, but for many moments they simply watched as Dagmar labored to breathe. His father closed his eyes, unmoving, save for the blood that he gargled, causing him to cough and sputter.

"Will you just stand there and watch me die, then? Let me bleed out my last while you gloat your victory over the man who gave you life?" Dagmar rattled.

Drast wetted his lips again, feeling tears swell in his eyes. "I cannot do it, brother." He looked away from his father and his brother, staring at the ground. "I cannot count the number of people I've killed, but I cannot kill him."

Tyran grunted. "I can."

Month of Ripening

Fifth of Warmth

1353 CE

Chapter XVII

Swathed in a veil of blue fog, Tyran crashed through the Grumadki, exiting the shadow world and once again entering the freezing atmosphere of the Netherworld. The cold stung at his cheeks as he adjusted his eyes to the strange haze. He squeezed his hand into a fist, reminding himself that Drast took the Alatir Stone before entering the last Grumadki.

He could not count the number of gates Kowin led them through since Dagmar's death. Within a couple days of exiting one, they were leaping through another, having no way to know if they were coming closer to Heshayol or not. And since the shadow world distorted time, he was clueless as to how many days or months they had traveled since leaving the Tower of Eresh.

He murkily examined the Grumadki behind him, wondering if Kowin would bother following this time. He suspected the god would eventually leave them stranded to fend for themselves.

Erzebeth had been missing since the battle against Dagmar. Tyran knew he should be more concerned about being abandoned by Kowin, but he held Ojenek, the key to Wolos's prison; he knew Heshayol was the destination; and he and Drast possessed the fortitude to withstand the Netherworld. Moreover, with the Alatir Stone in their possession, he and Drast were strengthened. In fact, he felt more and more like his old self with every passing day.

Moreover, and most importantly, his father was dead at last. Anything was possible.

He was hopeful.

Blinking away what felt like dust over his eyes, Tyran noticed the unwelcomed knot balling in his throat, another minor side effect of exiting the Grumadki. He tried to clear his vision with his fingertips. The discomfort experienced when stepping out from the shadow world to the Netherworld lessened since the first time. He was personally glad to be absent of the choking and excessive snot, but his nerves still rattled.

The other three should have been through already.

He was so focused on the Grumadki and the whereabouts of the others that Tyran barely heard the Bukavac's foot crunch against the ice behind him. He twisted to see the demon looming with a battle-axe gripped in its three-fingered hand.

The glimmering demon snarled.

Tyran forgot the mace on his belt loop, a battle cry ripping through his gullet. Holding steady beyond the crossed wooden beams, Tyran flashed flames at the giant beast. The fire blackened the frozen body wherever it touched. The Bukavac stomped a step closer with a wild roar, fighting through the flames. Tyran's eyes widened as the demon lifted its battle-axe above its horned head.

A magical arrow tipped with fire zipped over Tyran's shoulder, striking the Bukavac in the chest and causing it to stumble back, stopping the attack mid-strike. Tyran leaped to safety, rolling out of the way as a second arrow rapidly followed the first. "I have this one, brother," Drast snipped, stepping away from the Grumadki.

The Bukavac fell to the ground, dying softly.

Tyran winced, ignoring the demon and Drast. The metal shield on his back scraped against his upper spine. He made a mental note of taking the Alatir Stone from Drast to avoid the ache in his muscles. No doubt, the pain would be worse in the morning.

He leaned over and sat up as Kam and Kowin exited from the Grumadki behind Drast. Tyran narrowed his eyes at Kam, noticing how her dark hair now nearly covered her ears, and then Kowin, who sauntered through the gate with a smug look. He sucked in a breath, shoulders lifting, and let it out again without bothering to acknowledge the dead Bukavac or Tyran. An entire army could have lay dead and he likely would not have cared.

Kam lightly touched her hair and frowned, realizing its length. The behavior was typical whenever they exited a Grumadki now. With Tyran and Drast ageing backwards, Kam's hair had become the closest thing they had to an hourglass. "How long were we gone this time?" she asked weakly.

"Not long enough," Kowin replied.

Drast pulled the Alatir Stone from his pocket. "If we continue at this rate, we might have to pass this stone over to Kam. She keeps getting older, and I would rather not be a child when we reach Heshayol."

Tyran noticed Kowin's eye trace over the glowing white stone before returning to the horizon. He wondered how much more power Kowin would have if he held the Alatir Stone. He remained in his sitting position, trying to read Kowin's thoughts. "You will not have the stone."

His piercing sapphire eyes shot to Tyran with surprise. "I do not want *that* stone, mortal. Though I hardly think you two should have it either."

Tyran touched Ojenek through his pocket from where he lay on the ground, remembering Erzebeth's warning not to let Kowin have the bluish orb.

A low rumble from the fog and ground-shaking footsteps pulled Tyran's attention.

He flung himself to his feet, powering his movement

with Koldovstvo. Jerking his shield from his back, Tyran blocked the deathblow of another Bukavac who suddenly emerged from the mist.

The metal clanged, echoing in his eardrums. Tyran hit the Bukavac with his shield.

"I got it!" Kam shouted. She pulled her axe from her belt, swinging it back behind her ear.

Several magical arrows enflamed in fire sank into the Bukavac's chest, halting the Warden's attack. "I beat you to it, Small-tits." Drast grinned smugly. "Just stay back from battle until we ask for your help, eh? We do not need you dead before we reach Wolos."

Kam glared at him through half-raised eyelids, sliding her weapon back to her belt. "I would have thought the Tower of Eresh would have changed you."

Drast's face tightened, turning away from the skin-switcher. Tyran did not blame him. His own experience in the Tower was not something he wanted to reflect on any more than he had to. The experience was gut-wrenching.

"Where did these two Bukavac come from?" Kam asked, changing the topic. "I have not seen any demons since entering the Grumadki after the Tower."

Tyran scratched his head, looking at the giant bodies sprawled out at his feet. The Warden was right. They had bounded through shadow gates so fast, he scarcely had time to think about anything more than reaching their next destination.

"A few stragglers lucky enough to find their way through a shadow gate," Kowin said.

"You mean demons do not rove here," Tyran clarified.

"This is sacred ground; those who roam here do not survive long." Kowin cut between them with a grunt, slogging forward. "It doesn't matter. You will join their numbers at Heshayol. One way or another, even if I have to kill you with my own hands."

"Glad to know you will not use your swords." Drast

smirked.

Kowin curled his lip, unamused. "I have nearly found where Svarog hid my soul, and your endless banter is exhausting."

"Before you kill us, oh mighty Kowin, will you *please* reward us with a final word? I have been working on a magnificent speech; I would really hate to see it wasted." Drast pressed his lips together in a feigned pout before relaxing into a grin.

Tyran cut off his brother's nonsense. "Is that what you are waiting for, then? You have not found your soul yet?"

Kowin stormed forward. Tyran walked behind him with the others at his heel, listening closely. Kowin mumbled, "The only reason you march alongside me is because I have not yet retrieved it. Once my essence is back in my possession, nothing will stop me. I will annihilate each of you and then Wolos, and with a god of the pantheon gone—beyond the hope of resurrection—the other immortals will soon destroy themselves. They will have no way to restore balance."

"Wolos is not so easy to defeat," Drast said, "and if history says anything, you will find my brother and me to be more difficult."

"I was impressed with how you killed your father, but do not be mistaken. You are pawns," Kowin said.

"Why do you hate the thing you have created?" Kam crossed her arms at the far rear. "How can you be so callous?"

Kowin huffed under his crimson breastplate. "I did not create *you*. I created the immortals to oversee Aenar, to maintain the order I put into place—and instead, they made you worthless mortals. Not a single one of you is perfect."

"You are not perfect either," Kam argued.

"True, I am not, which is why I allowed myself to be held captive by the pantheon," Kowin said, stone-faced, as though the truth were plain and any righteous, intelligent being would have done as he did. "I have since learned from my failures. The imperfect cannot create perfection. In fact, they likely will create a less than perfect image of themselves, despite their intentions. The faults of any living being will inevitably seep into whatever they touch. Just as you are broken reflections of your father and mother, my children— the immortals—are fragmented shards of my being. They, too, are unworthy of *being*."

"So you wipe it all from existence?" Tyran asked.

"I will," Kowin answered. "The old-dark will return Aenar to chaos, and I will return to the cosmos. Any memory of you, the gods, your world will be forgotten."

"We will fight you," Kam said.

"You will try…fleetingly," Kowin replied. "Your nature forces you to persist, even when you might want nothing more than death. Living things in every world across Thrice Nine Lands are forged to *want* life, yearning for the next moment, ever-hoping it will be more glorious than the last; and then they eventually die. Fighting me, mortal, will be as hopeless as fighting time itself. You cannot defeat me. I am deathless."

"If you were not such an ass, I might like you," Drast said, giving Kowin a sidelong look.

"Like him? He is saying the gods failed when choosing to make us, and he plans to slaughter us like hogs," Kam cried, brown eyes narrowing. "He thinks we ruined his perfect world by being part of it."

"Yes," Drast said. "And when the time comes, I will be the first to punch him in his *godly* bits, but I cannot say I disagree with his reasoning."

"Me neither," Tyran said.

Kam scrunched her forehead as Kowin lifted an eyebrow at them. "See, you would fight me although you agree with me. Your nature is no mystery."

"Mm." Tyran rested his hand on his mace.

"I do not value my life or legacy," Drast said, clutching

his bow in his spectral hand and the Alatir Stone in the other as he walked. His face was full of mischief. "But if possible, I will do what I can to make sure your soul stays hidden and you are returned to Thrice Ten Kingdom, or I will defeat you in battle."

Kowin smiled thinly. "You know you cannot kill me."

"I do not know anything," Drast said, "but I am willing to find out."

Tyran's mind was peppered with thoughts of duty and tenacity and resolve. Everything inside him said that if Kowin found freedom he must fight against him, even though he felt his life was as meaningless as the god suggested. His mouth moved mechanically. "Me too."

"You cannot kill me," Kowin hummed, his voice eerily calm as they continued their pace through the fog. He shook his head. "There is too much of myself in you mortals."

Kam sighed. "And what exactly do you think you gifted to the gods that they should not have passed to us?"

"The desire to create, curiosity, free thought, the will to live…" Kowin said, pausing as if suggesting more could be named, but he was withholding for their benefit. "The members of the pantheon were meant to be the curators of Aenar and nothing more. Instead, they made mortals and instilled in them the components of chaos like passion and opinions and emotions."

"Here is a *thought* for you…" Drast said, "…you cannot lift a finger against us, and you are already claiming victory and perseverance. You sound like a boy bragging about the girth of his manhood before his balls have dropped."

"You three are hardly a concern," Kowin said, his chest swelling under the crimson breastplate.

"Oh really? Well, believe it or not, death has eluded us too, Kowin." Drast chuckled. "No matter how hard we try, we just keep marching on. I suspect we will keep *marching on*, actually, even after you are back in the Kingdom under Svarog's watch."

Kowin smirked. "I admit you surprised me when you escaped the Tower of Eresh, but do not think I will fail. I created the lands of mortals and the divine. I created the gods you worship; I know their minds." Kowin strained again as though he wanted to stop walking and could not; his feet scuffled against the ice. "They know nothing more than Aenar, their Kingdom, and the Netherworld. My soul is tucked away somewhere in your mortal world, and Aenar is a speck of sand compared to Thrice Nine Lands. The gods cannot hide it from me forever."

"They will not have to if you return to Thrice Ten Kingdom," Tyran said. "How much farther to Heshayol?"

"One more Grumadki," Kowin said, pointing to the crossbeams materializing in the distance. "Heshayol will be waiting on the other side. I will lead you into the ruins, and then I will return to Aenar to finish what I have started."

Chapter XVIII

"I thought you said Heshayol would be waiting here on the other side. I only see more of the same." Drast adjusted his empty quiver and traipsed on once again, staring at the less than impressive wasteland. Surrounded by frozen dirt and frozen mountains while gawping at an incessant frozen horizon, he internally muttered a series of curse words.

After surviving many long winters in Lairhein and then the frigid cold of Anaerfell, he would have given anything for the Netherworld to resemble a pit of fire. Disappointingly, he was held captive to frost and ice and snow.

The gods had no imagination.

"Where is Heshayol, Kowin?" Tyran rumbled, marching ahead of his brother. Tyran's now burly arms swung alongside his broad chest, and his newfound youth, acquired from passing through multiple Grumadki, was imposing. The shield on his back and the mace at his belt seemed significantly more dangerous in his possession. The elderly man who left Anaerfell and entered the Netherworld was gone.

Kowin took his time responding, lingering behind them, stepping away from the crossed beams of the Grumadki. The dismal fog washed over the erected poles. "Do not worry. You will never again see the shadow world."

Is he making a threat?

"He thinks he is clever." Drast squinted at Kowin over his shoulder. His stomach rumbled, reminding him of his ceaseless hunger. "The truth remains to be seen."

Tyran stopped his movement and turned around. "I did not ask about any Grumadki. Where is Heshayol?" he repeated, his rumble turning into a deep-throated growl.

"Forward." Kowin lifted his chin.

With a slight shake of his head, Tyran scowled and marched onward. Kam stayed at his heel.

Drast sighed heavily, meandering behind them with Kowin staying at the rear. They could do nothing more than follow Kowin's direction; at least, until Erzebeth found them again and told them how far from their mark they had truly strayed.

Kowin is taking you in circles, biding his time.

"Tell me something I do not know," Drast said. His mind emptied for a moment, and then the voice returned. The thought echoed inside his skull as though the words had been shouted into a canyon from a cliff.

The pantheon doesn't have the power to destroy.

Drast grabbed the side of his head to soften the sound of the voice, grumbling under his breath. The words reiterated Erzebeth's teaching some time ago. She had told them the gods were incapable of destroying and therefore needed to create humans to continue the cycles on Aenar.

"I think I knew that too, but why is it important?" Drast said. He rubbed his scalp as Kowin's long strides came in line with his own. The pantheon held Kowin's soul and, therefore, he followed their orders. The gods, however, could not destroy the soul.

He must not know.

"How could Kowin not know? I thought he was supposed to know everything," Drast said, his voice drawing the god's attention.

"Know what, mortal?" he asked.

Do not tell him! Hurry! Think of something else. Think of the ice. Think of Anaerfell. Think of the skin-switchers. Think of Small-tits.

"Uh..." Drast looked to Kam and grinned. "Why has Kam been walking this entire way? I am certainly sick of plodding along, but I do not have a choice. Can you not turn into a bird or something? Or are you only capable of twisting that lithe body into a hairy brute?"

Perfect.

Kowin grunted and sped away from Drast, unamused.

The Warden looked over her shoulder. "I could if I wanted. Though I do not know why you would think flying would be any less exhausting than walking," she replied. "Besides, I would not count on any of you carrying my belongings."

She has a point. You would probably drop them along the way, leaving her naked and without her weapon.

"At least I would have something to look at," Drast chuckled, winking at Kam, who gave him a steady, burning glare. Shrugging, Drast turned to look at the god's back as he stormed away, his black hair swaying against his mid-back. "How about you, Kowin? You are all-powerful, right? Why do you insist on stomping along like the rest of us mortals?"

Ahead of him, Drast noticed Tyran look over his shoulder. His brother shook his head slightly and raised his eyebrows, as though he were indicating Drast should end his talk with Kowin before it went any further.

Kam increased her speed, a sign she was escaping the conversation altogether.

Drast pushed his red bangs from his eyes. Like Tyran, the Alatir Stone had practically restored his youth through the many Grumadkis.

Kowin held his lips shut, refusing to answer the question.

He probably cannot turn into a bird.

Drast grinned madly, seeing every reason to entertain

himself with the so-called god. Kowin was not nearly as clever as he thought himself to be, being afraid of a pantheon whose hands were tied. A bit of chitchat would undoubtedly keep him entertained and make the miles pass quicker. Tyran was staring headlong at the desolate landscape ahead, joining the skin-switcher at the front of their irregular line.

Drast made sure to keep pace with the god.

"Are you troubled, Kowin? I mean, despite all your attempts to suspend our progress, we are still going to reach Heshayol and free Wolos. I bet we will reach our destination before the day is done."

Kowin rested a hand on the hilt of one of his two swords, grimacing at Drast's waggling tongue. "We will arrive at Heshayol soon enough. Are you really so eager to die?"

"Our chances of dying are drastically decreasing. I have not seen any more wayward demons since the two outside that last Grumadki," Drast said. "Seems we have stepped beyond death's reach."

"I told you the demons do not come here," Kowin frowned, "but you will die all the same."

He is even more dour than the God of the Dead, you know?

Drast slowed his pace to pick at Kowin. "Can you think of nothing more to threaten us with than death? We have seen and done far worse than anything death can offer." He tightly squinted his eyes, barely seeing Kowin through the slits. He displayed his few teeth between his spread lips.

Kowin replied, "You would be wise to listen to me."

You should listen to your brother. Nothing good will come from arguing with the immortal. You will say too much and he will use it against you.

"Rubbish. I enjoy arguing with you, even if you prattle on like a saggy-breasted harlot who only loves the sound of her own voice," Drast murmured, shooing the voice away with a wave of his hand.

"In a thousand years, why has no one cut out your tongue?" Kowin shook his head in amazement. "I speak of your death because mortals fear death and an eternity in the Netherworld. Yet you and your brother walk through this wasteland, among the forsaken, hardly wavering in its wake."

"I told you that you underestimated us," Drast cooed.

"The Alatir Stone in your possession gives you an advantage," Kowin admitted. "Though how either of you survived the Tower of Eresh with your minds intact remains a mystery."

He suggests your mind was once whole.

Drast laughed, agreeing with the voice in his head. "How could the Tower crack what is already shattered? If anything, the Tower only solidified fears already carried inside us. Tell me, what behavior comes without consequence?" Drast lifted his finger at Kowin. "You may not be imperiled by your actions, but every mortal is haunted by what they have done and, sometimes even more, by what they have not."

Kowin widened his eyes, seemingly amused. "I cannot know what you saw, but your argument is that you once before reflected on the events experienced in the Tower? The nightmares therein already haunted you?"

No.

"Yes!" Drast insisted.

You are lying.

"Surely not."

Yes, you are.

Drast grunted, shaking his head. "I knew all along, even if I did not want to admit what I knew."

Kowin said, "Through creation, you were woven into the framework of Aenar. Did you really think you could escape fate by lying to yourself? Ignoring your misdeeds?"

Drast bit his tongue, unsure what Kowin implied. Wolos seemed to clarify the meaning.

He is right. You do lie to yourself. You repeatedly forsake your

Drast grinned with discomfort, like a child feigning innocence after being caught pulling sweets from his mother's apron pocket. "You think I am evil?"

"I didn't say that. Good and evil are concepts created by mortals. You are simply inefficient." Kowin relaxed his hand from his sword's hilt, averting his eyes from Drast. "Though you Kaligulas show greater resolve than other mortals. I can see why the spirit chose you to come to the Netherworld."

Drast laughed, uninterested in reflecting on the motivations of Erzebeth. "You admire us, then?"

Kowin's face was emotionless. "Hardly. Your death will be as necessary as any other. I advise you to enjoy what you can of your final moments."

As expected, he ends with another threat.

"For someone who claims to be deathless, you spend a lot of time talking about death," Drast said, hooking his thumbs into his waistband.

Tyran stopped them suddenly, pointing to the haze of clouds hanging in the sky above them. "What in the Nine Lands is that?"

Drast crooked his head to follow his brother's outstretched hand. The frozen mist above them died out, revealing a pool of water suspended leagues into the air, well beyond their reach, swirling with murky black tendrils—possibly moss—dangling from the shallows. Thick roots, stretching like columns, emerged from the suspended water, dipping like stalactites from the heavens. Yet not a single root reached the surface of the Netherworld.

Drast covered his mouth to block the stench of decay that reached down from the water. The smell reminded him of the prolonged rot of bodies on a battlefield.

"When you passed through the Tower, you reached a space in the Netherworld meant for immortals and immortals alone," Kowin said, crossing his arms. "The

Tower of Eresh is meant to be a gate to deter mortals from seeing sacred sites such as this.”

We have different definitions of what is meant by sacred.

“Smells terrible,” Drast choked.

Kowin raised his head toward the spectacle, completely ignoring Drast. “Behold what remains of the Waters of Life and the roots of the Ash Tree, which in turn freed the Nithhoggr and set them loose upon the Netherworld. In time, the demons will make their way to the world of the living.”

“By the gods,” Kam murmured, shuffling backwards, holding her own nose. The skin-switcher, who had spoken of the Ash Tree’s destruction since the beginning, looked to be the most surprised.

“The roots appear to have been cut away,” Tyran said, gritting his teeth. “Why?”

Kowin almost sounded gleeful in his explanation. “Yes, the roots were severed after the death of Wolos. The Netherworld began to fill with demons and the gods became desperate for a solution. Your flawed pantheon hoped to free the old-dark to rebalance Aenar. A frantic attempt to remedy what cannot be fixed.”

Then why are we here?

“Why are we here?” Drast asked.

“Erzebeth told you,” Kam reminded them. “Mortals were given another chance to restore the world, but only if we could resurrect Wolos. He can mend the roots of the Ash Tree; he can cleanse the waters.”

“So they think,” Kowin said. “But the change in the plan has granted me freedom from Thrice Ten Kingdom. The Likhyi are growing stronger, and I will eventually be beyond the control of your gods. I will soon have my soul.”

“We will correct this,” Tyran said, walking away from Kowin. “Come on.”

Kowin pursed his lips, gesturing for them to continue.

For the many miles that followed, Drast found himself

trapped inside his own head. While he would have preferred to think of the decaying Ash Tree, he instead ruminated over the distressing experiences of the Tower of Eresh. From taking advantage of the servant girl to murdering the Kluk siblings to betraying Erzebeth and Tyran, Drast could recall very few positive events in his lifetime. He may have once pointed the finger at his father for guiding his hand against others, but now he could not ignore the number of times he acted of his own accord. Furthermore—even among the few cherished memories of spending time with his brother—he could not remember ever doing good for the sake of doing good.

He shuddered as he walked, clenching his fists with frustration. Although the Tower of Eresh lay leagues behind them, the thoughts and feelings of those he'd embodied stayed with him, no matter how deeply he wished to forget them. The moments he spent looking through Tyran's eyes were undeniably the most impactful.

Knowing Tyran felt joy multiple times in his life, whether alongside Maelili, Isolde, or Erzebeth, caused Drast's heart to fill with remorse. Even in the company of his brother, Drast never knew the bliss Tyran felt. The emotion was foreign to him.

He spent an hour or more attempting to discover an equal occurrence in his own life to lessen his self-loathing. Yet whether he was hammering Kura in his bed chambers or outfoxing an enemy on the battlefield, the level of gratification he found always fell short of Tyran's few instances of happiness.

With deeper reflection, Drast realized he was not so much disheartened that he never knew the same joy, but that he actively kept his brother from being immersed in what he repeatedly and readily found. The Tower revealed a truth about Drast he hated: he was not *good* like Tyran. Kowin certainly could argue the concepts of right and wrong were crafted by the lesser mortals, but Drast *was* mortal. And no matter how he wished to rationalize his behavior or conceptualize the cause of his morality, he was unable to ignore the cost of the destruction he wrought.

Are you trying to silence my voice? All this thinking is making it awfully difficult to speak.

"I thought about it," Drast said. He sucked in a breath and took in his surroundings. Kam ambled ahead of him, while Kowin and Tyran had fallen back.

They were all silent.

You deserve to suffer.

"Really? That is what you have been waiting to say? I expected you to say something deep and philosophical—you know, in your *godly* tone—but *I deserve to suffer.* Ha! Of course I deserve to suffer. Who doesn't? Mortals live to suffer. When we are bored, we create problems just so we might suffer another day," Drast said. He looked for something more to say to keep Wolos from hearing his own thoughts. "Come to think of it, even the gods cannot escape suffering."

Kam twisted her neck to look at him, her eyes narrowing.

"I am not speaking to you," Drast said, his eyes meeting hers briefly. He looked away, barely catching sight of her extended glare. She curled her lip rather unattractively, then refocused her attention to the front.

He grinned.

The skin-switcher does not trust you.

"Do you think I care? No, no, no."

Yes.

Drast scratched his head at the sound argument. He did not think he cared what Kam thought, but if Wolos believed he did, he supposed it could be true. "Maybe."

Your father really screwed you up.

"Every child could say the same," he replied.

Drast felt his heart sink at the silence that followed, overwhelmed by sudden doubt. He wondered if what he knew was the truth or whether he simply repeated the same lies to himself to ease his hatred. He spent years falling short of his father's expectations, telling himself he was unworthy to do anything more than strive for Dagmar's idea of perfection. He spent an equal amount of time reiterating the same nonsense to Tyran, as though his personal truth was fortified with his brother's reception.

Dagmar really had broken him. He made him into a monster. The corners of his eyes burned at the thought of what he might have been, knowing what he could never become. Somehow, Tyran had clung to some sense of good through the violence and maltreatment.

By the gods, Drast did not have the patience or the will to change now. The sudden desire to die danced between his ears. He wanted the agony he felt within the Tower of Eresh to disappear forever but, with a thought, the despair rushed over him, sinking into his stomach.

You deserve death more so than your brother. More than the skin-switcher. How long will you deny it?

He might have vomited if anything existed inside of him to throw up. His belly rumbled.

"First, I should undo what we did," he managed.

To me? What about what you did to everyone else?

Drast's head spun. "What I did to everyone else."

Why were you able to kill me and not your father?

"How is that relevant?" Drast huffed, shaking his head in annoyance. He adjusted the bow on his shoulder. His throat tightened at the possible answers he might give to the faceless voice. "Why would you even ask me that?"

We should think of all those you have killed through the years.

"I do not want—" Drast fought against the suggestion, but the simple words suddenly sent flashed images of the many faces he confronted while in the Tower of Eresh. Hundreds, if not thousands, of pained expressions tore through his visage.

Look at them, Drast. Were any of them like your father? Were any of them deserving of death? Was I?

Drast twitched nervously, unable to escape the words echoing in his skull. He formed his hand into a fist and forced his feet forward on the slick ice.

He needed to find something more to say. Anything to distract him from the noise in his head.

Why can you only destroy what is good?

Drast knew what Wolos was suggesting, even without the piercing question. Whether in war or for simple pleasure, he slaughtered men and women who had never so much as lifted a finger against him. He killed innocents. He murdered a god. Yet his father, who repeatedly manipulated him and abused him, was forever protected from his wrath.

Even in the final moments, Drast had to call on Tyran to fell the final blow.

Drast was weak.

He was not like Tyran.

You must save Tyran.

"I know, but I cannot save everyone," Drast said. "Just you, and maybe the skin-switcher if I have time."

You cannot save her. She must die.

Drast dipped his head, remembering Kam had to sacrifice herself for Wolos to be reborn and walk across the Kalinov Bridge. "She must die," he repeated.

But what if she dies before you reach Wolos? Who will free Wolos then?

Drast hesitated, turning to see Tyran lumbering behind him. His brother's red curls bounced over his blue eyes, his hand resting on the mace in its loop.

"I will. I must. Tyran will live."

Chapter XIX

Tyran could not count how many weeks or months came and went since they ventured away from Anaerfell to come to this strange place. He rested his shoulder against the towering rock column, gripping his steel shield in one hand and his mace in the other. The pillar stretched toward the purplish clouds, the top hidden from view in the suspended mist. He searched the skies for any signs of the Nithhoggr— or any other demon, for that matter—but as suggested, no demons wandered in this part of the Netherworld.

The skies were especially empty.

"This place is unnervingly quiet," Kam said from several paces back. "I can hear little more than my heartbeat in my ears."

"Mm." Tyran skimmed the large temple-like building stretching before them. The grounds surrounding Heshayol were ruins with broken rocks and columns as well as buildings crushed beneath the weight of time. Yet the central building withstood the elements: an enclosed stone colosseum standing almost thirty feet tall with a doorless entryway dead center. He crooked his neck to look at the chipped rock forming the angled rooftop.

Wolos surely resided within.

The piled rocks under their feet—some the size of

Tyran—shifted as the ground tremored. He bent his knees to hold his balance and leveled his gaze. Stones were disseminated in front of him across the uneven terrain, possibly the remains of old walls or a ceiling that once accompanied the stone supports. A few columns were intact like the one he leaned against, but the majority were broken and jagged, with the top half fallen and shattered into smaller fragments, adding to the strewn debris. Even after traveling through the wasteland of the Netherworld, he expected something more than scattered rubble and a standalone building. The place was more of a ruin than Anaerfell.

"Nine Lands!" Drast neared him, the ground moving beneath them again. He nocked an arrow on the string of his bow. "Unless my memory is mistaken, it has been a while since we felt any earth tremors. We are done with demons, right? This must be something more."

"Something is out there," Tyran agreed, though he could not say what exactly. Plenty of times he had felt the earth tremble under the footfalls of armies, especially in the Netherworld where demons ran amuck. This was different. "Kowin, what shakes the ground?"

The god was silent, standing a distance away with his arms crossed. He lifted his shoulders with a satisfied smirk.

Tyran scowled and rubbed his chin, staring into the darkness on the opposite side of the door. Nothing could be seen beyond the grey stones.

The earth rumbled again.

"This place looks ancient," Kam said, crouching down to touch the shaking rocks. "Could Heshayol have been some primitive structure built before this world was made into our Netherworld?" She looked to Kowin as though he might tell her any secrets he might hold.

He intentionally looked away from her, refusing to acknowledge her theory. His blue eyes darkened, scanning the thick vapor ahead, his long black hair whipping over his shoulder. The strands resembled wraith-like shadowed claws that gripped the curvature of his red breastplate.

"I do not think this is the time for a history lesson, Small-tits," Drast said.

Kam scoffed.

When he could see nothing stirring in the fog, Tyran stepped down from one rock to another, coming closer to the open doorway. "I thought you were planning to return to Aenar," Tyran said, hoping to gain some response from Kowin. "Do you not have a soul to locate?"

Kam clenched her jaw. "Why would you say anything about that to him? Whose side are you on, Red?"

"Soon," Kowin said, continuing to peer into the swirling fog. "First I will see what happens here."

Tyran stood rigid, hearing the forewarning in Kowin's tone. He followed the god's gaze to the doorway ahead. No doubt a trap awaited them.

Something moved inside; the rocks under his feet shifted once more.

Drast trailed behind Tyran, seemingly unaware of the distant movement, holding the edge of the rugged pillar Tyran had leaned against a moment before. He squinted at the skies, then scanned the darkness ahead. "Where is Wolos?"

"Inside," Kowin directed. "Go free him, if you must."

"We will," Tyran assured him.

He led the way into Heshayol, hearing the faint footsteps of Kam and Drast following him, expecting demons to leap from the shadows at every corner. Once the three of them were inside the structure, he used Koldovstvo to cast a magical orb of light. The dim yellow glow showed a ceiling stretching as tall as the building and more scattered columns. He was surprised to discover nothing immediately stirred.

"I have a bad feeling about this," Kam said.

"We all do," Drast said. "You don't have to vocalize it."

"Where have you brought us?" Tyran asked, moving

through the center of the columns. His voice was shakier than he would have liked, taking another step into the mist. Heshayol ran deeper than he would have imagined from the outside, tilting at a downward angle. The temple looked to be half-buried beneath the surface. In the limited light, he could barely see the pillars, let alone the stone floor. He warily lifted his shield in front of his body.

"*Heshayol.* As promised. What else?" Kowin gleamed from the doorway.

Tyran reached for his weapon. "We are not alone in here, are we, Kowin?"

Kam skittered to his side, her skin-switcher eyes catching movement farther within. She pointed to a large mass swiftly slithering down from a column. "No, we are not!"

The darkness eddied, revealing a pale, distorted form—as large as the stony supports—hurling itself at them through the dark.

"Gods! Shoot!" Tyran cried, fortifying himself behind his shield as a colossal white serpent head whooshed through the discolored fog and shadows. The lifeless eyes faded from view as the mouth opened—large enough to swallow him whole—and a forked tongue lashed out between two extended fangs. Stooping behind his shield, he heard Drast's arrow zip over him. He lifted his head enough to trace the path of the projectile, striking inside the creature's mouth, puncturing the soft pink flesh beneath an enlarged venom sack.

"A dragon!" Kam screeched. "No! We are here to free your father! Let us pass!" The creature threw its head back, emitting a venomous hiss, and whipped its triangular head nearly twenty feet above them.

"That is not a dragon. It's a snake," Drast said, lining three magical arrows along his bow. "Even I can see that, Small-tits."

"Osiscica," Kowin said melodiously, slipping back to

stand in front of the exit. He showed no interest in joining the battle. "She is the sentinel of Heshayol and the Keeper of Wolos. She will not let you take her prized prisoner."

Tyran glared over his shoulder at Kowin, who deliberately said nothing of this monster beforehand. The god had headed them into a trap, hoping they would be overrun by the giant snake. He may not have raised a hand against them, but he stayed to his claim that he would escort them to their graves.

"Tyran, move! Fly!" Drast shouted, the words a blubbered mess from his lips. "Now!"

Tyran did not bother to check Osiscica's whereabouts. He embraced Koldovstvo and took his brother's advice, leaping through time and space and flinging himself into the air. Magic surged through his veins, propelling him clear of the giant snake, which speedily belted underneath him through the columns. He could not see the end of the snake, but the sharpened spikes crowning deadened eyes and the slick body stretching hundreds of feet through the scattered rock and rubble sent a shiver through him.

Beneath Tyran, Kam moved to intervene with the monster, tossing her robe from her shoulders. The axe clanged against the rock. She hurriedly began transforming into the spawn of Wolos, the sacred bies. The coarse hair sprouted from her skin, while the bone and muscle in her face cracked and shifted to resemble the dark features of a bull. She grew several inches, layered with muscle from hoof to horn, and roared at Osiscica in defiance.

The long, spineless body of the reptile wound toward the Warden, ignoring Drast's many arrows tearing through its scales with little impact. The fog roiled over the snake's glassy form, the beast tasting the air with its blood-red tongue. Kam snorted, rushing at Osiscica. A moment before the monster revealed its deadly fangs, Kam reached out and grabbed its upper and lower jaw with a meaty grip, seemingly trying to hold the mouth closed.

Her muscles strained, a determined roar reverberating up from her gullet, but she was no match for the much larger fiend. Osiscica whipped its head, flinging the skin-switcher into a stone column effortlessly.

Osiscica charged the Warden, letting loose a growling moan as its body constricted.

A familiar green light tore across Tyran's vision in a sudden flash, blocking his view of Kam. He focused on keeping his orb of light illuminated, ignoring the sound of rock splintering and crashing to the earth beneath him.

"Erzebeth." Tyran lifted his hand to ward off the bright light. "Where have you been? Where is Wolos?"

"Do not let her die," Erzebeth said with hesitation, almost if she did not recognize the sound of her own voice. She spun around to look at the scene at their feet, scanning over Drast and then Kowin, who remained silent in the shadows.

"He means to kill us," Tyran said. "He *will* kill us."

Erzebeth looked as lifeless as Osiscica's eyes. "He thinks you are too weak to win. You must prevail, young Red."

"Mm," Tyran mumbled, realizing she was not going to answer his questions. She held as much vigor as an old man on his deathbed.

An inhuman howl resonated from Kam.

"She has been bitten!" Drast cried out.

Tyran descended away from the undead Vucari as Kam crashed through a pillar of rock, frantically clinging to the beast, arms wrapped around the upper jaw, inches from the poison-tipped fangs. Her brown fur was discolored where blood oozed from her muscular chest. A single fang, the length of its entire edge as sharp as a sword, had slashed through her flesh.

Osiscica's scales rubbed against each other, making a dry, raspy sound, as the monster raced along the debris, its mouth widening as if to make Kam fall down its throat. The skin-switcher's bestial hands weakly clawed toward the snake's eyes to no effect, coming short of reaching the silvery ovals.

"Keep it busy, Small-tits." Drast loosed several more arrows tipped with fire at Osiscica, which stuck ineffectively into the white scales before the magic faded. The snake hardly took notice.

Kam's head fell against the black nose slits on the snake, holding tight to the monster.

Tyran hurled his mace at the giant snake. The weapon missed the skull, hitting the side of the body as Osiscica twisted around a column. He pulled the weapon back to his hand with Koldovstvo. The beast solely focused on continuing the assault against the Warden.

Tyran moved to Drast's side.

His older brother smirked, hanging his bow over his shoulder. "The snake's shell is as concentrated as dragon scales. My arrows will not bring the beast down."

"Dragon scales…" Tyran scratched his head, recalling the black dragon they once battled outside Lairhein. "Remember when we fought against Torn'ash? We were able to break through his scales, and then you were able to fire an arrow at the heart."

"Dimly. I remember Torn'ash escaping." Drast creased his brow, waving his hand at Osiscica. "Besides, the anatomy of a dragon seems a bit more straightforward than a snake. I cannot say where the head ends and the tail begins on that *thing*, let alone find its heart."

"We must defeat it somehow," Tyran said.

"Alright, master strategist." Drast grinned, forming a magical arrow in his ghostly hand. "Go break through. But you best hurry before the skin-switcher is swallowed whole. If she dies, one of us will be forced to give our life for Wolos."

Kam crashed through another pillar. The rocks rained down over Osiscica, who seemed oblivious to the heavy boulders striking the length of its cold body. The Warden, still in the form of the bies, swayed weakly on the end of Osiscica's snout, her clawed grip slipping. She snarled, baring her teeth, while staring into its dead eyes.

"Get away from it!" Drast shouted at Kam, readying the arrow. He moved his red hair from his eyes, turning his chin to Kowin. "Please, take a moment to catch your breath. We will handle this."

"Your Warden will soon be dead," Kowin smirked.

Tyran rushed into the darkness, not waiting to hear the full of Kowin's reply or Drast's tireless snark. Empowering his being with Koldovstvo, Tyran attacked, weaving through the columns of stone. With all his might, he pulled the mace back and smashed the end of the weapon into the swift-moving snake as it slithered by. The weapon shook in his hand from the impact, the handle splintering above his closed fist; the aftershock vibrated from his wrist to his shoulder. He scowled, his fingers tingling and bicep flexing under the strain. Pulling the weapon close, he examined the useless handle.

It is broken!

The snake's outer core was tougher than Tyran's mace. Another hit against anything with substance would certainly snap the weapon in two.

Osiscica stopped its movement, rearing up the front half of its body, twisting through the air to face Tyran. Kam let go of the snout, falling twenty feet and slamming into the earth with a pained grunt. She attempted to lift herself up but fell back down. The form of the bies melted away, leaving Kam's naked body lying against the rock.

"Is she dead?" Drast cried.

Tyran slid his weapon back into his loop, readjusting his grip on the shield. He could not take the time to inspect the Warden. Though he did notice that the scales he struck were undamaged.

The snake coiled its long body behind itself, sliding over Kam's body, the weight crushing the skin-switcher against the rock.

Tyran swore he could hear her skull being crushed.

Osiscica attacked, its fangs lengthening with malice. The upper teeth hooked over the top of the shield, inches from Tyran's forearm, while the bottom jaw clasped to the underside. He gasped in alarm, jerking his arm free from the leather bindings on the back of his armament. Retreating several feet, he gaped as Osiscica tore the shield away; a second more and the beast would have taken his arm with the guard.

The snake thrashed its head back and forth, the silver gleaming between its gums for several seconds before flinging the shield into the fog. Quick as thought, Osiscica rotated back to strike at Tyran, its long body following behind, the forked tongue darting between its scaled lips.

Tyran unleashed fire at the beast from his hands, but Osiscica kept coming, tearing through the flames. He needed an escape from the charging beast.

Lightning zigzagged from behind him, hitting Osiscica over and over. Drast shouted with every burst of energy he released, but the bolts seemed to have no effect on the snake's thick skin.

"Kill it," Erzebeth said absently, moving beyond Osiscica without giving a second glance. The Vucari drifted through the bluish fog to where Kam had fallen, her voice a distant thought.

"Is she dead?" Drast yelled again.

Erzebeth descended to Kam's body, her tone void of all emotion. "The Warden is gone."

Chapter XX

Drast screamed, he laughed, and then he wept. Some mixture of the three kept him nearly blind as he flew to where the Warden's body was, falling to his knees as the tail of the monstrous snake scraped away.

"No! You lying whore! No, she isn't!" he screamed, laughter bubbling in his throat. His good hand touched Kam's face nervously, his other hand gone, unable to focus enough on the magic to keep it in place. "She is alive. She cannot be dead!"

Erzebeth floated near. "She is, Red. Help your brother so he does not accompany her."

She planned this. She wanted it to be this way.

Drast spun, tears blurring the Vucari's green translucence. "You did this. You wanted us to die. I knew it! I knew you wanted our deaths."

"Your brother is dying."

She wants you to have to choose. Your life or your brother's. One of you on the altar to return a dead god to life. You foresaw this betrayal.

He could feel his blood boiling. "You want us to be a sacrifice to your dead god because he was too weak to stand before us mortals. I am no mere mortal, skin-switcher! I am a dragon-man. I am a *god-killer*. I killed him and I can kill you!"

Erzebeth's form flickered.

"Drast!" Tyran's voice barely eked through his deafening heartbeat. "For the love of the gods, help me!"

No! Kill her before she escapes. Your brother is as good as dead anyway, no matter what happens here today.

Drast's head resounded with noise, like a mighty waterfall crashing against the rapids beneath. Deafening. Roaring. His broken pitch was unremarkable in comparison, a single drop splashing against the rocks. "No."

She has already seen to it that the final chapter of your story has been written, but you can have the final say.

Drast had no words for the voice, fighting the impulse swelling in his chest. Wolos's words shrieked inside his skull, nearly bringing him to his knees. He screamed as loud as he could until his throat burned in an attempt to silence it.

"Drast!" Tyran thundered when Drast's lungs finally fell short of air.

His mind went blank, attuning to the battle inside the darkened temple. The desire to kill the ghost twisted into an insatiable mirth. Madness.

"Coming, brother." He sang, giggling as he flew away from Kam and Erzebeth, his head scraping along the roof of the sunken temple.

Tyran stumbled away from Osiscica below, moving around a column, which was subsequently smashed to bits by the white snake in its pursuit. His brother skidded to a halt, returning his shield to his arm. The silvery guard emanated a cold blue light just as the snake struck with savage speed. Tyran grunted, rolling back from the blow and coming again to his feet in a crouch. He kept the shield raised. Osiscica moved to strike again.

With a low chuckle, Drast used Koldovstvo to crack the stone in a nearby column, pulling away chunks to send it teetering over, the roof creaking. The thirty feet of stone fell toward Osiscica, landing across its body and temporarily stopping its strike against Tyran. It hissed, curling and coiling itself, sending the rubble from the column rolling away from its contracting body.

Tyran looked up at his brother but said nothing. Drast could almost hear his grunting. Shield in hand, Tyran used his magic to hurl a chunk of stone at the massive snake, which bounced off its scales and rolled on. Osiscica hissed again, opening its jaws to strike at Tyran again.

"By the Nine Lands, Tyran, put some distance between you and it before you do something like that!" Drast shouted, half-laughing, unable to stifle his newfound merriment.

Tyran leaped backward from the snake, lifting off into the air, leaving the serpent striking at stone.

Erzebeth floated near, her greenish hue providing additional light to the orb Tyran managed to maintain. "Have you never killed a snake before? Aim for its head."

Osiscica's tongue flickered, tasting the air, its head seeming to bob sightlessly as it searched for the two.

"Shut it!" Drast retorted, raising his finger. After a moment, he added, "And yes, I am talking to you this time, skin-switcher."

At the sound of Drast's voice, Osiscica hurled itself forward, fangs dripping venom. He flew to the side, hoping the creature would fail to track his movement. Racing through the empty space, Osiscica crashed into the wall, coiling and rustling, hissing and spitting. The wall and roof cracked from the impact, causing large chunks of stone to fall on top of the serpent.

"Do not do that again." Tyran flew near. "Too many impacts like that, or if too many columns break, we are going to be buried down here."

Running out of options. You should have killed the skin-switcher when you had the chance.

Drast cringed at the sound of the voice returning. "Well, my arrows do nothing, your mace is broken, fire is useless,

and the only thing we have access to is the stone around us."
Drast pointed to Osiscica. "How are we supposed to kill the
thing?"

Osiscica hugged the jagged floor, recoiling from the
scattered wreckage of stones with its muscular mass,
ominously slithering toward Kowin. Hissing through its
mouth, the snake elevated its head several feet as though it
might strike the god. Kowin raised his jaw a hair and
sneered, jerking his head sideways to motion the beast away.

Drast growled as Osiscica turned obediently from
Kowin to refocus on him and Tyran. The beast approached.

"Use the rubble," Tyran grunted, using his magic to lift a
fallen chunk of rock and hurling it at the twining snake
beneath them.

The stone crunched into its triangular head, which only
seemed to anger it more. It snapped forward, faster than
Drast would have believed a creature that size could move.

Erzebeth amplified the color of her light to distract the
snake, but Osiscica tore past, unaffected, and snapped at
Tyran.

Striking too low, it managed to hit Tyran at the knees
with the top of its head, sending him tumbling into the
ceiling. He scrambled on top of the creature's head,
attempting to steer clear of Osiscica's fangs and to keep
from being crushed between Heshayol and its scales. Drast
watched in horror, but eventually he managed to fly off to
the side.

Osiscica followed with its tongue flicking.

"You are no help, skin-switcher," Drast muttered.

He quickly scooped up a stone as his brother did and
flung it the beast, striking her squarely in the eye. Pale yellow
ooze spurted from the wound. Osiscica belted her head at
him, rushing at him with fury.

He glided away, twisting to and fro, but Osiscica had his
scent, its tongue stabbing at the air and shadowing his every
turn. Desperately, he used Koldovstvo to pick up and toss

any rock or stone he happened to catch, but the snake barely seemed to notice the attacks. None were large enough to do more than bounce off its toughened scales.

Osiscica struck, one of the arm-length fangs piercing Drast's thigh.

Throwing his head back, he could not keep the wail from tearing through his throat. The pain seared through his flesh like fire. His hands instinctively fell to the wound, careful not to touch the lodged fang, gripping at his upper leg in despair. Almost immediately he could feel the venom burning through his blood. He struggled to extricate himself from the beast's fang, but the single sharpened tooth held him in place.

Tyran sprang to him, grabbing at his shoulder to keep him from being swallowed whole. "Drast!"

Drast tried to ignore the sting, breathing deeply.

"Free yourself," Erzebeth appeared by him. "Do not let her swallow you."

He grinned at Erzebeth. "I am tired of getting my ass kicked. I'll take my chances inside!"

"I don't think so." Tyran hooked his hand underneath Drast's arm, pulling hard and causing the sword-like fang to tear at his leg.

"Gods! Stop. Don't pull!" Drast was drawn closer to the snake as his brother followed his command.

"What do we do, then?" Tyran asked, holding on to him.

"Whatever you do, don't follow me." He forced a laugh as his legs disappeared into Osiscica's mouth. He looped one arm over the snake's snout, trying to delay the inevitable. He reached to his brother with his magical hand. "Alatir."

Tyran nodded, using Koldovstvo to direct the stone to his brother's grasp.

Drast sighed as his fingers closed over it, already feeling it go to work, the snake's gullet pulling at him, steady and relentless. He was already losing his grip, pulled almost entirely inside, the fang slowly extricating from his leg as it folded back to the roof of Osiscica's mouth.

With a relentless laugh, he pulled away from Tyran and let go of the snake to wave at his brother. "See you on the other side, brother!"

"Wait, Drast!" His brother's voice disappeared as he descended down Osiscica's throat, the soft pink mouth quickly turning to crushing blackness.

Hello, darkness, my old friend.

Drast giggled at the return of the voice—or tried to— but the weight of Osiscica's throat pushed the air from his lungs. His mouth opened and closed like a fish out of water trying to find more.

Something struck his fleshy cocoon from the outside of Osiscica, jarring him considerably, followed by a furious series of additional blows that probably caused him more pain than the snake. He twitched, trying to pound at the side of the snake's neck to tell his brother to stop the assault, but he had no mobility. Slowly, he was being pulled down farther into the breathless blackness of Osiscica's belly.

I am starting to think this was a really bad idea. He thought the words while mouthing them at the same time, but his lack of breath gave them no sound.

I could have told you that if you would listen. Kowin wanted you to be eaten. The skin-switcher, too.

A slow, creeping panic began to rise in his chest. The whacks and wallops continued, relentless and furious. Drast half imagined he could hear a scream of rage beyond the constricting muscles.

The crushing feeling in his chest had become painful, unbearable, stealing his attention from the agony in his leg. The Alatir Stone may protect him from actual physical harm, but the sensation of being eaten alive did not taper. Trying to focus his will, Drast used Koldovstvo to use the little air around him to press against the sides of Osiscica's throat, giving himself a momentary reprieve from the muscles that slowly and deliberately pulled him down. He took a single stale breath that started him coughing.

After several hacks, he finally gained control of his breathing, enduring the dry itch at the base of his throat. He soon found he could only manage by holding air in his lungs intermittently before taking another pained, short breath.

With a fingernail's grip on the magic that kept him from being compressed into the beast's next meal, he pulled the air around him into a singular mass and pushed it against the side of the snake's throat. Blinded by darkness, he could not see whether the attempt had any impact, but a sudden twist of Osiscica's elongated body, followed by a renewed pressure around him, told him it was, at the very least, a discomfort.

But try as he might, pressing his hands against the solid ball of air seemed to stretch the snake rather than cause any rupture or damage. He had nearly fully extended his arms, but nothing happened to give him freedom. Osiscica could probably swallow creatures ten times his size—his little ball of air was not going to do much.

Moreover, this small pocket of air allowing him to breathe turned so thick that each breath became a greater struggle. He could not find a way to satiate his need to breathe.

He became dizzy and tired. Wolos spoke in his head.
Cut it.

Drast blinked drearily and reshaped the air, trying to keep the element solid but transforming it to a sharpened point against the distended section of flesh. He hoped he was still closer to the head than the tail.

The pinned air tore a pint-size hole through Osiscica's skin and scales. The sudden burst released the pressure, causing the snake's innards to collapse back around him, removing the little air in Drast's lungs. Osiscica's blood gushed into the small space—Drast struggled to press his hand against the flow to keep himself from drowning. Finding the hole, he thrust his good hand forward, wriggling it until he felt the cold, fresh air on the other side.

As quickly as he could, he pulled the air through the small hole, filling the space around him and widening the gash in Osiscica's side. She writhed about in response, tossing him back and forth inside the space, which grew rapidly with the influx of air.

You may have been better off letting the poison kill you as it did the skin-switcher.

Drast angled his head, ignoring the voice. Breathing easily, with blood sloshing about—and a pocket of air large enough to hold him three times over—Drast felt a sudden reversal of the muscles pulling at him. Osiscica was attempting to heave him from its insides. With the pain and burning from the sharp fang still plaguing him, he fought against the snake's effort, shoving his magical hand back through the hole he created.

He hooked his other arm in the widened gash to prevent his ascension to Osiscica's mouth, while maintaining his focus on the pocket of air around him.

He was secure. He breathed easily.

A sudden tug at his arm dragged him through the opening up to his shoulder, and a subsequent tug nearly dislocated it. Realizing Tyran was trying to pull him out, Drast sought to further widen the hole, but the snake thrashed, twisting and turning. If it were not for the Alatir Stone, Drast likely would have lost his remaining arm.

He cried out momentarily against the pain, despite having gained no injury, and lurched away from Tyran. Pulling his hand back to the elbow, he giggled on impulse. Altering his magical arm into a jagged knife, he sawed at the muscle and scales of the snake.

With the opening expanded, Drast dove through with his hands above his head until he was hanging half out of the beast. Osiscica twisted around to face him. He grumbled, realizing how far away from the head he had slid down the body.

Halfway there.

Drast pushed the voice away again, noticing that his brother had been hard at work during his captivity. The snake's triangular head was bloodied and battered. The pale eyes were mangled, oozing yellow goop, mirroring the deep gouges and gashes along its horned snout and beneath its jaw.

"A little help, brother," Drast called out in desperation.

Osiscica reared to strike at him, a meal extricating itself from the snake's own body. The words were barely out of his mouth before he was yanked free with Koldovstvo. The beast behind him hissed and writhed in pain. A gaping, bleeding wound was left in its side.

Drast caught himself with Koldovstvo, flying in Erzebeth's dim light. Tyran's magical orb had disappeared.

Tyran eyed him, flying at the spirit's side. "We could have pulled you out. Was it really worth it?"

Oh, do answer him. Was it? I am not sure if it was long enough or pleasurable enough.

Drast grinned, trying to wipe blood from his eyes and cheeks. "Not even a little. A lot goes on when you're being eaten that you never really think about." Catching sight of Osiscica moving toward them again, he elbowed Tyran and flew back. "Here it comes!"

Tyran darted away and Drast flew down, struggling to find a stone that had not been broken to bits over Osiscica's head already.

You cannot ignore me forever.

"I can try," Drast muttered, searching Heshayol for anything to use as a weapon. "Oh, brother?"

"What?"

"Can we destroy just one more column? Maybe one at the back that no one will notice?"

Tyran's grunt as he zipped past, the snake striking after him, was all the confirmation Drast needed. Using Koldovstvo, he took an entire column, the roof cracking and crumbling, depositing a large mass of sand, gravel, and ice to the floor below. Keeping the column mostly intact, he melded it with magic into a stronger piece.

"Bring the beast back through!" he yelled to Tyran, smiling at the column. "And be ready to kill this blasted thing!"

Tyran used what larger pieces of rubble he could find to keep Osiscica's attention, pulling her through the underground complex toward Drast.

With the massive column parallel to the ground, Drast waited until the creature was nearly beneath it, dropping it to the ground with as much force as he could manage. Using Koldovstvo, he fused stone to stone, the column warping and bending, pinning the snake to the solid stone floor, its body and tail coiling, trying to push, pull, or lift itself free. Drast could feel the stone of the column cracking and breaking. He used stone magic to mend the rock as fast as he could.

"I cannot hold it for long!" he shouted, moving to hover above the snake.

"What is the plan now?" Tyran asked.

If you were not ignoring me, I might suggest blinding it.

"Blind it," Drast answered, groaning under the strain of holding Osiscica in place.

"It is blind!" Tyran growled.

"Its tongue, Tyran." Drast grunted in exasperation. "Its creepy, bifurcated tongue!"

Tyran zipped down and quickly latched onto the snake's tongue with Koldovstvo. With a deep-throated growl, he stretched it out between its scaled lips. "What now?"

Drast looked around and saw little besides Erzebeth floating uselessly and Kowin shuffling a step closer with a bemused look on his face.

Sword?

Drast nodded. "I know."

Dropping in front of the snake, he reached behind him

with Koldovstvo and yanked one of Kowin's swords from its sheathe to his hand. In one smooth motion, he swung up and over, cleaving the tongue in twain.

Osiscica reeled, shattering the stone column that pinned it, a large piece striking Drast and sending him skidding back, the sword readied in his hand. The Alatir Stone reduced the impact to nothing more than pain. Severe pain, but fleeting pain nonetheless.

From the corner of his eye, he saw the shadow of the snake slither close. He rolled clear and sprang to his feet, but by the time he turned around, Osiscica was gone.

Tyran was staggering toward him, bleeding from a gash on the side of his head.

Drast tossed the Alatir Stone to him, hobbling forward. "Where did she go?"

"Away." Tyran grunted, catching the stone and throwing it back. "We have some time to recover. Hang on to the stone for a moment." He rumbled in his throat, watching Drast catch the stone. "Nine Lands, what does it take to kill that thing?"

Kowin approached, ruthlessly ripping his sword from Drast's hand. "Do not touch my sword."

You would think you grabbed his bits.

Drast giggled, wheezing from exhaustion. "I just wanted to know what it was like holding a god's *sword*, if you follow me. It was *heavier* than I thought it would be, but certainly *shorter*. I nearly missed my target."

Kowin glowered, sheathing his weapon.

"Do you ever have that trouble, god?" Drast spat snake blood at the ground. "Pulling out your *sword*, ready to go to *work*, and missing the *mark*?"

"Watch yourself, mortal, or I will be the one who finally cuts out your tongue," Kowin threatened.

"I dare you to try." Drast stormed forward to throw another insult in the god's face and abruptly halted when Kowin vanished from sight. "Where did he go?"

Chapter XXI

"Did he really flee to Aenar?" Tyran demanded, fury beating in his chest. If anyone had answered him immediately, he would have missed it. His heartbeat pounded in his ears, his anger intensified by the wound on his head. With a growl, he hit a rock column with his open palm, ignoring the sting that burned into his wrist. "Nine Lands! The coward! I will kill him."

Drast did not respond, running his ghostly hand through his red hair and visibly biting his inner lip. He slowly approached Kam's bloodied and naked body, eyeing the Alatir Stone in his left hand. "I did not think she would die. She was not supposed to die. Not yet, anyway."

He paused, hovering the artifact over her body as though he was not sure what to do. He touched her hand with his glimmering sapphire-colored fingertips.

"The stone will not help her," Erzebeth said, hovering inches in front of Drast. The Vucari shimmered in the churning greyish-blue film as it filtered through her wraith-like figure. The only light in Heshayol came from her jade-colored essence. "She is beyond reprieve."

Drast glared at Erzebeth with a look that suggested he knew as much, considering Kam's shattered skull against the rock. Her blood and brains were difficult to miss, emptied beneath his feet. He grasped the stone in his fist, all white light fading from his eyes as he squeezed shut his eyelids. "We can resurrect a god, but not a skin-switcher? The girl must be lingering around the Netherworld somewhere. I say we find her and bring her back so she can resurrect Wolos. That was her charge. She said so herself."

"She is dead," Erzebeth said. "The process of bringing her back from the dead would be the same as resurrecting Wolos. One of you would have to sacrifice yourself to see her breathe again. The journey would be pointless, and you do not have the time."

Drast cursed.

Tyran breathed heavily, turning around as though some other answer might reveal itself. His anger distorted his vision; his ire was unyielding. He found little to ease his mind. The destruction of the inner building was obvious, with mountainous pillars of rock scattered in all directions and the dead Warden lying among the rubble.

He yelled in frustration.

"All this power, and we can do nothing?" Drast tried again, opening his eyes. He revealed the few thoughts Tyran could not seem to put into words. "This stone must have something more it can do," Drast said, lifting Alatir to Erzebeth, "or the one in Tyran's pocket, the Ojenek."

"Neither can raise the dead. Alatir heals and Ojenek unlocks. You were wise to keep the latter safe from Kowin."

Tyran stuffed his hand into his pocket, gripping the blue stone, the key to Wolos's prison.

"We have to do something!" Drast barked, a grin fighting to split his lips.

The undead Vucari was expressionless. "The Warden is dead, young Red. We can do nothing but go deeper into Heshayol. Wolos is all that matters now. He must be reborn before Kowin frees himself."

"How so?" Tyran spoke between his few gritted teeth. Blood oozed down the side of his face. His stomach rumbled from hunger. He already knew the answer to his rhetorical question. "You want one of us to sacrifice our life for Wolos because he needs to take a living spirit to walk over the Kalinov Bridge, right?"

"Yes," Erzebeth said.

"Have the pantheon force Kowin to do it. They have his spirit locked away," Tyran said.

"The gods cannot send their creator to die," Erzebeth said. "They would rather die themselves than ask him to sacrifice himself."

Drast cried out, "Then have one of them come sacrifice themselves!"

"That would not help restore balance. We would be no better off than we are now," she replied.

"Tell the pantheon to kill Kowin," Drast said, holding his laughter back. "I know. I know."

Erzebeth replied, "The pantheon cannot destroy anything. They have not the power."

"He wants to kill them," Drast argued out loud, though Tyran was no longer certain if his brother was speaking with Erzebeth or himself.

"Which would be no better or worse than before they were created. They are beings made to keep the cycles of the world, to maintain a specific order," Erzebeth said. "They do not have the capacity to understand the worth of what we call life."

Tyran huffed. "Because they do not see any difference between life and death."

"They are immortal," confirmed Erzebeth. "Regardless, the world was not broken by a god or an immortal. It was undone by mortals and must be fixed by mortals."

The smile drained from Drast's face. "We know, skin-switcher! Go away."

"We must discuss this, Drast," Tyran said. "I will—"

"You will not!" Drast shouted, staring at the ground, unable to meet his brother's gaze.

"I have to. If I—"

"*You* do not *have* to do anything," Drast growled. He swallowed. "When it comes down to it, I will."

Tyran grunted as if he had been punched in the gut. Silence ruled for a time while Tyran searched for an appropriate response. Eventually he found the words, his voice thick. "You do not need to do this, Drast. I do not think I can handle that. I thought…well, I thought you were not coming out of that snake alive. I cannot do that again."

Drast glanced at his brother. He looked winded. "I had the stone."

"Still—"

Drast spat blood. "You have a chance at a life that I cannot have, and so I will do what needs to be done. I am broken," he raised his stump, "and I know I am insane. We will see Wolos reborn." Drast stood upright. He looked off in the distance for a moment. He nodded his head and smiled wide. "I will make the exchange."

"Drast—"

He shook his severed arm at Tyran. "You have found your youth again with the Alatir Stone. You can still find a woman, settle down, and live a peaceful life. Nine Lands, you might even have children."

"What?" Tyran swallowed. "My life will never know peace, Drast. You, if anyone, should know that. We are brothers, and we stay together."

"No, I am not arguing this with you, brother," Drast said sternly. "You will try. You will promise to live a better life than what we have." Drast lifted his shoulders, breathing heavily through his nostrils. "If we bring Wolos back and stop Kowin, we undo everything Father did, and I want to see that happen. I have been ready to die for a while. I could not care less about glory or redemption or any of that nonsense, but sacrificing myself for a god sounds far superior than being run through with a sword."

"Mm," Tyran grunted.

"No grunts," Drast said. "You promise me."

Tyran could not imagine a life without his brother.

"Let me do this, Tyran. You live. I die." His jaw tightened with determination. "It should be this way. We should face the facts. You helped kill Wolos, sure, but I did the deed. I am the one who stopped his heart."

His mind flooded with ideas of how he might argue with his older brother, but he knew Drast would dismiss him with little effort. His mouth had always run almost as quickly as his mind. He reluctantly nodded. "Okay."

"It is settled, then," Erzebeth said. "Come with me."

Drast shadowed the spirit's ethereal form as it wisped through the patched fog and darkness. Tyran followed, casting another magical orb of light to hover over him. The yellow glow lightened the inside of the building, allowing him to quickly find his shield among the rocks. He recovered his guard with Koldovstvo.

Erzebeth took them to a wide stone staircase leading down into the earth, positioned at the back of Heshayol, nearly hidden among the collapsed columns. She floated carelessly to the bottom, while he and Drast treaded carefully along the slick steps. Once they reached the bottom, Erzebeth led them down an enclosed hall and then a secondary stairwell, almost hidden behind several larger pieces of carved rock, going beneath the earth.

Tyran's heart raced as he peered into the darkness below.

"I think it is your turn with the Alatir Stone. My leg is feeling better, and your head looks terrible," Drast said, offering the artifact to him. He nodded his appreciation and took it from his brother, feeling the magic immediately surge through him, healing his gaping wound. As usual, his skin turned as white as the gem in his hand. "If you have the stone, he will only be capable of killing one of us."

"Wolos?" Tyran asked.

"Or Kowin, if he returns," Drast mumbled. "Or

whatever beast we may face down here. The gods only know what other traps the skin-switcher has set."

"I think Erzebeth is on our side," Tyran said. Drast cocked a brow with amusement, scoffing under his breath. Tyran shook his head. "One way or another, I am not afraid of dying."

"I know," Drast replied with a short breath, easing down the stairwell, his good hand running along the wall.

A brush of cold air hit Tyran from the depths, along with the realization that Drast was saying more than what Tyran heard. He understood Drast loved him, possibly more than any brother ever loved another brother, but this was something beyond. Drast was afraid for Tyran. He was shielding him from hurt. He was protecting him from death.

He was doing what he had been incapable of doing for years under their father.

Tyran did not have words for his brother. The gravity of the emotion was foreign to him. Unnerving. He attempted to steer his attention away and, along with it, his thoughts.

The narrow passage under Heshayol was bitter cold, numbing his cheeks and stealing away any smell. After spending so much time at Anaerfell, he was familiar with the relentless breath of winter. Yet his gut roiled with uneasiness as they traipsed through the dark, the path brightened only by the green glow radiating off Erzebeth's ghostly form and his simple orb. Rooms and more hallways branched off in several directions, shadowed in more darkness. He hoped the demons, specifically the Strigoi, were truly absent from Heshayol. Without Kam, they would be unable to see the monsters coming for them.

What felt like hours passed, and then Erzebeth motioned for them to follow her through an open doorway. Their boots crunched over the rough floor, scraping against loose rock and cracked ice.

Tyran intensified the light of the yellow ball, hovering it into the air above him. He entered the room behind Drast, a room that barely resembled a prison or dungeon. Instead, the large chamber appeared to be an ancient library, absent the books, from the distant past.

Empty stone shelves lined the rocky walls in the circular room. The ceiling was carved into a blank dome without any decorations, a cut similar to the flat bare floor. The rock may have been smooth at one time. Tyran could make out scuff marks and deep gashes in the stone. He wondered what ancient battle may have been fought in the chamber to leave such markings.

The thought was fleeting when Tyran noticed the aged man with a white beard and bushy eyebrows strung up by chains in the center of the room. Despite his age, the strength in his broad shoulders and thick arms was unmistakable. Thick chains—as thick as Tyran's arm—wrapped around each limb and the neck of the man, glowing softly red, like coals burning in a hearthfire.

He stood upright, his back straight with his legs spread at shoulder width and his arms bound at an angle on either side of his head. The chains stretched through the walls and floor, shimmering with magical power.

Koldovstvo.

"This is worse than a Znaki," Drast said. Tyran shook his head. He did not want to think of the symbol that had kept them from wielding magic for the past millennium.

He neared the old man with Drast at his side. The twisted sand-colored horns beneath the man's long white hair were clearly visible in the yellow haze of Tyran's spherical orb. Even with a millennium gone and being touched by death, the Horned God remained physically unchanged.

The chains rattled as he raised his head to them.

"Wolos," Tyran said.

He responded, "I am the Horned God, the Protector of the Eternal Spring, the Guardian against the Frost. I am the God of Death."

Erzebeth bowed before her god. "Wolos, I have done all that you asked. The Ash Tree is safe, and the brothers have come to release you. The Warden perished on the journey here, but the eldest Kaligula has promised to give his life for yours."

"Really?" Wolos asked, turning to Drast with surprise.

"Which means you will not be in my head anymore, right?" Drast wrinkled his brow, staring through Wolos. "Tell me that you will not follow me into death. Despite your applauded sense of humor, I would prefer we go our separate ways. Let us just say it is not you, but me…"

"I have not been in your head, Drast Kaligula," Wolos croaked.

"Sure he has," Drast replied. He quickly looked over his right shoulder as though something were coming up behind them. "I know. You do not have to tell me. Just shut it already."

Tyran looked to the dark doorway behind them and saw nothing. Drast's madness returned tenfold with the Alatir Stone apart from him.

"How do we free you?" Tyran asked.

"He must swallow Ojenek," Erzebeth said.

Tyran gulped hard at the thought. The stone was smaller than the Alatir Stone, but would be more than difficult to stomach. "Okay," he hesitated. "And then what?"

"I will take us all to the Kalinov Bridge so you can return to Aenar, and I can return to my charge," Wolos said. "I will restore the roots of the Ash Tree. I will refill the Eternal Spring and the Waters of Life. I will lead the dead to their resting place in Thrice Ten Kingdom and keep them from the land of the living." Wolos swelled his chest. "I will restore balance."

"Listen, Wolos," Drast interrupted haughtily, louder than necessary. His face was twisted in discomfort. "Stop whispering your little words of wisdom in my head, you sick bastard. I do not want to play your games anymore.

Apologize to Tyran and me, we will free your *righteous* ass, and then you can kill me.”

Tyran blinked at his brother in confusion. He considered giving him the Alatir Stone back, at least long enough to set Wolos free.

“What should he apologize for?” Tyran asked.

“He said we could not kill him, and we did,” Drast said, rocking on his toes. “He was wrong to underestimate us and needs to say he is sorry.”

“Your strength was unforeseen,” Wolos admitted, his mustache rustling against his beard.

Drast waited, lifting his finger to his lips as if expecting more. When nothing was said, he smiled. “I suppose that will do. Give me Ojenek.”

Chapter XXII

The soul-searing atmosphere of Heshayol sent a shiver down Drast's spine, and the dim radiance of Tyran's light made the immediate chamber all the more haunting. Long shadows danced against the walls of the inner dungeon around him. He shivered, aware that the walls did nothing to protect from the bite of the Netherworld beyond the ancient stone. Anaerfell had been Drast's doom, but Heshayol would have been his hell.

With a smile, he wiped his hand against his trousers and took Ojenek from Tyran's extended hand. The glassy gem felt extra smooth. He then turned to face Wolos once more. He briefly thought about what the god must have gone through, being trapped in this desolate, hated place for the past millennium. A *dead* god likely did not need food, water, or fire, but the extended solitude would be unbearable. Of course, Drast was practically isolated with Tyran and his persistent muteness, but he, at least, could stare at his brother instead of looking eternally at a bleak wall.

The stone shelves did not even have books.

Even in death, there is no knowledge.

"I am hardly surprised," Drast replied. "Seems knowledge is always kept from us mortals, buried by the gods; that is, if there is anything to even know."

Erzebeth spoke from nearby. "Free him."

Despite her closeness, her voice was barely heard, like a distant thunderstorm hushed by the overpowering voice in his head.

Maybe the gods know something. Ask Wolos a few more questions while he is at your mercy.

"No. I have heard enough," Drast said, eyeing the Horned God. Wolos gazed right back at him with an eerie calm through his half-raised eyelids. Silent. Waiting.

You certain? Not every day does a mortal gets to question a god.

"Stop pestering me," Drast hissed.

"You will soon see me no more, I promise you," Erzebeth assured him.

Erzebeth's emerald hue was too close for comfort, shimmering against the shadow of the dungeon. Only now did he realize she was speaking to him.

She would ultimately be the reason for their deaths. He was certain of her betrayal more than anything. He spoke with disdain, sniping at her. "I look forward to the day I am no longer in the company of skin-switchers."

Clutching Ojenek in his good hand, he moved toward Wolos.

Kowin suddenly appeared in front of him. The god lifted his hand as if he might grab at him, but Drast jumped out of his reach.

"Nine Lands!" Drast shouted, pulling Ojenek safely behind his back. "Have you come again so soon? Eager to return to Thrice Ten Kingdom, are you? We will only be a moment."

Wolos rumbled behind Kowin, straining against the chains that bound him. They rattled and rustled under his might. "Do not entertain Kowin the Deathless, lest you wish the world to end."

Kowin leered. "Silence yourself, Wolos." He gave Drast a cold look. "Let the Horned God stay dead. The world should return to its natural state."

I suppose he means let the-world-return-to-primordial-chaos natural state, not the-dead-stay-dead-and-are-not-bubbling-up-from-the-Netherworld natural state. He must not have found his soul.

Drast cracked a smile at Kowin, drawing his attention to him. "Do you remain soulless? Have you been outsmarted by the Grandfather of the Gods? How embarrassing!"

Kowin growled, swelling his chest beneath his crimson breastplate. His hands swiftly fell to the hilts of his swords. "I only need more time. Wait for me to find my soul and you will be rewarded."

Reward you? Ha! He means to deceive you and destroy you.

"You would kill me," Drast said, looking at Kowin with fire in his eyes. "Do you even realize how mortal you really are? You have lived for an eternity and still you are no better than those you insult. You have been confined by the gods like water in a pot."

"The gods have my soul," Kowin said.

"And they will keep it," Tyran gave Drast a cautionary look but spoke to Kowin. "You have threatened us with death since the moment we met and nearly had us killed by Osiscica. We have no interest in helping you. Stand aside."

"You do not understand," Kowin insisted. "The world is better off being destroyed. Let the old-dark cleanse Aenar."

"From mortals, you mean?" Drast challenged. "I am really not up for that type of cleansing. I would be fine with a little sprucing up, however. You know, take out a few of the oddballs, maybe the *skin-switchers.*"

"Mortals are weak," Kowin said, rocking back and forth to block them from Wolos, seeming to ignore Drast as much as possible. "You two know this is true. You admitted the creation of mortals was a mistake. For a single moment, ignore your insignificant mortal nature and listen to those wiser."

Mortals are no more a mistake than the gods or Kowin himself. But you must crack a few eggs, you know? Serendipity and all that.

"Nothing exists without a flaw. Even you have faults,

Kowin," Drast said. He pulled his good hand from behind his back to shake his finger at the so-called god. Ojenek glimmered in his outstretched hand. The itch of a laugh lifted from the bottom of Drast's throat, adding mirth to his words. "You pretend to be all-knowing but cannot see the truth right in front of you. How can you call us ignorant when you are trapped inside your own head?"

You spend most of your days trapped inside of your head.

"That is not the point," Drast said.

You are not supposed to talk to him about his imprisonment by the gods, remember? You will make the skin-switcher mad.

"Stop talking, Drast," Erzebeth warned. She drifted between them, her eyes glowing. She hissed in his ear. "Keep Ojenek from him."

There she is, butting into the conversation. Kam is dead. She wants to see you dead too. She will have her moment soon enough. Do you not get a last word?

"I have plenty to say and I will say it," Drast argued. He rubbed his nose, tilting his head forward like he was sharing the deepest of secrets. "You are not bound to the pantheon any more than a priest is to his prayers."

"Ojenek! There is the gem I seek." Kowin gasped with recognition, seemingly not hearing the revelation. He reached through Erzebeth's ethereal form and grabbed the blue stone from Drast's hand. He drew back, his posture stiffening, looking forward incredulously.

"We are doomed," Erzebeth said softly, moving away as quickly as she had approached.

Nine Lands! What have you done? Does Ojenek hold his soul?

Drast blanched, repeating the question. "Oh, gods. Does it hold his soul?"

"No," Erzebeth said. "I told you Ojenek would unlock the wards on his mind. He is—"

Kowin interrupted her with sudden awareness. "The pantheon may have my soul hidden," he acknowledged shakily, his voice withering with disbelief, "but they are incapable of destroying it. They can only create, which is why they made you mortals. Mortals maintain the cycles of Aenar by delivering death. I have feared a lie, a fantasy, a delusion. I am free. I have been free all along." He bowed his head, shaking it slightly. "They locked away my mind." He lifted his eyes. "But no longer."

The god's eyes have been opened.

Drast pressed his lips together with concern. He spoke through gritted teeth. "If I happen to stumble across your soul—well, you are an ass, so I would definitely squeeze the life from it."

"Drast!" Tyran grabbed his arm to pull him away.

"Take Ojenek back," Erzebeth said.

Tyran let go of Drast to reach for Ojenek.

Kowin pulled back. "The gods locked away my mind. My reason. The scheming wretches. Nothing can force me to return to Thrice Ten Kingdom."

He will surely kill you now, and then your brother.

Drast did not have time to respond.

Kowin sneered at him. "I will take your miserable life, and then locate my soul. Once secured, I can easily destroy your world. No more god-killers."

A golden bolt of pure energy—unlike anything Drast had ever seen—ripped from Kowin's hand at Drast. He should have been dead, but the magic missed him by inches with Tyran anticipating the attack and shoving him clear. Drast hardly blinked but fell against the stone, the heat of the magic warming his back. In an instant, he rolled to his feet. Then, with an exasperated breath, he swung around to see the magic tear through the rock on the opposite side of the chamber.

"Kowin, do not do this," Erzebeth pleaded without emotion, floating past Drast as though her translucent form could protect him. "Give them Ojenek. Free Wolos."

Tyran cried out, unwilling to hear Kowin's reply, pulling his mace free from its loop. With a twist of his body, he stepped through Erzebeth and smashed Kowin in the face with the weapon, snapping the already cracked haft in two. The full force of the weighted end crushed everything from Kowin's forehead to his upper lip, sending his head whipping to the side and his body reeling over the chains binding Wolos.

He crashed to the ground in a heap with a muffled, gurgled cry, grabbing his face in both hands and somehow keeping his hold on Ojenek. The god struggled to pull his feet underneath himself.

Drast patted his own body to make sure he had not been hit by Kowin's magic. When he did not find any holes, he scowled and pulled his bow from his shoulder. He turned to make sure Tyran was also safe from injury and saw that his head had nearly healed from carrying the other artifact.

"Stone!" he shouted, holding his bow in his spectral hand.

If we could kill Dagmar, we can defeat Kowin.

Tyran tossed the Alatir Stone at him. Drast caught it in his good hand, while Tyran pulled the shield from his back and clung to the remaining portion of the wooden haft.

Tyran addressed Erzebeth, stepping forward. "We will not be resurrecting this god."

"No, we will not," Drast agreed, readying his bow with a magical arrow.

"Tyran, no," Erzebeth said, her features scrunching with concern despite her monotone voice. "You cannot defeat Kowin."

"Watch us!" Tyran growled.

Kowin all but got a leg under him when Drast released the first fire-engulfed arrow, hitting him in the neck. Two more followed, burying themselves into the side of his temple. Kowin warbled, spewing blood from his lips seconds before his legs bent and he crumpled back to the floor.

The magical arrows dispersed with his final breath.

Tyran neared Kowin with his shield and broken haft

raised. "I thought he would put up a fight."

I expected a bit more.

"So did I." Drast sniffed, cocking his head to better see the bloodied face smashed against the stone. Blood pooled around Kowin's cheek and eye as it oozed from flesh pierced by shattered bone. He formed another arrow with Koldovstvo. "Should I shoot him again?"

"Get the stone from Kowin, young Red, and release Wolos from his bindings," Erzebeth demanded.

Kowin's eye snapped open, meeting Drast's, breath refilling his lungs. He sprang to his feet with magic, shoving Ojenek in his pocket with a sneer.

"Here we go!" Drast grinned.

Drast shot. Tyran swung.

Tyran's shield arm flung upright against his will, catching the arrow before it could hit its mark. Tyran's attacking hand also paused mid-swing. He bellowed with frustration, being held by unseen strands of air, and then flew backwards across the room into a pile of rock.

Drast gritted his teeth as Kowin spun on him.

Shoot again. Again!

He shot arrow after arrow at Kowin. Pieces of rock lurched from the scattered rubble around the room, intercepting every projectile with ease, while Kowin trekked across the floor.

The god flared what was left of his nostrils in absolute rage. The bloody glare was horrifying, worse than any demon Drast had crossed. Red liquid seeped from multiple breaks in the skin. One of Kowin's eyes was swollen, pushing the eyeball beyond the socket, nearly ready to pop out from the pressure of the cracked skull. The small bones from his chin to his nose looked to be affixed by the gore leaking from his skin.

Kill him!

"I intend to," Drast said. He curled his lip, lowering his bow as Kowin neared. Fire rippled across the empty space like a broken web. Drast used magic to deplete the air in front of him, extinguishing the flames before they reached any further. He then darted in the opposite direction of Tyran, leaping across the room with Koldovstvo to settle behind Kowin. The room blurred around him as he readied lightning at the ends of his fingertips.

The spell never left his mind's eye.

The fist crushing into his face surprised him—Kowin had turned at the last moment and struck him. He wrenched his head to the side, withstanding the full might of the god, fully believing his left cheek met his right cheek inside his mouth through a gaping hole between his teeth. He straightened his neck, and the pain faded.

He cannot kill you. He cannot kill us!

Drast looked Kowin dead in his widening eyes and lifted the Alatir Stone in his clenched fist. "My turn."

He slugged Kowin in his injured face, powered with Koldovstvo, and knocked him back into the wall. The stone wall cracked; the chamber of Heshayol reverberated from the impact.

Kowin pulled himself upright just as Tyran's shield smashed him back into the wall with equal momentum. A shockwave boomed in the room, ringing in Drast's ears.

The god screamed in frustration, throwing Tyran's guard to the side. With a powerful cry, he released another bolt of energy, like the first, at Tyran.

Tyran extended his hands to block the deadly attack, but Erzebeth flashed in front of him, protecting him from the blast.

The light tore into her ethereal form.

She screeched, slowly evaporating from existence, until she diminished into a pile of blackened dust.

"Erzebeth!" Tyran shouted.

The skin-switcher is dead. By the gods, she is dead!

"Do not get too excited, brother. Remember, she was already dead." Drast smirked.

"Do not undermine her sacrifice," Wolos said. The chains binding him rattled again along with the sound of his deep undertone. "Your so-called enemy has been expunged from all existence."

Chapter XXIII

Kowin charged at him.

"Stone!" Tyran tossed the haft of his useless, broken mace to the ground and turned from Kowin. He pulled his shield back to his left hand, bracing under the soft light of the hovering orb above him. Drast chucked the Alatir Stone at him. Tyran stepped through the remains of Erzebeth—the black ash clinging to the sole of his boot—and barely caught the gem to his right hand, forgetting he could not use Koldovstvo to control the artifact.

The magical energy surged through him, promising him its protection.

The air in his lungs caught in his throat as Kowin's sword edge slipped along the back of his knees. He cried out, feeling the razor-sharp blade rip through him, cutting through each rigid tendon. He barely saw the god flank him. Like when the Nithhoggr clawed at his eyes outside the Grumadki, he could feel the pain, knowing the stone kept him from all physical harm.

His flesh remained intact.

Still, Tyran fell to his knees, the agony nearly paralyzing him, coursing through his senses as though the sword had actually crippled him.

Lifting his eyes, he met Wolos's cold stare. The Horned

God hung uselessly in his magically-infused chains, the key tucked away in Kowin's pocket. Regardless, Tyran suspected the god would do little to help them defeat Kowin. Erzebeth was clear that the pantheon had no concern how balance was restored to Aenar; they simply wanted the system to be functional once more. The pantheon was not concerned with self-preservation or life.

Not like Kowin, who wanted his precious freedom and the destruction of Aenar.

Kowin's bellow pulled Tyran from his thoughts, the blade cutting across his lower back before Kowin kicked him with full force. Tyran flew across the room, his skull cracking against the stone wall on the opposite end. The sickening sound reverberated in his eardrums.

He moaned, clutching the white gem in his hand.

The scuffling behind him drew his attention. He turned around to watch Drast blur across the room, using Koldovstvo to hurry his movements. Kowin's swords smacked against the stone floor where he stood defensively a moment before.

"Stone!" Drast screamed, hooking his longbow over his shoulder in a fluid movement.

Tyran lobbed the stone back to his brother, watching him snag it out of the air before Kowin spun around, energy crackling from his fingertips. Drast grunted as the magic hit him, stumbling back several paces.

The god glowered at the two of them, clutching the hilts of his two blades and standing upright. "How long do you think you can do this? I have watched you fight on the battlefield. We both know you will eventually grow exhausted and fall. I will not."

"Then we best make this quick." Drast scowled.

"You cannot kill me. I am not like this puny god in chains," Kowin said, gesturing to Wolos. "I hold the power of all the gods, the old and the new."

Tyran leaped across the void of time and space, flanking

Kowin in a heartbeat. "Funny," he hissed. "You talk as much as he did moments before we killed him."

Flames lashed out from his fingertips, striking the back of Kowin's head, igniting his long black hair. Drast followed his example, releasing fire from the opposite side to engulf Kowin in an inferno. The red and orange flames licked at his torso, melting his skin and blackening his sacred crimson breastplate. Kowin did not make a sound. He simply turned in the fire to face Tyran.

His blue irises melted away in the flames, bloodied pools draining from the holes in his skull.

Tyran did not see the flaming sword eject from the ball of fire until it sliced through his side and pierced his gut. He stopped casting his magic, dropping his shield and clinging to the sword. The sharp blade cut through his palms, the hot blood from his hands mixing with the red liquid flowing from his side.

"No!" Drast screamed, advancing on Kowin, intensifying the fire emanating from his raised hand. His skin was flush; his eyes glowed orange. Koldovstvo burned through him.

Tyran fought to stay on his feet, uncertain whether he should pull the weapon free or leave it lodged in place. He slowly moved his hands up to the hilt, gripping the wrapped handle in desperation. Kowin took a step closer, ignoring Drast's flames. Wherever the god's skin was visible, Tyran saw grotesque flesh blackened and bloodied, splitting from his bones like meat left too long over a campfire.

Kowin did not seem to care.

He would kill them.

Tyran embraced Koldovstvo to pull away, but Kowin struck first, using magic to throw him into the rear wall several paces away. Tyran whipped by Wolos and smacked into the old stone of Heshayol, landing on the ground on his shoulder. The sharpened blade shifted against his stomach with the impact, slicing farther through his body until stopping against his opposite hipbone.

He could scarcely make a sound, thrashing momentarily before finally lying still. The room dimmed.

"Gods," he murmured.

Drast's howl echoed. He faintly saw Kowin smack into the wall in front of him—likely from Drast's outburst—with immense force. Every bone should have been broken. Drast's footsteps trailed after, smacking the ground in front of him.

Tyran saw Drast's youthful features for a moment—a flash of teeth and blue eyes. For a moment, pain disappeared as Drast shoved the Alatir Stone into his hand.

Tyran pushed it away. "No. You—defeat him."

Drast nodded with a pained expression, holding onto the artifact and turning away.

The room went black, the din of ongoing battle rang.

The ground quaked. The stone shelves shook.

The room cracked.

The grunts and cries of his brother seemed endless, as though Tyran listened for an eternity. When his eyes fluttered open again, he shrank back from the patches of frost and dust lingering over him. The room had quieted and turned pitch black. The sound of battle was now distant, beyond the stone walls of the dungeon.

Tyran attempted to sit up but was stopped by his aching side.

He groaned, his hand resting against the blade lodged inside him. He raised his hand. "Light," he muttered, creating an orange orb over him, illuminating the hollow of Heshayol.

He must have been holding his wound when he fainted, because his fingers were sticky with blood, thick and dark. His stomach roiled with nausea; he could sense the taste of copper in his throat.

He could not die. Drast needed him.

"Free me," Wolos said. "I can take us to the Kalinov

Bridge, and we can be done with this."

"Kowin has Ojenek. It is hopeless," Tyran struggled to say, blood slipping over his bottom lip. He rubbed his lips with the back of his hand but did not bother trying to see the god through the floating debris. The wall nearby was broken, stone torn away from the earth and shattered. The staircase leading from the room was in shambles too, with fragments of rock sticking in every direction. He bit his inner lip, wondering how long he had been unconscious and how much more of Heshayol was destroyed.

"Get the key," Wolos said.

"What good…is your rebirth…if Kowin is free?" Tyran asked. "He has unlimited power. If we do not defeat him, everything will be taken. Everyone will be destroyed. Hate will rule." Tyran's mind swirled. "My father has won."

"Your father?" Wolos hummed. "Your father is dead."

Tyran groaned, catching blood in his throat. He hurried to swallow a mouthful of bile.

Wolos's voice rumbled. "The gods seek balance, not eternal destruction. Kowin was bound by the pantheon because he held too much power for the mortal world. If I return to my seat among the gods, balance is achieved, and Kowin, again, becomes too great a risk for Aenar."

"You will fight him? The pantheon would fight him?"

"No," Wolos admitted. "But threads will be woven to see him returned to Thrice Ten Kingdom."

"You mean to say you will use mortals to do what you will not." Tyran scowled at the Horned God. The sharp blade burned against his flesh. He winced. "We are but pawns to you gods, and you wonder why we set out to kill you."

"This is how balance is kept," Wolos rasped from the center of the room, his chains rattling. "If you do not wish it, then let Kowin win. Certainly, the death of everything will be easier, Tyran Kaligula. You have the choice."

"Mm." Letting Kowin succeed meant his father's love

for hate would also win. "I never did well with *easy*," he said, pulling his foot under him to stand. He held his side and the sword as though it might keep his insides from spilling out.

Blood pooled around him. The sight made his head light.

Drast bolted from the staircase with the Alatir Stone held in his good hand. His bow and quiver of arrows were gone.

"Tyran!" He rushed to his side in a huff, eyes wide with madness. Drast did not have a scratch on him. He grabbed Tyran's hand, planting the gem in his palm. "I think I wore him out."

The power of the stone surged through Tyran, illuminating his body in white light. He gasped, the energy taking his breath away. He could already feel the power beginning to stitch the wound in his side. He stood a bit straighter, and although he continued to bleed, he no longer felt the pain.

Drast offered a faint apology, and then ripped the sword mercilessly from Tyran's side.

"Gods. It hurts," he slurred, grasping Drast's shoulder to steady himself. Tyran eyed the room and quickly found his shield. He pulled it to his left arm with Koldovstvo to cover his wound. "Where is he?"

Drast pointed back the way he had come just as echoes of footsteps came down the stairwell. Kowin's laughter could not be mistaken, echoing into the chamber.

"I can see why Erzebeth favored you, saved you at Anaerfell and guided you to the Netherworld," Kowin said, entering the room. The god was more dead than he was alive, his blackened breastplate hanging on smoldering flesh and bone. The black strands of hair and pointed nose were gone, his skull partially crushed from whatever happened in the battle with Drast. He stomped forward, looking at Wolos, shaking his head with what may have been disapproval before turning to the brothers. "The darkness inside you lent light for humanity's best chance at life. You have spirit—a tenacity unlike anything I have seen in mortals—but it changes nothing. Despite all your strengths, you cannot escape death."

"You speak as if it's over." Drast smiled.

"Oh, it was over long ago."

Drast snickered.

The three of them touched Koldovstvo, moving quicker than the eye, a series of shadowed movements in the dim light.

Tyran stepped in front of his brother, blocking the first sword swing with his shield, then letting loose the guard and holding it in place with Koldovstvo. He began to leap behind Kowin as Drast zipped around the room in a flash to attack Kowin with the sword that had stabbed his brother.

Kowin grabbed the shield, ripping it from Tyran's concentration and propelling it at Drast. Tyran stopped, attempting to pull the shield back to him with Koldovstvo. The mental struggle between the two ended up flinging the steel guard into the broken wall.

Kowin twisted, swinging his sword's edge at Tyran. He feigned back, nearly forgetting he held the Alatir Stone, and only remembered when Kowin reversed his steps to unleash a second attack at Drast.

The blow was swift, barely missing his brother's neck before being deflected by the other sword. Kowin advanced three more times, swinging high and low, powered with Koldovstvo. Drast was no swordsman, but his luck held true in parrying each blow, moving the weapon to his magical hand.

His smile widened with each success, growing so close to Kowin they had no room to swing their swords. Kowin grabbed Drast's sword hand, and Drast wrapped his arm around Kowin's smoldering frame. Tyran raised his hand to pull Kowin back before Drast was stabbed, possibly using a strand of air, but Drast was quick to shove Kowin away.

Laughing, Drast spun out of reach from the god, ever light on his toes. He revealed Ojenek in his left hand, having pulled it from Kowin's pocket. "Ho! Should we make this interesting and free Wolos? What do you say, Kowin the *Deathless*?"

Kowin scoffed. "Wolos will not raise a hand against me."

"Free him, Drast!" Tyran cried, reaching for his shield again. If they were going to die here, they could at least hope for reprisal through Wolos.

Drast followed Tyran's instruction, flinging Ojenek at the Horned God. Wolos opened his mouth to catch the gem.

"No!" Kowin bolted, having no ability to pull the stone to him with magic. The god dropped his sword to catch the shimmering blue stone with both hands, inches from Wolos's parted lips.

Tyran reached out to pull the blade to him with magic but stopped with a gasp, seeing Drast flank their enemy.

His brother caught Kowin off guard, seizing his right shoulder and impaling the second sword through the back and into the heart. The blade effortlessly tore through the god's chest. Kowin's went rigid, helplessly dropping Ojenek at Wolos's feet. His hands remained outstretched on either side of his body. He twitched, turning his chin to look at Drast behind him.

"You gods are so predictable," Drast leered. "Live through this." With a cry, Drast empowered his attack with Koldovstvo, twisting the blade sideways and ripping it free.

Kowin the Deathless fell to the stones, his body shattering like a Nocnica into a thousand pieces.

Chapter XXIV

Drast exhaled, collapsing to what remained of Kowin. His spectral hand vanished, the bloodied heart falling to the stone floor with a splat. His mouth dried and exhaustion won him over. He glanced at the bulbous organ to ensure the thing did not have a pulse. To his relief, the heart was unmoving.

His fingers on his good hand shook beyond his control, trembling without reason. Koldovstvo no longer surged through him, but his body spasmed from the veins in his neck to the end of his toes. He warily reached for the small flakes of what had once been living flesh. The mix of gore and black soot painted the edge of skin.

"We killed him," Drast said in disbelief, twisting his hand to better see the grime of the god. "We won. We should not have, but we did."

You doubted yourself? You were fated to succeed.

A shaky breath exited his frame again, causing his chest to quiver. He did not believe in fate. "We did not deserve to win. The Warden should have survived. Not us."

"Kamila Artur fulfilled her charge. Once I am freed, she will no longer be a demon. She will be taken from this place."

Freeing me from death was never about you.

"Shut up. You are not Wolos," Drast murmured.

The real Wolos grunted above him. "I am Wolos. You are not being misled."

Tyran's foot stepped on the rock at Drast's side, and he knelt to grab Ojenek from where it had fallen. His brother's wound continued to dribble blood, but the Alatir Stone seemed to keep him from the pain. His skin glowed under the power of the magical artifact.

He grunted, scooping up the blue stone in his hand.

The shimmering, glowing chains holding Wolos clinked and clanged as the god straightened to accept Ojenek. His bushy eyebrows pinched together, and he turned his head so that his curved horns glimmered in Tyran's light. "Feed me the stone, and I will take us to the Kalinov Bridge. We will finish this."

Let's hope the gods are not vengeful.

"I am ready for his wrath," Drast mumbled in a strained breath. He twisted his neck to look at the dilapidated walls and debris scattered through Heshayol. The prison was meant for death. "I am tired."

Wolos opened his mouth as wide as he could, splitting mustache from beard. With a shaky hand, Tyran pressed the stone into the God of the Dead's mouth, barely fitting the oval gem into the opening.

Drast lifted his eyes, fascinated. Heaving and gagging, Wolos struggled to gulp Ojenek down, the lump of the orb visibly sliding down his throat. He fought for air as he worked the stone down, his muscles flexing in the binding chains. With each forced swallow, his face turned paler, a dark shade of blue tinting the muscles in his neck until Ojenek entirely disappeared from his gullet.

You have to give it to him. Swallowing it like that; he has a godly fortitude. I would have spit the gem out a thousand times over.

Drast smiled. "Well, that diminishes any delusions of your godly nature."

"Not the time for jokes, Drast," Tyran said.

Drast smirked weakly, only half parting his lips. "I will soon be unable to make any jokes. Have to take what opportunities I have left."

Tyran grimaced but said nothing more.

One by one, the thick chains binding Wolos lost their magical glow and tumbled to the floor. The noise echoed in the enclosed room.

The Horned God gasped for breath, his eyes flashing with renewed power. He whipped his head to Tyran and then Drast with a respectful nod. "Let us return balance to Aenar."

I guess we will not be receiving any form of gratitude.

Drast gritted his teeth.

A flash of light burst in Drast's mind like a glorious sunrise, stealing away all other sight. His mind flooded with thoughts of what he knew was inevitable, along with visions of what he hoped would come to pass.

To his relief, the voice in his head was briefly silenced while he mused.

Wolos could not be reborn unless he or Tyran offered their life in return. If being a martyr meant Tyran would live, Drast was more than willing to sacrifice himself, but he could not make himself think of dying yet. Instead, he thought of Tyran experiencing a life of peace and affection, which brought Drast a sense of calm he had never known. A life involving a wife, children, and a regular profession bored Drast to tears, but he knew such monotonous daydreams thrilled Tyran.

For all they had suffered over the past thousand years, his brother deserved whatever happiness he could find.

Drast had never forgotten his verbal exchange with Wolos during the battle at Anaerfell. The simple words burned into Drast, more so since walking through the Tower of Eresh. The Horned God said Tyran's charge in life was to find love. No doubt, Tyran was given chance after chance to do so, only to be thrown from his path by either Drast or

Dagmar. Now, with their father dead, Drast was comforted in disappearing too, so Tyran would see his purpose fulfilled without his brother to muck things up.

Tyran would not be held back any longer. With his brother's youth restored by the Alatir Stone, he would have another lifetime ahead to achieve what Drast and Dagmar kept from him.

Drast lurched forward by whatever magic Wolos used to transport them. The spectacular light blinding Drast suddenly vanished.

He snapped back to reality, his mind swimming as though he had been jolted awake from a dream. The blue mist and purplish sky enveloped him in the Netherworld once more as he knelt against the frozen soil in the same way he had at Heshayol. Wolos stood boldly in front of him, and Tyran's wide frame could be seen from the corner of his eye. None of them had changed their position, simply the location. Whether the journey took a moment or a hundred moments, he could not say.

I, for one, am glad we did not have to walk the length of the Netherworld again.

"No one asked you," Drast said, rolling his eyes upward to address the voice.

"What?" Wolos lifted his bushy eyebrows.

"If we only could have traveled to Heshayol in a similar manner." Drast rose to his feet. "Could have saved us a lot of trouble. Could you not have brought us to you?"

"My power was limited in Heshayol under the magic of my bindings. Kowin could have skipped you to Heshayol, if he so chose," Wolos stated, turning around to overlook the landscape. "Clearly, he did not."

"No need to worry about it. We are done now," Tyran said under his breath. "Kowin is no longer our concern."

The earth rumbled under Drast, the ice and rock in front of them falling away into a familiar chasm. His first thoughts were of Kowin returning from the dead, but he realized they simply were back at the starting point. He watched the Kalinov Bridge form across the expanse, leading to the other side where the rope bridge to Babejega, and then Aenar, awaited. By some miracle, he managed to stay on his feet this time.

Tyran stepped nearer to the bridge. He peered over the edge, searching for Zyem, no doubt. "How do we do this?"

Wolos reached for Tyran, placing a gentle hand on the back of his shoulder. "I will take one of your spirits and cross the bridge, using the essence to give new life to my soul. You will no longer be living."

"And you will take mine," Drast snarled. "Take your hand off my brother. You will take me!"

Wolos lifted his hand and faced Drast with a raised eyebrow.

"Drast..." Tyran began.

He still thinks he can be sacrificed instead.

"Do you think I do not know?" Drast shouted, turning on his younger brother. "Hold your tongue, Tyran. I already told you that I will be the one to cross the bridge with Wolos. My mind is spoiled, and my arm is gone. I refuse to live the rest of my life ham-fisted. But I want some assurances before he has his happily ever after." Drast spun on Wolos. "Erzebeth said we would gain entrance to Thrice Ten Kingdom for freeing you. I want to hear the truth of it. Did the skin-switcher lie?"

Wolos stood in silence for some time, watching Drast and Tyran with consideration. Drast twitched, almost buckling under the silent gaze. He could not stop Wolos from swooping him up and taking him over the bridge against his will. The god did not have any reason to answer him.

He wants to kill you.

Drast did not engage with the voice, grinding his teeth until they hurt. He did not think Wolos would simply kill him or Tyran. Though he did wonder whether Wolos held the power to clear them of the brutalities they committed during their lives. Or whether any of it even mattered. Perhaps the god speculated over their capability to enter the Kingdom. Then again, he might simply have been forging a new lie to convince Drast to willingly forgo his life.

"No," Wolos said at last. "You will not enter Thrice Ten Kingdom for saving me from Heshayol, nor will you be rewarded for resurrecting me from death. The nature of your charge, given to you at your creation, does not change as events unfold during your life." Drast opened his mouth to protest or to curse Erzebeth's betrayal, but Wolos spoke louder to prevent any interruption. "However, you may enter Thrice Ten Kingdom yet. If you recall, your charge, Drast Kaligula, was to be a champion for your younger brother. You were meant to protect him, guide him, and give him the means to fulfill his purpose. None of the fell deeds you have done during your long life will count against completing your charge. Sacrificing yourself so your brother might live to complete his as well will keep you from the Netherworld."

"And Tyran will meet me there?"

"You already know the answer," Wolos said. "He would be free to return to Aenar and complete his charge. If successful, he could then meet you in the afterlife."

Drast eyed Tyran with hesitation; Tyran gazed back at him with wide eyes. His brother knew this was the best way. "Will it hurt?" Drast asked.

"Yes," Wolos said, clamping his hand onto Drast.

Maybe we should rethink this. I do not want to die…again.

"Promise me you will live your life, brother," Drast said, keeping the tears from his eyes and embracing Tyran. "And promise me that you will meet me in the Thrice Ten Kingdom."

"I will. I promise," Tyran struggled to say, his voice low.

"Good. Ale and wenches will be waiting." Drast swallowed, breaking free.

He looked to Wolos. "Come, god, let us end this so that

my brother can get on with living."

Wolos nodded and turned to walk across the bridge.

The pain was sudden and brief, a thousand pinpoints marking where his soul was extricated from his fleshy cage. He felt it for only an instant before darkness closed.

Epilogue

Wolos disappeared over the bridge, leaving Drast's figure sprawled out where he had fallen, his piercing scream still echoing in Tyran's mind.

He kneeled, the cold of the earth stinging his knees through his trousers. He crossed his brother's hands peacefully over his chest, looking momentarily at the chasm stretching ahead of him.

The thin land bridge extended over the abyss. His life awaited him, though he truly did not know how he would find the correct pathway home.

Regardless, he promised Drast to live it.

He wondered whether he should lug his brother's body over the Kalinov Bridge and back to Aenar or leave him where he lay. Truly, he could see no purpose in returning the body to the world of the living. He and Drast no longer had a home, let alone a place dedicated for burial. He did not even know where he would go.

He supposed the Netherworld was as good a resting place as any. Besides, his brother was dead. *Dead.*

The word echoed in his head, and he embraced the sound, despite its immediate implications. He dared to think Drast finally found peace. He almost longed to join him.

Silently, he wept.

For a time he did not move, only trying to keep his shoulders from shaking while he watched his brother's lifeless form, willing him to rise again. Eventually he swallowed his grief and gritted his teeth until the tears stopped.

"Wolos better have told us the truth," Tyran muttered, wiping his face. "If I find you have not been brought to Thrice Ten Kingdom after what we have done for the world, I might have to slay him a second time."

He smiled despite himself, knowing his threat was empty.

God-killer.

The voice of Zyem boomed inside his skull. Wind whipped against Tyran with the mighty beating of the dragon's wings, pushing the red strands of his hair back over his ears. The massive black dragon rose from the gorge beneath and neared him.

Tyran sprang to his feet, standing protectively in front of Drast's corpse to face the dragon. The three heads of Zyem snaked through the air with a deadly ire. "Wolos has risen." Tyran gestured to Drast's body. "My brother sacrificed all he had."

So he has. Zyem hissed in his mind. *Yet you still carry something that belongs to me.*

Tyran's hand fumbled in his pocket. He pulled the Alatir Stone free, revealing the glowing, pasty artifact in his palm.

Give it to me and I will imbue you with the insight to know what road will take you home.

"Home?" Tyran repeated. The word had little meaning to him anymore. And while he admittedly longed to know it as he once had, he could not say Aenar filled him with warm feelings. In fact, nothing about Aenar called to him, yet where else would he go?

He sighed, feeling the power of the Alatir Stone churning through him, keeping him safe from illness, old age, and physical harm. With the artifact in his possession, he could go anywhere, be anything. He could rule nations or rule nothing, powerful and unstoppable. He would be a god among mere mortals.

His heart swelled at the thought.

Do not be foolish, mortal. Stay the balance you have fought for, and go home. Remember your onus.

Tyran pulled his arm back and threw the mystical gem at Zyem, gasping as the magic of the stone fled from his body, the white glow fading from his skin. He collapsed to his knees with a whisper. "Take it."

He was certain Zyem took the stone, although he did not watch the exchange. Instead, the knowledge of his pathway home burned into his mind like a map traced in the sand. Over the Kalinov Bridge, into the nexus, and the rope bridge—

A sword tearing through his chest cavity punctured his lung and stole what thoughts remained in his head.

Tyran gurgled with surprise, dropping his chin to see the thin blade coated with dark blood. Before he could react, his fists clenching, the cold sting of a second blade touched his neck.

He bent his neck to look for Drast, only to have his sight obstructed by the spectacle of crimson armor and a flash of white teeth.

He could not speak.

Kowin leaned over him, whispering in his ear, "I told you I was deathless."

ABOUT THE AUTHOR

Joshua Robertson was born in Kingman, Kansas on May 23, 1984. A graduate of Norwich High School, Robertson attended Wichita State University where he received his master's in social work with minors in psychology and sociology. His bestselling novel, *Melkorka*, the first in The Kaelandur Series, was released in 2015. Known most for his Thrice Nine Legends Saga, Robertson enjoys an ever-expanding and extremely loyal following of readers. He counts R.A. Salvatore and J.R.R. Tolkien among his literary influences.

J.C. lives in the Midwest with his wife and two dogs and has an M.A. in English Literature. The first novel in his world, *Blood and Bile*, was released in 2017. Before completing junior high, J.C. had received his first box set of Dungeons & Dragons and devoured J.R.R. Tolkien's *The Lord of the Rings*. Since, he has been heavily influenced by a myriad of fantasy authors, such as Weis and Hickman, Robert Jordan, and Ed Greenwood.

www.ingramcontent.com/pod-product-compliance
Lightning Source LLC
Chambersburg PA
CBHW050604190726
48283CB00007B/2271